Piercing the Fold:

Book 1

Venessa Kimball

Published by
Crushing Hearts and Black Butterfly Publishing, LLC.
Algonquin, IL 60102

Published by
Crushing Hearts and Black Butterfly Publishing, LLC.
Algonquin, IL 60102

Edited by Elizabeth A. Lance
For Crushing Hearts and Black Butterfly Publishing

Cover by
Riley Steel

This book is dedicated to Greg, Dylan, Lauren, and Ethan.

Prologue

A hazy, dusk-filled night approaches me. As I run, I watch the darkness challenge the light, bringing an indelible silence as it slowly creeps into the world. The unhurried sunlight retreats beyond the sidewalks, the grass, the trees, the buildings, the houses. The darkness wins the challenge. Fear envelops me.

I run with panic weighing heavy on my chest. The pound, pound, pound of my heart and feet are in harmony. My breath is silent, but fast; I can feel it. I feel the urgency to get home to save them, my parents. Wet, glossy asphalt shimmers on a dimly lit street as I climb the familiar hill just before turning left toward my house. I can see mist gathering at each lamppost down the long road. Nervousness and fear slip into my mind. The urgency to get there faster is my singular thought that is festering up to the tip of my tongue as I mouth the words, but no sound escapes. Out of the sheer silence, I hear a man's holler and a woman's scream.

The voices are so familiar at first, then distort.

Mom. Dad.

Even though my muscles burn, I move with speed and strength as the hill's elevation becomes almost too steep to bear. At the crest of the hill, I see my house. No lights, except for the one room upstairs. Incomprehensible speed gets me to the front door of our house in seconds. I brace myself with one deep breath because I know what is coming. Even though I have dreamed this nightmare countless times, I still feel the blood drain from my body. My throat constricts in preparation to bar any sound coming to my aid. I feel a dark, evil presence all around me, thick with a terrorizing and intimidating presence. It knows that I am listening for it. I feel the rush of the dark force block my path. As I attempt to pass and climb the stairs, the sensation of walking through deep snow kicks in. I push myself to press on, having had repeated these same attempts and failures time and time again in this vicious, cyclic nightmare. I am up the stairs two steps at a time with unearthly speed. My kick to the door cracks the door frame and startles Dad. His head snaps up to look at me, and then he promptly returns his disturbing gaze to Mom. They are huddled, holding each other in a corner between their bed and nightstand. My mother is writhing and convulsing in his arms. My father is holding her, weeping and quickly speaking under his breath, a prayer, I think. I feel the heavy, intimidating presence in the room with us now. I cannot see it. I can never see it in my nightmares.

"Leave this house," comes out of my mouth, crackly and muffled with no strength behind it, like my mouth is stuffed with cotton.

I close my eyes and focus on my strength. I put every ounce of volume behind my voice. "Leave my house, my family. With all my strength, I com—"

Then my mind shifts; I hear the audible reality. "Command you to leave!"

3

The sound of my voice wakes me.

I am drenched in sweat, yet shivering and cold. I cannot move my body. I can only look around. My legs feel like they are being sat on, and my arms feel as if they are chained to the bed. I move my eyes to the window by my bed. It is still dark. The trees are casting dark shadows on my bedroom wall. I am breathing rapidly. I try to slow my breath down.

Don't panic, Jes.

More frequently than not, when these very physical nightmare occur, it takes a while for my body to regain the ability to move. In my adolescent years, the doctors remedied my parents concern by naming this bizarre episode "sleep paralysis". The nightmares became more intense as I got older and so did the paralysis. My breathing is slow and deep now. I can start to feel a tingling in my legs and arms. I lie there, waiting for the paralysis to pass. Three times this week. I can't help but think, like so many times before, that these nightmares could be a vision. A warning or sign of some kind. I look at the clock; it is 3:34 a.m. Too early to call Mom and Dad. I always talk with them after "an episode". Since I can remember, Mom and Dad have been either physically at my bedside or available by phone to comfort me after the nightmare. I suppose it is their way of bringing me back to reality after the horrific unreality of it all. Now, I am hesitant since the increased occurrences of the nightmares; it would only worry them. The frequency of these nightmares is beginning to worry me as well.

4

Chapter 1

Sunny skies and cool, brisk breezes. Leaves, in a multitude of colors, tumbling down from the trees and onto the sidewalks and streets. I've lived in Marietta, Georgia, my whole life. Last year, freshman year at Southern Polytechnic State University, I moved into my own apartment. My parents wanted me to live at home and commute, but I was determined to give it a go on my own, to proclaim my independence.

I was adopted as an infant by Roan and Delilah Sera. The Sera's waited many years to try to have children. They discovered that it was not possible for them to have their own, and that is when I arrived. Mom and Dad said that my birth mother, Anna Gershon, had an accidental death. They said they did not know the details of her passing. When I was three, Mom and Dad were surprised with the birth of their daughter, Bethany.

The memories of my childhood were wonderful. As small children, Bethany and I were rarely left alone with a sitter. It was always a very close and trusted friend left to watch us. My parents were never far from my sister or me. I guess they were cautious with us in that sense. When I was in elementary school, Dad and I would take long hikes in Kennesaw Mountain National Battlefield Park. As I got older, I was able to hold my own better on the rough terrain near the foothills. Dad and I would run the trails there. The lake near the national park was also a place of great memories. Mom, Dad, and I would get up early on Saturday mornings to fish and bring home our afternoon catch for cleaning. Bethany liked to sleep in, so she never joined us. Dad taught me how to clean the fish we caught. I always joked with them that I should have been their son.

He always reminded me, "Strength is not a variable only applicable to masculinity. It is your strength, Jes, that will define and defend your femininity."

Mom was always the reminder of my femininity. In my tween years, girl time included shopping and pedicures. In elementary and middle school, Mom and I spent special alone time taking field trips of our own to local libraries, museums, zoos, aquariums, and planetariums. At night, Mom and I would sit out on the back porch and talk about the good and bad of the day and stargaze.

* * *

I remember a conversation from second grade.

"Jes, how was your day today?"

"All right. Sandra told Janice and Beth not to sit with me at lunch, and she said it in front of me. She knew I was there!"

Mom coyly asked, "And how did you handle that?"

I looked up at Mom, puffed my chest out, and said, "I planned to sit with Sarah today. It didn't bother me one bit."

Mom congratulated me on taking the high road in the discussion with Sandra.

Mom continued. "But remember, Jesca, sometimes it takes a stronger person to walk away from a confrontation and remain righteous than to stay and battle."

"Mom, where is God? I mean, I know He is everywhere. I know He is in Heaven, but where is that? Is it in space? Is He in our universe? Is He in our galaxy? Or is He beyond all of space?"

"Such a visionary, Jes."

Mom stopped, looked up, then at me, and decided what to say. "Jes, God is everywhere and somewhere. I believe that He is not as far away from us as some think. I believe that God will reveal our ability to physically reach Him when it is our time to pass over."

We lived a Christian life. Attending worship regularly was part of our weekly routine in the Sera home. However, Dad and Mom made sure that we respected many of the scientific theories and their link to God and Christianity. In my parents' eyes, there was no reason to deny science and scientists their due respect as visionaries of biology, physics, astronomy, and so on. Our pastor, Daniel, was a visionary of Christianity. And I was taught to appreciate both and see the inevitable harmony they could harness together as a union. Dad and Mom taught me that it is the scientists' and pastors' different interpretations as visionaries that will eventually intersect, producing one singular, indisputable truth.

On cue, I would ask, "And what would that undeniable truth be?"

Mom would say with a smile, "Well, if we knew, then there wouldn't be much of a purpose for all of the visionaries we are blessed with, would there?"

* * *

I am their first child, so it is understandable why they didn't want to let me move out. I was so ready, though. I was becoming more involved on campus and with specialty coursework now; I need to be close to campus.

I open the curtain to the window in my apartment: sunshine. The light shines clarity on every object in my visual range. Still groggy from the long night of unrest, I put my undercover, Jackie O sunglasses on. My hazel eyes resemble a bloodshot mess. I started my sophomore year about two weeks ago. My apartment is about two blocks from campus. The first couple of weeks of a new semester are always tough: getting your schedule regulated without tearing all over campus like a maniac, waiting in long lines with fellow students to purchase books that are so pricey the hard covers should be made with gold filament. Let's not forget the supplies for the courses. Oh, and the collegiate paraphernalia. I may sound jaded, but I enjoy the campus life and the feeling of camaraderie with fellow students.

As I walk, I button up my blue peacoat. My dark brown, wavy hair is whipping across my face. I quickly tug on the rubber band secured around my wrist and pull my hair up into a high bun. I'd absentmindedly let it grow out over the summer. I desperately need a trim. I start calculating the number of nights I have not slept due to the nightmares. Crap, this is the sixth time in two weeks. It may be the new semester. The stress of settling in to my coursework. The new apartment. My part-time job. The multiple responsibilities could be taking a toll on me.

That sounds exactly like something Mom and Dad might say to precursor an offer to take some of that stress off my hands by coming back home. I can do this, though. I have always been headstrong and confident and never backed down from a challenge.

I come to an intersection just on the fringe of campus. In my peripheral vision, I see a dark green jacket and a baseball cap, traditional garb for campus. Feeling the urge to acknowledge the person, I look over. This guy is looking at me with these dark, angry eyes. No other expression on his face, devilishly catatonic. Then his face shifts. I instantly feel a surge of energy run through me. Everything starts spinning. I put my hands out to try and catch myself. I feel him grab my arms. I'm about ready to wale on him when I look at him again. The eyes, they are normal, quite beautiful, actually. Light green and gorgeous, to be exact.

What the hell just happened?

He is still holding my shoulders to steady me. "Are you all right? You almost fell into oncoming traffic."

I stare at his face for a moment, searching for a change in it. "Uh, yeah. Sorry."

That is all I could think of, really?

9

He let go of my shoulders and quickly darts across the street ahead of me. I try to catch up to him to get another look at his face. I can't get the first image of him out of my mind.

I tell myself it didn't happen.

It is just your mind playing tricks on you, Jes. You're tired.

He has his head down as the majority of people on campus do, extremely focused on getting from point A to point B. He takes a left at the forked path where I need to take a right. I pause just a bit to watch him walk. I'm so tempted to run up to him and look at his face once more. The wind suddenly picks up, bringing along with it the frigid cold. Feeling the sharp cold in my bones, I turn and head to Shakespearean Lit.

It bothers me all through my first class. Maybe I am hallucinating because of the lack of sleep. It could be the change in weather. The shift in barometric pressure could account for the dizzy feeling.

When he touched my arms, the shock was so strong, though.

What about his face?

My vision has always been perfect. It has to be the lack of sleep: hallucinations, headaches, dizziness. All are symptoms of lack of sleep. This reasoning calms me enough to get through my next two classes.

After my classes, I head off campus, stop for a Starbucks', and walk to work. I work at a bookstore, Benson's Book Store. Benson's is about three blocks from campus. I love how close my apartment and my job are to campus. It makes me feel safe and secure to know my life could be wrapped up into a six-block radius. Benson's is a small-town, privately owned bookstore. My best friend, Elisha, and I have been working shifts there since high school. The owner, Todd Benson, is a retired English professor from the university. He started up the bookstore after retiring since he loved the college environment that buzzed around downtown. He didn't want to give that up. He was very visible at the store for many years. Then, his health started to fail, and he handed ownership over to his son, Todd Jr. Todd Jr. is a hippy, literally. Once a week, he walks in with no shoes, torn jeans, and a half-buttoned flannel to "take care of business", look at shipment records for new orders and delivery records for old, check the registry for purchase and sales accuracy, etc. He is in and out in about six hours since we aren't a huge conglomerate.

I cross in front of a side-street alley. Whispers catch my attention, and I turn to see two people in the alley. The situation looks off. I duck around the corner so they won't catch me listening in.

A gruff voice whispers, "See, it works like this, I help you out, and you help me out. 'Kay?"

I hear a rustling bag being pulled between them.

A woman's voice whispers back. "I know how this works. I'm not new to this, damn it. Just give me my boyfriend's stuff. I've got your cash."

I can't help my curiosity. I slowly peek around the wall I am leaning against.

God, why am I getting involved?

A middle-aged man, dressed in slacks and a leather jacket, and with greased-back, blond hair, is groping this much

11

younger girl. She must be in high school. She looks too young for college. She is holding a small baggy with one hand. She is pushing away the man with the other as he tries to kiss her.

The sinister, slick, male voice whispers, "Oh, sweetheart, I think you know that cash won't cover this."

I feel anxious for the girl. I want to help her. She must have felt me looking at her because she looks up at me. Her eyes meet mine. Her mouth doesn't move, but I can hear her speak to me. *Go away! I'm fine. Mind your own business. Go!*

I stand there for a few seconds in shock from the interaction they are having and what she just said to me without speaking an audible word. I slowly turn, back away from the alley, and lean against the wall. My heart is racing from anger and frustration. I want to help her out of this, but she doesn't seem to want it. I can't help but think what she would do for her boyfriend and his apparent addiction. The more I think, the angrier I get. I have to get out of here. Frustrated, I push myself off the wall, fold my arms around myself for warmth, and walk away.

How could I hear her voice in my head?

Maybe I was just thinking of what she would say.

But it wasn't in my voice. It was in hers.

I start feeling nervous.

What is going on with me?

I walk into the store and immediately head to the back to put down my backpack and get a coffee. It is pretty vacant in the store at this time of day. The rush usually starts around 5:30.

All was quiet except for Elisha, who was listening to her iPod at the cash register, tapping her pen on the countertop and chewing gum. We have been friends since kindergarten. We are inseparable. She has been my partner in crime in many juvenile pranks. We grew up going to the same church and youth group. We have been through each other's dramatic boyfriend issues. We went to prom with our dates together. We graduated together. We both got part-time jobs together. We both go to the same university.

We have different majors, though, way different. Elisha has always been the free-spirited one. She is into art, writing, and music. I stand in front of her for a second and smile as she taps to what sounds like *Silversun Pickups*. She looks up at me with a do-I-have-something-on-my-face look.

"Let me ask you something, Elisha. Do I look okay? I mean, do I look different?"

"You look fine. Hey, there was some guy in here earlier asking if you worked here. Said he knew you from class. I told him that I was new to the job and didn't know all of the employees yet. He's pretty gorgeous. Are you holding out on me? Do you have a 'special friend' you haven't told me about?" Elisha smiles coyly and sits back in her chair.

I'm paying little attention to Elisha's banter. I'm thinking on everything that has happened today. It occurs to me that it isn't just today. My hearing voices happened a couple of times last week, too. I thought it was just my thoughts. But what happened just now makes me see it in a different light. I wasn't hearing my voice at all.

Elisha touches my shoulder. "Hey! Jesca! Earth to Jesca!"

Elisha obnoxiously pops her gum. I quickly download the day's happenings to Elisha. The freaky details about the cutie that I almost lashed out at and the crazy drug trafficking going on in the side alley by the Starbucks.

"Jes, you have always been 'out for justice'. Maybe today was the token vigilante day of the week for you. This crap goes on around us all the time. Maybe you're just sensitive to all of it today. You may be looking for it in some weird way. I mean, you are pretty weird when it comes to scoping out the not so obvious. It's like you have radar for it or something."

I don't want her to explain it away that easily. Something is going on with me.

"What about the freaky face on that guy?"

"Easy, Jes. Something on TV last night triggered that image, and it popped into your pretty, little head this morning because you are so tired from not sleeping. By the way, your mom and dad are pretty concerned about your lack of sleep. They keep calling me and poking around to find out about their baby girl. You need to give them a call. Apparently, you haven't called them in a week. God forbid!"

I bat my hand at Elisha. "'Kay, I got it! I'll call them tonight!

I start to walk to the back room and turn toward her once more. "And I have not always been 'out for justice'!"

Elisha responds with a half laugh. "Yeah? Okay, Super Girl."

The Art History and Economics sections need restocking. I get to work on the boxes. I vaguely hear the front door open to two soft-spoken guys. Elisha and I both look up. Elisha greets them, then turns to me. Elisha's blue eyes are wide. She is relentless. She mouths, "Hotties!"

I smile, roll my eyes at her, and turn back to continue stocking. I hear a clicking sound and then humming. It sounds like the air-conditioning kicking in. I stand up and go over to the air-conditioning vent to see if that is where the sound is coming from. Elisha leans over the front desk and looks at me.

She mouths, "You okay?"

I whisper, "Can you hear that humming sound?"

She stops chewing her gum and looks up while she listens. "Uh, no. Do you?"

I look at her, then close my eyes. "Never mind. I thought I heard thunder." I walk quickly back behind the stacks.

I lied to my best friend. I don't want to explain to her what I hear, especially when I don't know what the hell I am hearing from the get-go. I feel my heart flutter with nervousness. The hum is now taking on a physical presence in my body, a vibration in my chest. It starts small, like a flicker of a sensation. Then the vibrations radiate to my arms. Then to my head.

I hear a thick voice. "She knows…"

I feel the little hairs on the nape of my neck shift direction. Someone is near me, behind me. I turn around quickly, but no one is there. I can still hear whispers, but it is far away now. I

15

slowly shift to the other side of the aisle and peek between books to try to find where the voice is coming from.

The thick whisper comes again from a different voice. "She won't say anything."

I close my eyes and try my hardest to clear my thoughts of everything but the heavy whisper. I search for the sound that I caught and lost a few seconds earlier.

The hair on my neck shifts again. I can feel someone, no, two people now. It is like these two people speaking are on either side of me. My breath comes faster.

"Do you realize how destroyed her reputation would be if anyone knew what she did with five of us last night? She won't say a word, IF she remembers."

I am tempted to open my eyes and look for them, but I don't. I keep my eyes closed and calm my breath so I can stay focused in the moment. If I open my eyes, I will lose the voices and what they are saying. What did they do to this poor girl? I wanted to get up, find them in the aisle they are conspiring in, and confront them. The feeling of solid flesh next to me slowly begins to fade. My anger is distracting my focus. I refocus on calming myself. I need to hold on to the voices. I need to hear the rest. I need to know if she is all right.

"Man, I don't know. Are you sure we didn't hurt her? When we left, she was crying a lot. What if someone found her and got her to talk?"

All I can feel is hate for these two guys. I feel tears on my cheeks. The feeling tilts my focus, and I start to lose the conversation again.

16

"We are not having this conversation any more, man. Jana said she would cover for us. Make her think she knew what she was doing and was okay with it! We are clear, man. We are golden."

I hear one of them scoff. It is amazing how one small sound can set you off. My eyes pop open. I start to move forward to find the voices when the dizziness hits me like a ton of bricks. Then the nausea hits. My stomach feels like it is knotting up.

I close my eyes, but that makes the spinning feeling worse. My body has a mind of its own and is pulling me down; I am out of control. I lean against the stacks for balance. I feel myself slide down until I am sitting on the floor. I open my eyes, but all I see is flashes of light.

Oh no. I am going to pass out.

I hear the bell at the front door.

I mumble loudly, "Elisha. Don't let them leave."

My voice sounds tired and breathless.

I hear Elisha rush to me. "Jes! What are you doing?"

"Those jerks were just talking about…they were with this girl, and there were five of them, and…"

Elisha puts her hand on my head. "You're burning up, Jes. Hold on." She leaves me for a minute. I hear water running in the bathroom; I figure she is getting a wet cloth for my head.

I open my eyes. She is back with the wet cloth and puts it to my head.

Elisha has a worried look on her face. "You are so pale, Jes. Just sit here for a minute. I will be right back."

I am too weak to ask her where she's going.

17

She is gone for a bit. The cloth on my head is helping. My stomach is unknotting, and the dizziness is going away.

I want to try standing. I push my hands under me and start to pull my legs up to stand when Elisha comes back; she pushes me back down softly.

Elisha sits down in front of me and looks at me. Her look is uncomfortable.

"What?"

Her smile weakens. "Jes. I'm your best friend, and I love you. That is the only reason why I'm telling you what I'm about to tell you." She puts her hands on both of my arms. "I think you may be on the edge of insanity. I mean, you are acting really loco!" She lets out a short laugh.

I push her arms away slowly and roll my eyes.

More seriously, Elisha says, "Look, you need to go home. You pulled in extra hours last week. I will cover you. Just take care of yourself! I know those nightmares have come back full force. Your mom and dad told me. And now you're fainting at work. I don't want my bestie being put away in a loony bin when she has her whole life ahead of her!" Elisha gives me a weak, sarcastic laugh. I can hear some fear in that laugh, too.

Elisha sits with me until I feel somewhat normal again. I pack up my things in the back room and think of how insane I must look to my best friend. I can only shake my head.

Chapter 2

I feel like I slept for days. Truthfully, it is almost a full day. Twenty-two hours, give or take. I woke up around 8:30 a.m. long enough to use the restroom and get a glass of water. The sound of the heater turning on is what finally wakes me up from my self-induced sleep marathon at 3 p.m. It is so strange how the smallest, yet distinct sound can catch your attention. The click of a heating system as it kicks on. The sound of the warmth moving through the air ducts above. As my body wakes, my eyes remain shut, taking in the sound. I imagine being the heat moving through the aluminum, swaying from one side of the piping to the other, like I am on an inner tube on a crazy water ride. I open my eyes. The sun is retreating behind the almost-barren trees. I lie there thinking of the events of my life lately. It seems like a distant, crazy, insignificant set of circumstances that I could chalk up to being sleep deprived. I am hoping the sleep I have gotten takes care of the craziness in my life.

I feel energized enough to head out for a run. Mom always said that running brought me to my center. It definitely helps me work things out in my head. I desperately need that time right now. I leave the apartment and head northwest toward Kennesaw and the lake. It is a good distance, about seven to eight miles round trip. It is a familiar trek, though. Running it reminds me of the fun and comforting times with Dad.

The concrete turns to gravel, then dirt, and then rock. I enter a trailhead in the Kennesaw Mountain National Park. I descend into a more densely wooded area. The sun is shimmering on the fallen leaves and damp mulch. The cool air that hits my face and legs is much appreciated. I focus on my breath, on the ground, on the music, and on the movement of my arms and legs. All my senses are centered, and I am aware of everything. Dad and I used to call it being "in the zone". This is different, though. It feels like every part of me is hypersensitive and hyper-focused on what is around me and inside of me.

Then, I hear the humming. Then twigs begin to break close by. I stop and look around. I feel the vibration start as soon as my body stops moving; it is strong. I feel my heart flutter in my chest and my stomach twitch. The dizziness doesn't come this time. My heart is pounding. Not just from the run, but from anxiousness. I see a dark flash out of the corner of my eye. It is upright, not low to the ground like an animal. I turn my music down just to be more in tune with my surroundings. I pick up my pace. My legs begin to take larger, faster, stronger, unnatural strides. My vision and hearing is fine-tuned. The crumbling, bright green leaves under my feet sound like a trash compactor crushing plastic. My arms work quickly to push away stray shrubs, twigs, and twine in my path. I sense something, a presence coming up on me. It is closing in quickly. I have had this feeling before in my nightmare.

I quickly look behind me while running. I see a black, smoke-like entity. It doesn't have a face or details to reveal if it is human. It is like a blur of darkness in the landscape. Its quick movements and ability to shift around the wooded obstacles heighten my anxiety. The humming is even stronger now, clouding my thinking. I can feel the vibration throughout my body like a jackhammer. I see an opening to the trailhead, a clearing.

It has to be the lake.

I put more power into my pumping arms and stretching stride. The sunlight becomes brighter as the trees open their canopy to unleash me from the woods. The pull of the darkness from behind releases me like a rock in a slingshot.

I am out of the trail. I stop and turn to look back into the wood. I am close to the ground.

That's odd.

I look down at myself. I am in a combat crouched position. My breath is ragged sounding. I try to focus on calming it.

I stay crouched for a while. Nothing appears in the shadows at the trail's edge. Just rustling leaves on the rocky ground. I stand and slowly pace in front of the opening to the wood, looking, watching, and waiting as my breath becomes more even. I must look like I am stalking prey with the way I am pacing. The humming sound is diffusing quickly, and the vibration is minimal compared to my racing heart.

I turn and look out at the lake. A man is staring at me from a boat.

Mr. Ezra Kahn?

I feel my cheeks get hot from embarrassment.

I was crouching like an animal.

21

I look down and turn away from him for a minute. Maybe he was baiting his line and didn't notice my animal-like behavior. Damn it, I have to acknowledge him. I turn back and smile.

"Hi there, Mr. Kahn."

Mr. Kahn tips his fishing hat to me. His light brown hair is ruffled under his cap.

"Jesca Gershon-Sera. You okay?"

He saw it all. Crap. Why did it have to be Mr. Kahn?

* * *

I ran into him, literally, last semester before my class with him. He was a few inches taller than me. When I ran into him, I bounced off like I was running into a wall. For a professor of academia, he was quite sturdy. I thought then that he must have worked out. He quickly pulled me up with one hand. His light brown eyes were terrified that I had gotten hurt. "Are you okay? I'm so sorry."

"I'm fine. Just fine. I wasn't watching where I was going. I am trying to find the physics department."

As we made small talk, he led me to the physics department, his department. He was the reason I decided to pursue coursework dealing with cosmology, astrophysics, and quantum physics this year. Yes, it sounds boring by title, but the content was mind boggling.

* * *

"Yes, it's Jesca. Hey, have you seen anything or anyone odd running around before I came out of the woods?"

Looking more concerned for me now, Ezra says, "Yes, I did see a man heading into the woods about ten minutes ago. Is everything all right?"

I feel my nerves heighten again. "Yeah, yeah, everything is fine. Well, it is nice seeing you. I better head back."

Ezra smiles. "You too. Be careful heading back, all right?"

I wave as I jog along the exterior of the woods to enter from another trailhead. I head along the edge of the woods, not wanting to get too deep into the forest. I fall back into my normal pace quickly.

I can't help thinking about the coincidences of seeing Mr. Kahn around town lately. I wonder what his life outside of campus entails. Did he have a family? A wife? Did he live alone? Divorced? He seems like a nice enough man to have a family and maybe a couple of children. Contemplating Mr. Kahn's life freaks me out a bit, but it passes the time perfectly to get me home without too much thought on what I experienced in the woods.

* * *

Back at the apartment, I take a much appreciated hot shower. The air turned frigid very quickly near the foothills, making the run home colder than on the way up to the lake.

After my shower, I decide to head into town to see Elisha at the store. I dress quickly, bundling up with a scarf and hat for the short, but chilly, walk. I hadn't talked to her since the twenty-two-hour sleep marathon. I owe her a big thank you since she covered for me.

On my walk, I put a call in to Mom and Dad and get voicemail.

"Hey, Mom. Hey, Dad. Just wanted to let you know that I'm doing fine. Have caught up on some much needed sleep. I am feeling so much better. Love you. Bye."

Well, it is partly true. I did catch up on sleep. And for now, everything seems fine. Well, other than the eerie, dark someone chasing me in the woods. Oh, and the supernatural, high-velocity running I apparently possess now.

Chapter 3

I make it to the store just before Elisha locks up.

"Hey there, Jes. What are you doing here? Shouldn't you be home sleeping?"

I stutter a bit. "I just wanted to say thanks for covering for me so I could rest."

I reach in and give her a hug.

"Don't be silly, Jes. We don't need you collapsing at work or falling asleep during lectures, do we? You call your mom and dad? I love your parents, Jes, but you need to talk to them. They have left me eight messages and four texts in the last twenty-four hours."

I respond with a small smile. "Already done."

Elisha finishes locking the door. "Where are you heading now?"

"Back home. I wanted to make sure you knew I was okay. You know, in person. I think you were right about all the stress and no sleep thing."

Elisha's face seems to relax. That was my intention for her, since I didn't truly believe what I was saying myself.

You don't believe that for a second, Jes.

Elisha sighs. "Well, my mom and dad have requested me for dinner. Hope they aren't going to spring another surprise on me. Like, 'Sweetheart, we are considering renting our house and traveling around Europe for a year.' Seriously, I don't know how they can be so spur of the moment. Such a carefree and liberal lifestyle. I mean, really, c'mon."

I laugh a bit, amused by Elisha's attempt at a serious conversation about her parents. "Love you, Lisha. Hey, I'll be in tomorrow at noon after class, all right?"

"Sounds good. Go home and sleep!" Elisha smiles, turns, and starts walking in the opposite direction.

I yell after her with sheer sarcasm. "Yes, ma'am."

I turn to head in the opposite direction. I begin humming a Christmas jingle as I walk briskly to beat the chilled air.

As I walk, I recollect something my mom and dad always told me when I was in a rut. Sometimes life gets set off balance. Sometimes it's a good thing, and sometimes, not so good. Remember to keep your guard up and push through the rut. Never back down or away from seeking and surfacing the meaning, the purpose of the imbalance. It is the seeking and surfacing that will help you transcend it.

I'm distracted by the humming and vibrating sensation that shoots through my body. It feels like an electric surge from my toes, up my spine, and into my head. I hear someone walking a few steps behind me. I turn just enough to see peripherally. Nothing is there. I walk more quickly. The whispering comes again, quick and raspy.

It is impossible to decipher the words. Waves of people are passing me on either side, walking in the opposite direction.

Could I be catching pieces of their thoughts, internal conversations?

A woman passes to my right. *"Soymilk, Tums, and meat tenderizer."*

Then, a man passes to my left. *"Tommy needs to finish his project by Saturday."*

A young couple is ahead of me with their heads down, walking toward me.

"Why is she being so unreasonable?"

"I don't know why he is being so quiet. What did I do?"

I feel like I am under attack. I need to get inside, away from the voices. I look for a shop that is still open. Small-town shops close pretty early around here. I hear the raspy voice again, very deep and very close.

"Jesca."

I see a light two doors up on the left and rush for it, Margot's Deli. A cowbell rings me in at the entrance.

It is very quiet, except for the music, *The Doors "People are Strange"* playing in the background.

I walk quickly to a booth and sit on the side facing the front door. I eye the door as I tap my finger on the countertop. An older waitress named "Sally" brings me a menu and a glass of water. We exchange smiles, and she leaves me to browse the menu.

The cowbell sounds. My eyes dart over to see Mr. Kahn taking his jacket off. He hasn't seen me yet.

He looks back toward the kitchen. "Hey there, Stan. Slow tonight?"

Stan must be the cook I see through the serving window over the bar. Stan comments on the dining traffic, but I am still looking beyond Mr. Kahn. I am looking for a sinister person to pass on the sidewalk, when Mr. Kahn steps in front of me. "Jesca. What brings you here? This is my hotspot in town."

I am caught off guard by his presence. "Uh, hi there, Mr. Kahn."

I start fidgeting with the peeling corner of the menu.

Kahn smiles, and it immediately takes the edge off of my anxiety.

"Ezra, please. We're not on campus. And even if we were, I would feel more like myself if you called me Ezra." Ezra must have picked up on my awkward feelings about this and quickly adds, "Most of my students call me Ezra."

I blink, realizing I hadn't answered his original question.

"I was walking from the bookstore where I work and got, um, got hungry."

Ezra shifts his satchel to his other arm. "This is a great deli. They have the best Ruben sandwich in town. And their peach cobbler is amazing. Are you meeting someone? You keep looking at the door."

"What? Oh. No, just me."

Ezra hesitates a bit, and then asks, "Can I join you? I mean, unless you would like to be alone."

I feel kind of bad for him. He looks eager for company. And his being close to me at this moment in time is kind of comforting.

"No. I mean, no, I don't want to sit alone. Please join me. The company would be really nice." I crack a smile again to make him feel welcome. I eye the menu absently, still on edge from the earlier event.

Ezra looks at me with concern. "Everything all right?"

I'm pretending to focus on the menu. "Yep. Just fine."

Ezra returns to the menu, but I can sense his concern.

Sally, the waitress, comes back around to our table. "Are you two ready to order?"

All of a sudden, she sighs upon seeing Ezra. "Ezra! I didn't recognize you, my boy. I guess it's because you are always sitting alone." Sally winks at Ezra and pats his shoulder with her hot pink fingernails.

Sally looks over at me accusingly. "Oh. Is this one of your students?"

I'm mortified. I know what she is thinking.

I hope she is one of his students, little vixen. She can't be much older than twenty-one. She's gorgeous. Oh, Ezra. And here I thought you to be an honorable man. This young spring chicken is...

Ezra starts in immediately. "Now, Sally, this is Jesca. She is one of my students from the university. She seemed lonely over here, and I thought I would accompany her, being she is new to your deli. Plus, the only gal I sit with at this deli is you."

With that comment, Ezra winks at me.

Did he hear her, too?

Sally giggles and puts her hand on Ezra's shoulder again affectionately.

She is awfully touchy.

Ezra shoots me a look just as my thought sprung from my mind. I shrink back in my seat.

"Oh, Ezra Kahn. You are young enough to be my son. You are such a charmer!"

29

Sally looks over at me with soft eyes this time. I meet her eyes with mine. "Well, sweetheart, what would you like to eat?"

I look over at Ezra then back at Sally. "The Ruben and peach cobbler, please."

Sally turns to Ezra.

"Good selection. I'll have the same, Sally."

Sally takes the menus. "Coming right up, chickadees." Sally gives me a wink and a smile.

Ezra starts, "Sorry about that. It was mortifying for me as well."

I laugh it off, but wonder what a coincidence it is that his emotions are the same as mine.

"Jesca, you seem really tense. Is everything okay? Is the semester going all right?"

"The semester is fine. I just have…I have been…" I shake my head.

I can't lie to him. He is not interested in my drama.

I lean forward and lower my voice. "No. I am tired and nervous and fidgety and anxious, and it is pissing me off. I have been having these thoughts, dreams, whatever, about this dark thing, and now I'm feeling it, seeing it, sensing it, hearing it in real life, I think. Oh, and the fact that I'm seeing all of the unsavory behaviors of the public around me magnified. And I feel like I'm going nuts! I'm not sleeping. I'm hallucinating and seeing people's faces contorting to faces of monsters. And…before I saw you at the lake, I was hauling ass with crazy, ultraspeed through the woods trying to escape this, this thing!"

30

I stop and look up to halt the tears from falling down my cheeks. I take a deep breath to clear the lump that has developed in my throat. I close my eyes for a second and breathe. "I'm sorry. I don't know why I just unloaded all that shi…stuff on you. You don't need to hear all of that. I just…never mind."

Ezra looks at me with sympathy.

All of a sudden, I see a change in his facial expression. It turns from sympathy to something neutral and emotionless. "Is there anything I can do?"

Noticing the shift and a bit taken aback by it, I scoff. "I doubt it. Can we pretend like I didn't just unload the last week of my life on you and start over with something more academic?"

I know that will be a safe topic, void of emotion.

Ezra smiles with understanding. "Sure."

I shift my mood for Ezra's sake.

"Okay, so tell me what your latest graduate lectures have surfaced from the theories of the universe, time, space, etc."

Ezra's eyes light up. "Well, let's see. Have you heard of the Einstein-Rosen bridge theory?"

I look at him with a vague nod. I remember catching something on The Learning Channel about it once.

"Well, in short, this theory deals with quantum physics. The potential of negative mass being harnessed and used to fold space and allow a wormhole to open to other worlds. Worlds already in existence and worlds not yet discovered."

My face must have "skeptic" and "confused" written all over it, since Ezra gets out a pen and grabs a napkin.

"Imagine this napkin here has a point A and point B. A is one edge of the napkin representing world A. B is the other edge of the napkin, representing world B. If I fold this napkin in half, fold time and space with negative energy and mass, this will create a dense weight on world A. The weight will be so strong that it will pierce the fold to the other side of the napkin, hence connecting world A to world B. That is what will bridge the distance between the two worlds. It's called a traverse wormhole."

I am curious. "But isn't it impossible to find negative mass anywhere on the Earth. Even engineering it has posed barriers. How can you say that a hole could be created big enough to teleport a human, let alone an atom. Teleporting from world A to world B quickly, safely, and smoothly. How can that be?"

"That is where Einstein and Rosen left off, and years later, physicists expanded the theory into numerous ideas and possibilities to achieve negative mass."

I am eager to hear. "What are they?"

"Well, that is a conversation we can have another time." He ruffles his unruly hair and blows out his lower lip.

Moments later, Sally returns with our Ruben sandwiches and dishes of cobbler. I frown a bit, feeling cheated out of an intriguing conversation. I always loved it when Dad and Mom talked about theories. This conversation with Ezra brought back good memories.

Ezra smiles and takes a huge bite of his sandwich. He says through the bite of food in his mouth, "Your food is getting cold. Eat up."

Ezra is right; the Ruben is fantastic. The cobbler doesn't disappoint either. We eat in silence, enjoying our meal thoroughly.

My cell phone vibrates on the table. It is Mom texting to make sure I call when I get home.

Ezra eyes my phone curiously.

I respond, "It's just Mom checking on me. They have been worried about my stress, lack of sleep, and the invisible me over the past few weeks."

Ezra looks at me with sympathy again. "I can completely understand their concern. I mean, life can get pretty intense. Your parents want to be there for you, just in case you…if you need guidance. That is their purpose." He drops his gaze to his plate.

"Yeah, I know. With this, I just think…I think what I'm dealing with is beyond what they can handle. Even though talking to them relieves the stress for a short time, I keep falling back into this, this rut. It's like the twilight zone lately with these intense experiences. My dream state is bleeding into my reality." I blow out my lower lip and snicker. "Just lock me up and throw away the key." I scoop up the last bit of vanilla ice cream and peach chunks on my plate.

Ezra brushes his hand through his dark hair and sits back. "Jes, you aren't experiencing anything that I would consider you needing to be institutionalized. You need to practice some relaxation techniques, imagery, to help you. And you need to buy some chamomile tea and drink it before bed to relieve tension."

Did he just call me Jes?

33

I shift in my seat a bit. "So what is this camel tea that can help me sleep? Where do I get it? It sounds exotic."

Ezra laughs. "It is chamomile tea not camel tea, Jesca. And you buy it at the market in the tea and coffee section. Now, on to imagery for relaxation. Have you ever tried it?"

I think back because that word "imagery" sounds so familiar. "Yes, my parents showed me how to use it to calm my nerves before bed. I was very anxious the nights following nightmares, so we would practice together. You know, I haven't even considered it. Thanks, Ezra."

My phone vibrates again. It is Mom texting me.

Mom: We will be waiting up for your call, honey.

Translation, we will wait up all night and make you feel guilty if you don't call. So call us now!

I look up at Ezra. "Thank you so much for the company. I'm glad we ran into each other. Believe it or not, you made me feel much better about the things that have been going on in my life lately."

Ezra sighs. "Well, I'm glad I could help. Wish I could do more. And dinner is on me, so get out of here and call your parents already. This is the second text in under thirty minutes. They will not give up, believe me." Ezra smiles.

I reach into my pocket to find my spare cash. "At least let me leave the tip. I don't want to feel like I didn't contribute."

Before I can get my money out, Ezra puts his hand up. "Nonsense. My treat. Be safe on your walk home. I will see you around campus, all right?"

I sit back, thinking on that for a second. "Yes, I'm sure you will. Seems like I've gotten to see you more regularly lately."

Ezra gives me a look of awkwardness.

I quickly correct myself. "I mean it's not a bad thing. I really like your company."

God, I hope that didn't sound weird to him.

I genuinely feel comfortable in his presence, like you would with a dad or uncle.

Yep, that sounded weird.

I mean, he's practically a stranger. I only know him through classes at the university. It isn't like we've known each other forever.

Ezra's awkwardness clears, and his face lights up. "Not at all, Jesca. I feel the same way. It is nice to talk with you and listen to your dilemmas, no matter how mundane you may think they are. Life will definitely not get easier. But you will get better at it. Does that make sense?" He looks at me with hope in his eyes. A desperate type of hope for me to really understand what he is saying.

I really didn't. I hated to burst his bubble, though. "It makes sense. I hope I get better at life sooner than later. This part of my life is kind of sucking."

Ezra says, "It will, Jesca, sooner than you may realize."

We say our brief goodbyes, and I grab my bag and head out the door, walking quickly toward the market.

Chamomile tea.

I never knew the market had a whole section on teas for relaxing. I get the tea and head home. The walk home is quiet. Not many people wandering the streets at this hour. I decide to call Mom and Dad to keep me company while I walk.

"Hi, Mom. Yes. I'm fine. Just had to head to the market for some chamomile tea. Okay. I will add a touch of milk."

Gross.

"All right. Hey, is Dad around?"

Dad gets on the other line. "Remember the imagery we used to practice with you? I hope you have been using it. First breathe deeply in. Then out. In. Then out. Now, close your eyes and imagine your favorite peaceful place."

I interrupt, "I remember the rest, Dad, thanks. Uh, I've got to go. I just made it home. I'm going to try and get some rest."

Before hanging up, they both ask me to promise to call if things don't get better. I halfheartedly promise.

I sit in bed with my cup of tea in hand. Sipping and flipping through a magazine. I close the magazine and sit the almost empty cup of tea down.

Okay. My favorite place. The ocean. The sand is warm from the afternoon sun.

I continue to set the scene in my mind as I close my eyes. The sea breeze is blowing steadily, as I sit on the beach, facing the hypnotic waves. I begin synchronizing my breath with the consistent ebb and flow of the waves.

"Breathe in. Breathe out."

I become limp. Each muscle from the tip of my big toe to the tips of my ears feels numb. I slip into sleep, and I'm at peace for now.

Chapter 4

I'm running in the woods. I hear the low, dull humming vibration coming from all around me. I'm not sure if it is coming from inside of me or outside of me.

"Jesca. You are safe. I am with you."

The voice is so familiar, but I just can't pinpoint it. I don't feel vulnerable, though. I feel the breath of this guiding voice on my shoulder; I turn to find nothing but wooded terrain. I do not feel the sinister darkness that I have felt in the other nightmares and visions. All I feel is warmth, a shielding embrace. I'm running faster, out of the woods into the clearing near the lake. Just a few strides and I flash to treading on familiar concrete heading back to Mom and Dad's old house. The mist is seeping in on the streetlights.

I'm back in the nightmare.

The warm voice comes again. "You are ready to learn the truth."

Flashes of the nightmare come crashing into my mind. For a moment, my anxiety rises. Then I remember the voice and feel its presence. Calm and relief wash over me. My pace slows as I come to the front of my house. I hear the yelling from Dad and screaming from Mom.

The voice interrupts my brief anxiety spike.

"They are fine, Jes. You have done this many times. See the truth. This time look into the darkness. Face it, and fight it."

My heart is pounding frantically. I want to run for the door, but I hesitate.

The voice comes again. "Jesca. You are in control. This time see what you fear. See why this vision is tormenting you. Nothing can hurt you or your parents right now. Your physical body is at home in bed; you are sleeping."

My breath becomes more even as the voice of reason soothes me.

My hand reaches for the doorknob. In the blink of an eye, I'm in the entryway with the door shut behind me.

This speed thing is pretty convenient.

I start to sense the heavy, musky dark crawling around me on the wooden floors. I feel it creeping onto the walls. The darkness begins the pulling from within me. It is like a magnetic feeling drawing me toward it. I pull back against it slightly.

"Jesca, push back. You have done this before. You have this powerful force within you. Wield that power; use your energy."

I push back as I have always done in this nightmare. I am praying to God under my breath.

"Create a shield of white light around you, Jes. Imagine a white powerful light surrounding you."

I focus my entire mind on drawing this shield around myself. I feel this force of light reverberating off of me, molding around me. I sweep my arms to the right, then the left. The dark shifts away at my every move. I head up the stairs slowly.

It's working. The pull isn't as strong now. I am breaking its hold on me.

In an instant, I am in my parents' room.

The terrible scene. My mother convulsing on the ground, struggling to remain herself. My father praying over her, tears and anguish on his face.

"Encircle your parents within your shield. Surround the three of you."

I whisper, "I don't think I can." I feel like I am sinking against the door.

The voice is at my ear now and more forceful than before. "Yes, you can. You have the strength. Now do it!"

I shiver at the sternness of the voice and the lingering feeling of the warm breath on my ear. I close my eyes, walk toward my parents, and focus on spreading the energy from within myself around my mother, father, and I.

All of a sudden, the chaos becomes silent. My eyes shoot open, fearful that I have done something very wrong. My parents are looking at me, faces contorting into terrible, monster-like beings. Their eyes are jet black with no whites to them; they don't look human. Their expressions are full of hate, anger, and a yearning to attack me. I am their prey. My heart and stomach begin to twist and burn with fear. I feel my focus slipping.

The voice comes again. "Don't, Jes. Don't let your energy slip away. You need to save them. The dark entity is pulling at your fear. Take it on."

I lean in to my mom first. She looks like she is going to attack me, but I don't back down. I close my eyes.

Dear God, save me.

I feel the white-hot energy spill from me onto her. I grab hold of my father by his shoulder. I press them both against me. My shield is encircling us. I open my eyes and see my mom's face as her own.

Her eyes are filled with tears. She mouths to me, "You did it, Jes."

My father's holding on to my mother and me.

He says, "We're safe. You are safe, Jes."

The powerful shelter I created is still radiating from us. I can feel that the dark presence is still pushing against me.

Why is it not backing off?

The voice responds to my thought. "It is waiting for our weakness to show. Any sign of it and it will attack again. Your energy is still strong. Now imagine yourself turning up the energy slowly, building it inside you until you feel like you need to let it burst from within you."

I whisper, "How the heck do I do that?"

"Your mind, Jes, can do so much more than you are aware of. Just do as I am telling you. Your mind will know what to do."

I shut my eyes and feel heat bouncing from me to my parents.

That must be the energy radiating from me.

I breathe in, imagining I am taking in the energy around me from everything, the earth, all of it.

The voice confirms my actions. "Yes, that is it. You've got it."

I feel the air around me. It feels intensely electrified. The warmth of the energy is pure, electrifying energy. I open my eyes to see what effect it is having around me. The energy is a pulsating wave moving around us in time with my racing pulse. Every pulse I feel a wave of pure energy roll around me, my parents, and the darkness. My pulse quickens out of fear of what is happening.

I'm doing this?

The energy synchronizes with my pulse instantly. I quicken my pulse with determination now.

I'm doing this!

The energy waves roll over the room in a consistent hypnotic flow; quicker and quicker until there is a silent flash every second: flash, flash, flash. The darkness falls back as the strength of my energy drowns it. I don't move from my mother and father. We are holding on to each other. All I hear is our breathing.

Chapter 5

I wake breathing fiercely, and my heart feels like it is pounding out of my chest. I am unable to move, though.

Damn it, sleep paralysis.

I lie there and try to recollect the dream step by step before it slips away. I am physically exhausted even though everything happened in my sleep.

I quickly shift my thoughts to the voice, my guide. The voice was so strong and protective. I felt safe for the first time in there, remembering the words that this comforting voice gave to steer me through my nightmare to save my family.

My family!

I look at the clock, 5:30 a.m. I am able to move my arm very slowly if I concentrate on it. *The numbness is fading quicker this time.*

I pick up the phone even though it may be too early to call. I need to talk with them. The nightmare is still so fresh, so intense in my mind. I need my parents to separate the ethereal and reality that are intermingling in my mind.

Dad picks up on the first ring. "Jes. Is everything okay?"

I answer quickly, "Everything is fine. I just wanted to hear you. Are you guys okay?"

I hear Mom in the background. "Is she okay?"

I answer before Dad has the chance to relay her message. "Yes. It was the nightmare. This time it was different. I made it through. I can't really explain it all. But I saved you and Mom. I know this sounds crazy, but I think it was a test."

I hear Dad walking as he listens.

"Dad? What are you doing?"

Dad is speaking to someone else, not Mom. I hear muffled voices as if he is covering the receiver.

That makes me anxious.

"Dad? What is going on over there?"

Dad quickly uncovers the receiver. "Jes? Sorry, um, Mom was answering the door."

I wait for Dad to elaborate, but he doesn't. I'm irritated by his unwillingness to give me an explanation.

"At 5:30 in the morning? Who is it?"

Dad dodges my question. "Hey, do you think you could come over for breakfast before you head into work. We, uh, need to talk about something."

Dad quickly adds, "Everything is fine. We just need to talk about some decisions we are making."

Wearily, I agree. "Sure. I'll be over in a couple of hours. I go in to work at noon today."

There is a silence between us. In the background I hear rustling and other voices. I can't help but pry. "Are you sure everything is all right over there? Do you want me to come over now?"

"No. Just take your time, honey. We are just getting up and about. We have a friend that just popped in. So we have catching up to do before you get here. Take your time." He sounds more himself now, which brings relief to my flighty emotions. We say our goodbyes and hang up.

43

A friend at 5:30 in the morning?

I crawl back into bed. I can't help but wonder who the friend is and why he or she is over at the house so early in the morning.

I close my eyes, still tired from the active dream state I was in for most of the night. I felt so strong and in control of myself and everything around me. I think about the terrible nightmares and hallucinations. The people that I have encountered over the past week. How the dreams have become more intense, severe, spontaneous, and chaotic almost. Somehow, I was able to find stability and control in the chaos.

The guide's voice helped me.

The comforting feeling comes over me again. I feel empowered and confident for the first time in a long time. Maybe I will be able to sleep now that I have this energy within me to protect myself. I'm curious if this ability, this energy within, will bleed into my waking hours just as the visions and hallucinations have found their way into my reality.

The ability to hear even the smallest whisper found its way in. The speed I possessed in the woods found its way into my reality as well. The humming sound and vibration around my body, like a shield warning me of impending danger, has found its way in. What if I have unlocked a part of my mind that has been hibernating, until now.

What has awakened this inside of me?

I fade back into sleep.

Chapter 6

I head over to Mom and Dad's around 12:30. Mom and Dad got me a blue 2001 Mazda CRV on my 16th birthday. I remember being so excited. I had just gotten my license; that was a liberating moment. My car is reliable, practical, nothing fancy or sporty. I only use it to get to Mom and Dad's and when the weather is beyond wind and light drizzle.

I turn on the radio. The national news fills the car's speakers. I am partially listening just to have some background noise as I drive. The news is riddled with global warming theories, upcoming elections, living green eco tips, earthquakes, tsunamis, unstable weather conditions setting unprecedented records this decade. I turn it off before I make it to the turn onto my street. So much is happening lately. Or maybe I was just more aware of the events in the news.

Why the awareness now?

I arrive on my street, and immediately the anxiousness turns to a dull burning, starting in my head to my heart, then stomach. It is like that burning sensation you get when something scares you to the core.

Damn, I hate this feeling!

My dad says it is called the flight or fight reflex.

The vibration in my head, my body, starts. I take some deep breaths as I pull into our drive.

Chapter 7

The first shock—a sign in my yard reading FOR SALE in red letters. The second shock—a plaque of even bigger red letters lies diagonally over the previous red letters stating SOLD.

The third shock—the Wise Guys moving trucks being loaded by four burly men dressed in navy blue jumpsuits.

I feel vertigo and clammy. I storm from the car and run past two men moving a desk out of the house. I don't bother excusing myself as I push past and through the front door.

I holler, "Mom! Dad!"

Boxes line the entryway. No response, just silence.

I yell louder, "Mom!"

I begin to walk from room to room. As I pass, I see boxes and plastic wrap on furniture. I head to the master bedroom. Dad is removing the bedding, and two movers squeeze past me, with a lamp in one hand and a pillow in the other.

I look at my father, dumbfounded. "What is going on, Dad?"

His face is so serious.

Mom comes out of the closet. "Jes. Honey, I know this is a little shocking…"

Sarcastically, I respond, "Just a little, Mom. Where are you going? When did all of this happen?"

Dad and Mom both look at each other. Then they look at me. They approach me and lead me out of the master bedroom toward the living room.

Dad starts, "Jes, Mom and I decided a few months ago that we were ready for a simpler and smaller life. We are going to be empty nesters soon, with Bethany going away for college next year. We don't need this huge house anymore. We decided that Colorado is a great place for us to retire."

Dad looks at Mom for reassurance. Mom's smile is small. She continues, "So we put the house on the market, and a week later, we had a contract on it. The couple who bought the house are moving in next week and are expecting their second child in May. This house is perfect for them. We're sorry you had to find out like this, honey. We just haven't found the right time to tell you, with all the stress you have been dealing with."

Dad adds, "The lack of sleep, nightmares, school, job, all of your responsibilities...we didn't want to throw in something else for you to worry about."

The vertigo feeling subsides. But the humming is still audible.

Something is off, not right.

I try to force myself to believe. "It's fine. I just wish you guys would have warned me. I thought you were getting divorced or something worse like..."

Dad jumps in. "No, no, sweetheart. We are so happy to make this move. We think that we have been hovering too much over both you and Bethany lately."

Dad looks to Mom. Mom adds, "Dad and I need to find ourselves again. Enjoy each other and travel. We have found the cutest little condo that will allow us to travel and not have to worry about home maintenance."

Wow. I mean, I did want my mom and dad to back off a bit with the hovering, but I didn't think they would pick up and move.

"What about Bethany? What is she going to do for the rest of her senior year?"

Mom and Dad look at each other again.

"Bethany will be staying with the Sanford's, Serena's family, for the remainder of her senior year. She will spend the summer with us before attending college at the University of Colorado. She already applied and was accepted. She won't be staying with us; she will need her space to spread her wings."

I am floored. My parents are allowing my sister to stay with a family for the rest of her senior year? My parents had really changed. How long had I been out of the loop with them?

And Bethany, she didn't clue me in to any of this. Well, I hadn't taken the initiative of picking up the phone to call my little sister either, so I couldn't shift the blame entirely on her. She is probably pissed at me for being so distant. And I completely understand if she is.

"Sweetheart, why do you look so sad?"

"Well, I am a little sad about the house. I mean, we have lived here all of Bethany's and my life. I'm going to miss this place." I clear my throat. "But I'm so excited for you guys.

48

You are finally living a life for you two. You have dedicated your lives to raising Bethany and me. It is your time to live now."

I give a brief smile through my welled up eyes and quivering lips.

Dad and Mom both smile and hug me.

A gruff voice from behind us interrupts our moment. "Excuse me, Mr. and Mrs. Sera. We have all of the items that are going into storage. We will be back Tuesday of next week to move you folks to Boulder."

I take that moment to clear the air. I wipe my tears and force a laugh. "It's not like you'll be in another country. We'll see each other on holidays and stuff." This was true and pretty much how often we were seeing each other now. So it wouldn't be very different from life as we knew it.

Dad adds, "It seems like things are coming together for you, Jesca. Last night's breakthrough with your nightmare is a huge step."

"Yeah, things are coming together. I'm really doing much better."

Even though the slight humming is still present, I give my parents a smile to reassure them that I am fine.

My parents have a few loose ends to tie up with the movers, so I excuse myself. I tell them I will be stopping by on moving day to see them off. Then, realization kicks in. Everything is coming together for me at the exact same time my family is moving apart. How is that a good thing?

Something is off balance.

It's like that feeling you get before lightning strikes. My smile turns to a stiff lip of wonder at the coincidence as I walk away from my home.

Chapter 8

The cliché cowbell rings as I enter Benson's to start my shift.

Elisha looks up and sarcastically says, "Hey there. What's up with you?"

I reply sarcastically, "Well, hello to you, too." I roll my eyes, as does Elisha. We both have a brief scowl of annoyance that quickly fades into coy smiles. That's just how it is between us.

Elisha follows me to the back room, where I set down my things.

"Seriously, Jes, what's up? You look different."

I look up at Elisha and sigh. "Well, my parents have sold their house and are moving across the country."

Elisha's eyes bulge. "What? When did all of this happen? What about Bethany finishing high school? Is she going with them? God, I thought my parents would have been the first to do something like this. Why didn't they tell you?"

I shake my head in agreement. "I know, right!"

I sit down on the stool nearest her. "I'm happy for them, though."

"Really, or are you just saying that?"

I look at Elisha, waiting for her to elaborate. She catches on.

"I mean, don't you think that is bizarre. Your parents have been overly worried about you for the past two weeks. Rightfully so, I might add. They have been calling me and

51

calling me since you were dodging their phone calls and texts. Then, BAM! They decide to move hundreds of miles away from you, and they aren't one bit nervous or worried about you? This move is happening so quickly, so spur of the moment. Something else is going on here."

Now that Elisha has reiterated the quickness and coincidental nature of this move right around the time of all the chaos within the past two weeks, I am not taking my earlier episode of concern lightly.

Like clockwork, the six o'clock wave of customers heads into the store. It's not just a weekday thing. I've watched the natural flow of this behavior over the years. People are out to dinner and in town. They decide to stroll and window shop after dinner. They pop in and out of the stores, running into friends, colleagues, neighbors, associates here and there. There is always room on a nightstand for the latest bestseller or classic that was once read in high school or college. That is when they come into our store.

We are in the middle of the wave. I am making brief exchanges with the browsing customers. The vibration starts. It is very slight. Almost indistinguishable. Then the low humming begins. I try to refocus and remain busy with customer conversations. My heart starts to beat faster with nervousness, knowing that this is just the beginning of something that never ends well for me. I check out those that have made their selections, trying to remain busy and distracted from the giant elephant in the room.

7 p.m. rolls around, and the humming has intensified. The vibration in my body has turned into strong tremors. Then the

whispers start. The whispers are like swishing in my ears, creating brief dizziness. My heart feels like it is going to burst out of my chest. I feel like I am short circuiting.

I try to fight back by breathing slowly, closing my eyes periodically. The whispers subside briefly. Then they come back with intensity.

The whispers are coming from them, the people here.

I start having hot flashes and feel both nauseous and claustrophobic at the same time. Brightly lit spots start multiplying in my peripheral view and then move over my entire area of vision. Everything begins to spin.

I'm going to pass out.

I hear the cowbell from the front door ring. I turn toward the sound, but by this point, everything is dark. I can't see anything.

I feel like I am blind. People are talking. The humming becomes louder. The vibration is so strong my skin is tingling with pins and needles. I hear Elisha to my right whisper. "Hey, Jes, you don't look so good. You're white as a ghost."

I feel my body begin to shake.

Then nothing.

When I come to, I hear Elisha talking to someone.

"I don't know. One minute she was fine. The next, she was walking toward me, white-faced and tipsy. I thought you said her transition would not be so haphazard? Her mind and body will melt down if she keeps going like this, Ezra!"

Ezra?

Someone is pulling me up. I feel warm arms and smell a leather jacket. A cold hand runs over my forehead. I blink my eyes slowly. Elisha is standing in front of me, shooing the crowd away. "Okay, everyone. She's fine, just a low blood sugar attack. Crazy college students think they can live on one meal of ramen a day." She laughs a little to try to make light of the situation. "Please keep shopping, and I will ring you up. Our friend Jesca is going to get some real food and rest."

When I am able, I set myself upright and look at the one comforting me.

Ezra.

"Hi there, Jesca. Did anybody ever tell you that food is a necessity? Elisha says you haven't eaten today. Tsk, tsk."

Ezra helps me to my feet.

I look at him with frustrated eyes, but decide to play along. My voice doesn't hide my anger, though.

"Well, I planned to grab something small after we closed."

Elisha has her arms crossed over her chest like a protective mother hen.

"Closing time has come and gone for you, sweetheart. Your prof is going to get you some grub. Right, Mr. Kahn?"

"Yes, we're going to get some food right now."

The game that they are playing pisses me off. I grit my teeth. "Enough. I heard you while I was coming to. I know that you two know each other."

Ezra and Elisha look at each other with guilty eyes. A man interrupts from the checkout counter.

"Excuse me, Miss."

Elisha looks over her shoulder then back at me. She puts her arm on my shoulder. "Hey, text me when you get in, okay."

She gives me a sorrowful look filled with apologies. I nod and look away. I don't want to look at her right now. I might say something I will regret later.

Ezra leads me out of the bookstore. The crisp air hits me as soon as the door opens. It helps bring me out of the dizziness I am trying to overcome.

Ezra is on my heels. "That Elisha is a very good friend, Jes. I mean, she seems like she really is protective of you."

I start to walk more briskly from Benson's toward Margot's Deli. "She has been my best friend since we were in kindergarten. She knows everything about me...obviously."

I give Ezra a sharp look.

Ezra looks down at the concrete as we walk. He blows out his lower lip and messes his hair, making it more out of sorts than it already is.

I see I have ruffled his feathers and decide to push the issue. "What did I say? Oh, you didn't think I was naïve to the fact that Elisha obviously knows more than she has let on about me. I mean she has been your personal spy, right?"

I growl out of ultimate frustration. "Ahh!"

Ezra steps in front of me to stop my brisk walking.

"Here, let's get some food at Margot's. The Rueben is good, but the Club is phenomenal." Ezra takes hold of my shoulder and leads me into the deli.

Ezra orders for me. He makes sure that Sally packs them to go. I don't argue. I know that he wants to talk to me about what just happened back at the store, so I let this domineering attribute be for now.

We are walking out of the deli ten minutes later.

"Where are we going?"

Ezra walks briskly, holding the brown sack with our food and drinks. I try to keep up with his long strides.

Why is he not answering me?

I stop in the middle of the sidewalk. "Uh, hello? Where are we going?"

Still walking, Ezra answers me. "We are going to campus. We can eat there and discuss what I should have told you sooner."

I jog a bit to catch up. "Wait. What did you say?"

I feel the burning start in my throat and travel quickly to the pit of my stomach.

He stops, turns, and looks at me firmly. "We will discuss it when we get there."

With that, he turns and keeps walking. I follow him closely now. My heart is pounding, wondering what he is going to tell me as soon as we get to his office on campus.

Chapter 9

Ezra's office is substantial for a professor. It looks more along the lines of a dean's office. We sit at Ezra's desk opposite each other and eat in silence. I finish quickly, wanting to get on with what he has to say. I stand and clear my side of the desk as the cue to start the conversation. I dispose of my trash and browse the shelves in the office as Ezra eats. My interest settles on an ant farm.

I mumble sarcastically, "Friends of yours?"

I remember having one when I was eight or nine years old. I would sit for long episodes giving each of them names, personalities, and story lines. They each had a distinct job in the farm. Their purpose was dictated by survival. There were bad days with death or a trapped ant that needed saving. There were good days associated with the cooperation of the ants for the greater good, digging a new passageway to the unknown. I was always so excited for the ants when they cleared the new passage. I knew the big picture of this ant farm. However, I was still so proud of my ants' victories in their small world.

"They are fascinating little creatures, aren't they?" Ezra is standing a few feet from me. He walks back to his desk and clears his side. "They are creating their own world in there. Each has a purpose. Each has a significant part in the functionality and nature of their survival individually and cumulatively. Some make good choices and some make bad ones. The natural balance of good and bad reveals itself in everything at some point in time, doesn't it?"

I look at Ezra, now standing next to me peering into the little world he has given to these ants.

Ezra turns and walks around the room. "You know, we are much like those ants."

I respond with a hint of skepticism. "We are? How is that?"

Ezra turns and walks toward the wall of books on the other side of the room. "Remember our conversation the first time we ran into each other at Margot's?"

I nod. "Yes. You were talking about wormholes and how they are not impossible and completely plausible with the right amount of negative mass, like a black hole's event horizon."

Ezra eyes me with pride of my recollection. "Well, these little ants are in a pursuit just as many of us are. They want to cut out a new tunnel to something different, better, or greater. Sometimes they tunnel and find they have gone nowhere. Sometimes they tunnel, get trapped, and must be saved. Even more, sometimes there is mutiny against the one that is trapped and injured trying to tunnel. The others either save it or kill and eat it to keep their expanding world unpolluted, no barriers or blockages."

I let out a sound from within. "Ugh. That is disgusting."

Ezra says, "Yeah, but haven't we as humans done such abominating actions throughout history? Concentration camps. Elimination of the perceived weaker of the human race."

I nod and wave my hand. "Okay, point taken. The ant farm analogy is getting a little heavy, don't you think?"

There is silence for a few moments. Tension instantly becomes thick in the air. *Lightning striking at any moment.*

I can't wait any longer. I walk toward Ezra and stand in the middle of the room with my hands up. "Okay. So hit me with it. Let's discuss."

Ezra extends his hand for me to sit. "Have a seat."

Ezra sits in his oversized side chair. I sit on the love seat and lean forward in anticipation.

Ezra holds his folded hands over his lips for a few moments. Then he slowly lays both of his hands on either arm of the chair. His gaze is steady on me.

"As a child you were adopted by the Sera family. You have a younger sister, biological to the Sera's. Her name is Bethany. You were raised in the Christian faith. You were raised to respect the arts and sciences. Your best friend is Elisha Montgomery, who also works with you at Benson's Book Store. Since you were young, you have been having a reoccurring nightmare. One that has become more frequent and vivid in the recent weeks. You are also experiencing unexplainable abilities and advantages..."

I put my hand up to stop him. "Whoa! What? You mean the warped visions and the high-frequency hearing I have are abilities? How do you know about me? My life? My family?"

I feel so violated. I don't really know Ezra Kahn, other than he was my professor one semester and has been making regular appearances in my life lately. This man could be a stalker, for all I know. He has been following me around town, expressing growing interest in me. I feel the urge to leave quickly. I know that Ezra feels my urge as well.

Ezra puts his hand on his forehead and lets out a half laugh and half cough. "Jes, I'm not stalking you. I am old enough to be your father, for God's sake. Your parents and I…Well, let's just say we are very old friends." Ezra's face and tone instantly become serious again.

I'm silent, feeling sabotaged all of a sudden. First, my parents are leaving. Then I discover Elisha's espionage. Now Ezra knows my parents.

My voice quivers with anger. "Okay, you better start explaining your side of this story. I'm about five minutes from getting up and leaving! Enough on what you know about me! Who the hell are you, and how do you know my parents?" I feel my face getting hot and flushed.

Ezra starts, "I am Ezra Kahn, a guardian."

I wait. I deserve more than that. "Guardian of what? From what? For who? Me?"

Ezra leans forward in his chair. "You took my introduction to physics class. You remember my lengthy unit on quantum physics and time. World to world travel?"

I sit back into the love seat and cross my arms, giving off the vibe that this better be good, because I have no idea where he is going with this.

Ezra continues, "Substantial theories of plausible wormholes, other worlds, space travel. See, Einstein and Rosen's theory was the catalyst that inspired others to 'tunnel' further and pursue the possibilities of such theories."

Ezra points to the ant farm. "Just as our little friends, there, have been those that have failed to create tunnels, wormholes, because they didn't have the knowledge. But there was one who had the knowledge. He created a traverse wormhole that could sustain its opening long enough to allow humans to pass to other worlds and galaxies."

Arms still crossed, I probe where he is going with this. "Why isn't he sharing his creation, his knowledge?" I shake my head, trying to grasp for a clearer explanation. "What does this have to do with me?"

I get up, grab my bag, and turn to leave.

Ezra raises his voice in an effort to stop me. His sternness makes me turn to look at him. "It has everything to do with who you are, Jes. On this Earth there are those that have chosen pursuits without a care for humanity. And there are those with the purpose of guarding and protecting humanity from the careless. We are the guardians, your parents, me, and you."

Chapter 10

Ezra has my attention. I drop my bag at the door and head back to the sofa.

The look on my face must have told Ezra that I am still completely lost in this fantastical story that he has thought up.

Ezra shows his irritation. "Do you believe in Heaven and Hell?"

"Yes. Of course I do."

"What if I told you that I have a theory that Heaven and Hell are very real and could have been created during the metaphoric clap of God's hands creating the ripple called 'The Big Bang Theory'. That clap of His hands was enough mass to spawn multiple universes, galaxies, and worlds. Two of those spawned worlds could very well be Heaven and Hell."

He pauses to let me think on that for a minute.

"What if I also told you that I believe that Jesus was the first traveler between this world and Heaven as he ascended after his crucifixion. My theory is His death created enough negative matter to open a wormhole, allowing His ascension to join His Father in this other world, Heaven."

My chest feels heavy as I take in the fascinating visuals of possibilities coming from Ezra's theories. Still, in the back of my mind, I am wondering where this is all going. *What in the hell does world jumping, negative matter, and humanity's salvation have to do with me?*

Ezra leans forward in response to my thought. "I will tell you," he says and continues, telling me the story of Sebastian.

* * *

In the early 1940's, a physicist by the name of Sebastian Onoch became very interested in pursuing Einstein's research, especially the traverse wormhole theory he developed with Rosen. The potential of creating traverse wormholes to other areas of space-time through the Casmir Effect of creating antigravity, electromagnetic waves, and negative energy was his fascination. His career as a physicist for the US government was very mundane and uneventful, filled with pencil-pushing and routine standards expected of him on a daily basis. He lived for his passion of physics outside of his day job.

Sebastian lived here, in Georgia, with his wife, Dobria, and their two sons, Caleb and Balthazar. Caleb was the oldest son. He was very athletic, intelligent, a people pleaser, and kind hearted. Balthazar was also intelligent and precocious, but lacked the social intelligence and personality his brother had. Balthazar spent much of his time reading, researching, problem-solving, and studying. They were both very strong-willed children. And they shared one other common thread. They were both starved for Sebastian's attention, acceptance, and love.

One day Sebastian received a call late in the afternoon. It was the boys' school. The director said that Dobria did not make it in to pick up the boys and asked if he could come get them. Sebastian picked up the boys and headed home. The entire drive home, Sebastian was in a fog, wondering where Dobria could be. When they arrived home, there was still no sign of Dobria. The house looked undisturbed. Dishes from the morning breakfast were still in the sink. Sebastian paced the floor while the boys ate dinner.

After dark, a knock at the door stopped Sebastian's pacing. The boys had already prepared for bed. Sebastian rushed to the door. The boys rushed to the stairs in hopes of getting a glimpse of their mother, bright eyed and smiling with open arms.

Two state troopers were standing where Dobria should have been.

"Mr. Onoch?"

Sebastian cleared his throat. "Yes. I'm Mr. Onoch."

Sebastian knew something was wrong with the presence of the troopers at his front door.

The shorter trooper stepped forward and whispered, "Mr. Onoch, can you send your children to their rooms. We need to speak with you privately."

Sebastian put his head down. "Of course." He turned to his boys, who were peeking from the staircase. "Boys, please head up to your rooms. I will be up soon."

Balthazar started, "Dad, why can't we hear what has happened to Mom?"

Sebastian cut him short in a raised tone. "Balthazar, do not argue! Upstairs, please!" Sebastian stopped himself, realizing his tone. He resumed more calmly. "I will come up and explain everything to you after I have talked with the troopers."

Caleb held Balthazar's hand, and they both retreated to Caleb's room. Caleb and Balthazar sat on the bed, statuesque, waiting for their father.

Sebastian let the troopers into the living room, where they sat quickly.

Sebastian did not waste time. "Where is she? Where is my wife?"

The tall, lanky trooper responded, "Mr. Onoch, your wife was found not far from the lake this afternoon around 2 p.m. She was…"

Sebastian stopped them with his hand. "No! My wife does not go near the lake, let alone the woods, without me. You must have made a mistake. She probably has…" Tears began to well up in his eyes as his quivering voice was working hard to convince them and himself that Dobria was fine.

The short trooper interrupted, "Mr. Onoch, we know it is her. It appears she was taken into the woods and left to pass. Her identification was found not far from…the body. It looked like there had been a struggle at the abandoned car."

The troopers sat in silence as Sebastian took it all in. The tall trooper added in a quieter, softer tone, "Identification is not necessary. We already have the positive ID."

Sebastian cleared his throat and wiped his face abruptly, like he was wiping away the memory of what he just heard.

Stoically, Sebastian dismissed the troopers. "Thank you, officers. If you could please leave me with my children now."

The troopers nodded and let themselves out. Sebastian stood at the foot of the stairs for a moment, looking up toward the bedroom door that held the only remaining union of himself and Dobria. He was contemplating how to tell his boys what has happened.

The month that followed was what would be expected of a family thrown into a tragic loss. Sebastian and the boys walked around the house in a fog, boxing items and labeling them for storage, goodwill, or Colorado. It was like their lives had been confined to a bowl; their lives had the momentum of Jell-O. Sebastian knew the moment he told the boys that nothing would ever be the same again. The life they had created here was centered on Dobria. They needed to move and create another life.

Chapter 11

It took a while. Two years had passed before the Onochs found normalcy in Colorado Springs, Colorado. Dobria's case became cold and was never completely brought to closure for the family. Sebastian and the boys had set up home on an estate near the first set of mountains. The Onoch Estate was more of a compound. Sebastian hired a full staff, consisting of a full-time nanny, one full-time butler, two gardeners, and tutors for the boys. Sebastian resumed his career as a physicist for the government. The position paid very well even though the work continued to be mundane and uneventful once again. The benefit was that it left Sebastian time to obsess over his passion for quantum physics, astral physics, and the cosmos.

Caleb and Balthazar had everything they could possibly need. They did not have the one thing they wanted most, though, their father's love. Sebastian had filled his open wound of loss for his beloved wife with his obsession. It left his boys always at arm's length. Sebastian muted his painful feelings by filling all of his spare time with the possibilities of new discoveries in the cosmos.

While muting these painful feelings, he also muted his compassion and love for his family. Sebastian was fascinated with Einstein's research on wormholes and the possibilities of multiple worlds being accessible through such portals. Einstein spent years, until his death, researching the possibility that the Bermuda Triangle was a naturally occurring wormhole. The continued and growing obsession of Sebastian's began to spawn grander concepts and theories. After work, Sebastian would come home, greet the boys, make small talk, and then retreat to his office for continued research on his passion. Sebastian even had a small detached office commissioned so that his experimentation could be performed without the concern of privacy being breached.

The office was built with untraditional materials for the time. Steel-studded walls covered with sheetrock and masonry brickwork was the foundation of his experimental lab. Bulletproof doors and shatterproof windows, these were materials that were not widely known in construction yet. To avoid any breach of the construction of the office, Sebastian acted as foreman and contractor on the project. Sebastian had avenues through which he could get the materials needed. The crew hired was screened personally by Sebastian. Every crew member was well accounted for on the job and in society. Sebastian knew everything about those that he hired.

Sebastian was careful with his work, his journals. He also was very careful to keep the boys clear of this part of his life.

Years passed. Sebastian was researching, exploring, and engineering experiments. Then finally, it happened. Sebastian had a breakthrough. He discovered a way to manipulate negative mass into an object, making the Casmir Effect a sustainable reality. He created the first traverse wormhole through the gravitational waves of negative matter.

* * *

I stop Ezra. "Wait a minute. When was this? 1960's or something?"

Ezra replies, "Actually, it was 1965. While the world of physics was still a newborn, Sebastian was already years ahead of his time creating wormholes. It is mind boggling, I know."

I try to collect my thoughts. "So, Sebastian kept all of this a big secret. He didn't want to spread his theories to the physics world? Why didn't Sebastian want to bring light to his findings and spread the knowledge to the public? He could have advanced the research of space by decades! Kip Thorne, Stephen Hawking. Sebastian could have been collaborating with them to create great advances in physics!"

Ezra shakes his head. "Yes. He could have. But at what cost? For the greater good of humankind? To explore beyond the edge of our observable universe? To find new life? To find different lives? Aliens? Worlds? How many? Infinite? Jesca, where do you think the line should be drawn for playing God?"

I have no retort. I am intrigued and visibly eager to hear more from Ezra. "So what happened after his discovery? What was this object that Sebastian used to create and harness the negative energy waves to create, let alone, hold open the wormholes?"

Ezra sits back and smiles. "Ah, spoken like a protégé physicist."

I roll my eyes at his comment.

Ezra continues Sebastian's story.

* * *

Sebastian coveted his experiments, failures, and successes. Keeping close notes on all the occurrences. He became more reclusive and secretive with his findings. He designed, engineered, and experimented on himself so that his findings remained his own. Sebastian realized that copper was the key to conductivity of electromagnetism.

We have copper in our bodies, but it isn't enough. He worked to find the link to create electromagnetic radiation with the combination of copper inside and outside of the body through a mechanism, a conduit. This conduit would possess electromagnetic propulsion capabilities with electrons and protons moving at faster than the speed of light to create antigravity. The object as well as the individual conductor would both possess the antigravity needed to create the opening of a wormhole.

This object had to be very portable, which is what took the most time. He created the object, the Copula. The Copula is the size of a half dollar. The exterior is made of shatterproof material. The interior of the Copula has a very tedious design.

The workings inside resembled that of a clock; a copper disc shaped in a concave nature with a stabilized motor smaller than that of a black bean. Atop that is a spinning gear axis with two arms or rods with paddle-like discs the size of a lentil off-shooting the rods. The motion of the arms of the Copula are propelled by electric current from an external force. Once propulsion begins, the arms form a figure-eight motion. This energy synthesizes with the energy within the body due to the copper conductivity between the Copula and that within the body. The exterior force and interior force synchronize and become one large object of antigravity. The catch—synthesis can only happen with the body when it has an external charge. It needs a jump start.

* * *

Ezra is quiet for a moment.

I am on edge. "What is the jump start?"

"An electric shock. A small contained surge of electric current to set the Copula into motion."

I sit back, creating a visual of how the scene of this surge would play out in reality.

Ezra sighs, knowing my mind was putting this together. "Beyond that, Sebastian had to will his body to release the energy within himself needed to synthesize with the Copula. This took months and months of study and practice. At that time in history, metaphysics was a practice in Eastern philosophy, so he had to travel to Asia to access a healer that could teach him how to harness his inner energy. He persuaded the coach to travel back to the United States and remain with him as an employee of his estate until their training was complete. The healer was honored and immediately took the offer. The healer and Sebastian trained daily to heal him of the sorrow of his wife's passing and to combat any physical ailments in his body. Sebastian also trained to gain metaphysical abilities like astral projection and extrasensory projection. All of this training was superficial in the eyes of those around Sebastian. The true intent of the training was for his experimentation with the Copula.

"The object was initially worn by Sebastian in the first generation of experimentation. He created the object to be the size of a half dollar. As the Copula draws energy from the human that wears it and the human increases the release of his inner energy, it creates faster than light propulsion. The speed of the propulsion creates antigravity. In turn, negative matter is formed. That antigravity pierces a whole through this world creating an opening to another for travel, a wormhole."

My mind is whirling. "He harnessed negative matter? My God."

I can't wrap my mind around how long ago Sebastian had pioneered this scientific miracle and how so many have tried and failed since then.

"Okay, so he has one opening. How can it remain open without harming him as he passes through?"

Ezra touches his chest. "The copper naturally within our body combined with our life force being expelled. We all have internal energy. That energy force within us is the other half of the equation of keeping the wormhole from pinching closed. We are the necessary ingredient to pass from point A to point B and pierce the fold in space."

I ask, "And where was that? He didn't know where he would end up?"

"Leap of faith. Sebastian believed wherever he ended up, his point B, would reveal his greater purpose. And the point B world was not like our world."

Chapter 12

Sebastian took every precaution to make sure he was well suited for any conditions that he may encounter; extreme environments containing high levels of sulfur among other elements. Gases that our earthly bodies were not accustomed to. Sebastian had planned his travel gear. He needed to make sure his gear was portable. Expedition gear would be a good comparison.

Among the gear were two tanks of oxygen harnessed and attached to his fiberglass and steel protected torso and to the helmet that channeled the oxygen through the interior. Plastic metal materials made up the helmet for the unimaginable conditions that could present themselves in space. Yes, Sebastian was in a space suit, just as if he was ready to board a shuttle for launch. He would be able to breathe clean oxygen for approximately four to six Earth hours. He was aware that being prepared may not matter; he may never need those hours. He may never get to point B alive, and when he got there, he may never be able to come back, suffering a terrible death after the oxygen ran out. The leap of faith was great.

Getting his hands on this gear was a small, undetectable matter of pencil pushing that Sebastian performed regularly, due to his rank and status as an experimental physicist. Test tubes for collection of specimens, camera, composition journal and writing materials. Of course, the Copula, which he wore securely around his neck. Prior to his travel, Sebastian made the arrangements necessary for his boys, his estate, just in case he did not return.

The first time he traveled, he made sure it was in the middle of the night. His detached office on the estate was well suited for withstanding the possible noise and energy that could be emitted from this event.

Sebastian connected the defibrillator to the Copula. Within seconds of the electric charge, the Copula was in motion and Sebastian was experiencing the pull from within. Once the wormhole was open, it felt like every ounce of his being was on pins and needles. It also felt like Sebastian was being pulled. Kind of like the feeling you get when you wake from a good night's sleep and you stretch to wake the partially atrophied muscles and tendons.

The travel time was quick, a few blinks of the eye. Piercing point A was a pull. Entry to point B was like a rebound effect. The entrance was such a powerful rebound, Sebastian blacked out upon landing in the world.

He didn't know how long he had been out. The sound of wind whistling through a tunnel woke him. It might have been a reflection of traveling through the wormhole; he wasn't sure, though. He looked around for the after burn of the wormhole, but there was nothing. The environment was only dust and gravel. The atmosphere's air appeared dense and heavy. Sebastian looked up to find a source of light. A sun and moon were almost invisible in the atmosphere.

He had charted constellations for decades. He was familiar with the charted galaxies and moons that existed in our universe. His eyes traveled the atmosphere above, looking for any familiar constellations. The space above was whirling with a yellow-tinged gas just thick enough to hide any noticeable design of stars.

The temperature readings, well below freezing, would not support life on this hard, barren, tundra-like terrain.

* * *

I interrupt, "So it was a lifeless planet. No alien life?"

Ezra questions me. "Aliens? What makes an alien? Just that if the traveler is the foreign being? We are all alien in that respect."

I nod once, acknowledging his reasoning. "Point taken. So, there was no sign of life?"

"Like I said, on the surface there was no sign of life. Subterranean life existed, though. Sebastian found burrows an hour into his expedition.

"The burrows were wide enough for a grown man to climb down. In the burrows, about fifty yards below the hard ground, there were open caves and caverns with springs. Sebastian steered clear of contact with the springs, unsure of the liquid's composition and elements. Among the edges of these springs, Sebastian found plant life and fungal spores. They were exotic in appearance, a deep shade of purple and luminescent blue. Life existed in the springs as well. Below the crystal clear surface were iridescent green fishlike organisms."

Ezra looks at me. "Can you imagine being somewhere that you want to learn so much about, but your time is limited? Sebastian was running out of time quickly. His oxygen level in his suit was already low, reading forty-five minutes remaining.

"Sebastian needed to move quickly. He collected specimens and documented his findings. Sebastian also brought supplies to construct a grander scale Copula to attach to this world.

"The Copula would be the tag, a homing device, for this world for future travel. The Copula around his neck and the Copula on this world would always be linked, a union with their own unique coding. All that remained for this expedition was the naming of this world. He looked at his left hand. Still encircling his ring finger was the gold band signifying his wife and his union. He named the world Dobria."

Chapter 13

I take a sip of my diet Dr. Pepper. "Did he get back?"

"Yes. But he could not wait for his return to Dobria. After the first expedition, Sebastian spent days researching where in this universe he could have ended up. How far was he from our galaxy? What galaxy was he in?

"After analyzing the crystal-clear liquid the organisms in Dobria were swimming in, which turned out to be H20, Sebastian knew it had to be a world with earthlike qualities and elements. This only made him want to travel to Dobria again to discover other similarities.

"His return travels to Dobria were more methodical and calculated. With the programming of the Copula, he was able to determine the coordinates of the galaxy that contained Dobria, the Andromeda galaxy. He had programmed a link between the Copula in Dobria and the Copula he wore so that the wormhole would be controlled for consistent travel. Sebastian spent days at a time in the new world. Days in Dobria were weeks on Earth; properties of time differed so radically. Consequently, Sebastian's body began to adapt to the alteration of time. The more frequently he traveled to Dobria, the longer the stays, the less he would age. Other alterations began to take hold. Along with the new environment he was studying and the multiple organisms that were being discovered on Dobria, Sebastian was experiencing physical and metaphysical alterations within himself."

I interrupt with a snicker. "Like what? Could he levitate and read minds?"

Ezra chuckles. "Yes, among other capabilities."

My sly smile turns stiff quickly, remembering my own recently acquired capabilities.

Ezra continues, "His physical strength increased as well. This prompted Sebastian to start testing his blood after every travel to and from Dobria. The level of copper in his blood was increasing after every trip. The rising level was not toxic. It did explain the advantageous capabilities that Sebastian was gaining as the level of copper increased within his body."

For a moment, I consider my experiences of speed and strength while running in the woods last week.

Why would my levels be heightened, though?

I put that thought in the far corner of my mind. I don't know if I did it out of pure denial or overwhelming fear.

I question Ezra, "How was he getting increased levels of copper in his bloodstream?"

Ezra replies, "Sebastian discovered that the more connected his body became to the Copula, the more smooth the entrance and exit from the wormhole. He decided that a second generation Copula needed to be engineered as an implant. A battery would be inaccessible and unnecessary upon implantation."

Ezra blows out his lower lip and tousles his hair; a small idiosyncrasy that clued me in that his stress level was increasing.

Ezra knows my question before I ask.

How would he use the defibrillator to start the Copula then?

I suck in my breath, realizing what Sebastian was doing.

Oh!

"He electrocuted himself!"

Ezra leans forward in his seat. "Well, yes and no. Think of the second generation Copula in terms of a modern-day pacemaker that needs to be charged at times. All of his vitals were monitored as a safety precaution. The charge initiated the electromagnetic propulsion in the Copula. His body only reacted to the Copula, not the charge. The Copula's release and synthesis with Sebastian's body was much greater with this generation. It also increased the Copula's release of copper residue into Sebastian's body after each travel, thus the increase of copper within him."

Ezra leans back in his seat. "Sebastian knew he needed more minds to filter through the immense amount of discoveries he had encountered up to this point. He handpicked close and trusted colleagues and associates he had known for years to begin traveling with him. These colleagues needed to have respect for the necessary balance of science, humanity, spirituality and nature.

"Sebastian wanted a variety of associates to explore, discover, analyze, and develop Dobria. The list included biologists, botanists, geologists, and scientific engineers just to name a few of the credentials. He also made sure the people he had chosen were agreeable to the inevitable plan, which was to eventually live, develop, and fully experience the superior capabilities and advantages that came with living there. Only those that agreed to the plan were implanted with the Copula."

Ezra pauses and looks at me for a long time, silently.

I become self-conscious. "What?"

He continues, "Nothing. There was one day, one event, which changed everything. That very moment in time shifted everything for the Onoch family and the cosmos.

"Caleb and Balthazar were in London attending University. Balthazar decided to come home for a surprise visit during fall session break. Balthazar had followed in his father's footsteps. He had received accolades for his past and current dissertations as a budding physicist. He had just been awarded an internship with NASA in the States and was eager to tell his father. Balthazar was always seeking acceptance through Sebastian's eyes, which could sometimes be perceived as an aggressive and competitive nature."

Chapter 14

Balthazar entered the Onoch Estate.

"Hello? Miss Sasha? Mr. Edmond?"

He walked into the lounge.

"Father, are you here?"

Balthazar slowly approached the lab outside of the main house. Even though this area was off limits to Balthazar as a child, he was an adult now. Part of Balthazar was eager to tell his father of his success. Part of him was eager to see what had been hidden behind this fortress for years and years. Those childish thoughts quickly dissipated as he knocked on the heavy, metal door. The door shifted under his knock. He gave it a shove, and it opened a hair.

Balthazar pushed the door open wider.

"Hello?"

Sterile counters, sterile walls, and minimal furnishings. Beakers, metals, and maximum welding machinery. Computers generating data, downloading and auto-saving like an electronic record keeper. And the smell of a hot, metallic residue.

Balthazar couldn't resist taking a look at some of the contents of closed cabinets and drawers. Balthazar accidentally bumped the keyboard as he sat in the chair. The desktop on the computer was still active. Balthazar looked around suspiciously for signs of his father.

Smell of hot metal?

Leaving open access to his data?

What had his father just finished doing?

Balthazar noticed a file folder on the desktop that was open. The file within the folder that stood out was labeled "Onoch's Blueprint of Travel".

Balthazar rolled his eyes, recalling his dad's eccentric ways.

Balthazar clicked on the file, expecting to see his father's recorded data of his travels over the years. Balthazar anticipated seeing some sort of excel spreadsheet.

Balthazar stopped breathing for a second and sat back. It was not a spreadsheet at all.

The folder revealed all of Sebastian's notes, theories, engineering specifications, experimentation notes, and results of successful travel through wormholes. Balthazar remembered the times his father was too busy in his lab researching, experimenting, and theorizing.

"Oh my God. So this is what encompassed your life for all these years, you bastard."

Balthazar leaned into the screen and read.

Chapter 15

Ezra takes a sip of his drink and shifts in his seat. "It's not what you think. Sebastian was not traveling to Dobria while Balthazar was picking through his lab. He was attending a debriefing on current and future space travel missions at his department. His appearances at the department were becoming fewer and fewer.

"Debriefings were one of the few appearances that Sebastian had to be at in order to alleviate any suspicions about his frequent absence and insistence of working from home."

Ezra leans back and continues.

As he pulled into the estate, Sebastian noticed the parked car upon the drive at the main house. He quickly parked and walked to the front entry. He moved from the entry to the formal living room.

"Hello?"

Sebastian continued to walk through the downstairs rooms, looking for any sign of an intrusion. He stopped and closed his eyes. A moment later, he sensed Balthazar's presence and moved haphazardly to his office.

Balthazar was still sitting in front of the desktop when Sebastian entered.

Sebastian paused at the doorway and spoke calmly. "What are you doing here, son?" Uncharacteristically calm for someone who had just had his life's work violated.

Balthazar turned in the chair to face his father. Balthazar held a small, black floppy disk in his hand that he quickly slipped into his shirt pocket.

"Father. You have been busy over the years with all of your travels. Tell me, what have you found out there?" Balthazar's smile was filled with both quandary and envy.

Sebastian dropped his head in disappointment. "This is not for you, Balthazar."

Balthazar interrupted, "For years I have followed in your footsteps, desperately wanting to be your protégé. You know of all my honors as a budding physicist. I know you are aware of my accolades even if you have never shown acknowledgement of them."

Sebastian stepped through the door and shut it tightly behind him. "I do know. You are truly growing to be a great physicist."

Balthazar stood. "I was coming to tell you about my most recent internship. NASA wants me to assist the aeronautical physicists on future launches for a year."

Sebastian showed genuine astonishment. "Son, that is wonderful news!"

Balthazar said, "You know what would be wonderful news? To hear my father tell me that I am worthy enough to become his protégé, his right hand."

The two silently stared at each other. Sebastian knew what Balthazar had discovered.

Balthazar gave way. "I want to be a part of this, Dad. I know what you have been pursuing. You have succeeded where so many have failed or not even fathomed attempting, for that matter. You have traveled to another galaxy, for God's sake. I want in."

Sebastian rubbed his head. "Balthazar, this is not for you."

Balthazar was seething. "Oh. And you are so sure of this?"

"You are not ready to be a part of this. You are young and impressionable. There is an imbalance you can create in our world by opening paths haphazardly to other worlds. I was naïve when this began. Now, I wish I could take back what I have put into motion. It is not too late to stop what imbalance can perpetuate from here. I'm ending all of it."

Balthazar moved to the exit. "I lack the knowledge? All I have is knowledge. Not love. Not nurturing. Not you." Balthazar reached into his pocket and pulled out the floppy disk. "Dad. Knowledge. That is my power."

Sebastian looked at Balthazar with sorrow in his eyes. "Don't do this, son. Don't start something you know nothing about."

"Like the way you put 'something' into motion years ago. Taking your children to another city far from what they knew. Having them raised by the nanny and butler. Depriving them of your love? What about that delicate balance?"

Sebastian could not respond. It was true, he had failed in that realm of his life.

Balthazar pushed past his father. Sebastian could only focus on what would become of the knowledge that his son just acquired from his lab.

I stop Ezra. "What a jerk of a kid. Sebastian did all that he could with his family's situation. Yeah, he was a little obsessive and eccentric. So what? He was brilliant."

Ezra carries on, "Balthazar fled back to London. He delved into Sebastian's research, riding on his coattails. He began building his own design and performing experimentation with the Copula blueprint. The programming of the coordinates of the Andromeda galaxy was a bit tricky, but not impossible for Balthazar."

I interrupt, "Well, what about the implant? Why didn't Balthazar use the second generation Copula?"

Ezra smiles coyly. "Sebastian had not included the second generation Copula design in the original file. Sebastian never left all his eggs in one basket."

Ezra and I exchange a brief smile.

I whisper, "Good for you, Sebastian."

"Within months, Balthazar is traveling."

"Did he travel to Dobria?"

Ezra answers me in a matter-of-fact tone. "He can't!"

"Why?"

"Remember, every Copula is coded and paired. Sebastian had put the coordinates of the Andromeda galaxy into the file Balthazar took. Sebastian had programmed his implanted Copula to synchronize with the homing device in the world he was traveling to, kind of like a cosmic string linking point A to point B. Balthazar could not access that information. It was only coded on the Copula in Sebastian."

I smile and whisper again, "Two points for Sebastian."

My mind begins to wonder. "So why would he need programming for a specific planet? It would only be necessary if he was attempting to have multiple codes, locations. I mean, he is only traveling to Dobria, right?"

I silently fear his answer as I look into Ezra's eyes. Ezra pauses. "No. He is not."

Chapter 16

I sigh out of mental exhaustion and reach for the rubber band around my wrist to tie my hair into a bun. My hands work quickly. "All right, this is getting heavy."

Ezra folds his hand together and leans his forearms on his knees. "Well, it gets heavier. Balthazar has found a world in the Andromeda galaxy. Balthazar saw the need for the stationary disc at point B just as Sebastian had. He also saw the need for other colleagues to be a part of the discoveries in this new world. This is where Balthazar's lack of judgment and respect reared its ugly head. Balthazar lacked caution and respect for the nature of things. His team was a hodgepodge and rough around the edges group. Balthazar's assortment of colleagues did not contain the strong morality of Sebastian's team. Balthazar had inhabited a world quite different from Sebastian's as well.

"Sonde was a sulfuric, volcanic environment. The surface was rocky with tall stalagmites emanating gases with high concentrations of acidity. The bubbling, liquid solvent that quick, eel-like life forms were darting through was infused with low levels of ammonia. But ammonia still. The liquid was murky and iridescent, purple swirls of chemical scattered over the surface. On the surface, this planet appeared uninhabitable by human life. Sulfur levels were significantly dominant in the sense that Balthazar and his team detected methane and ethane gases in the environment. Balthazar named the planet on the first visit, Sonde.

"Just as Sebastian had, Balthazar found signs of subterranean life.

"Balthazar encountered beings after his second expedition. By that point, he had already commissioned an astrobiologist, astrophysicist, and another physicist with whom he had a romantic involvement."

I snicker. "Is this the part where you tell me the aliens…I mean beings, had three eyes, green skin, and spoke in an unrecognizable tongue?"

Ezra looks at me and says, with a snicker of sarcasm, "No. They barely resembled humans."

I question him, "Barely resembled humans? How can you barely resemble something?"

Ezra looks more seriously at me. "They were able to shift into beings that would appear less threatening for the 'visitors'.

"The first time Balthazar wrote of his encounter with a being that had not yet shifted…"

Ezra trails off. He blinks a few times and rubs his hand over his mouth and chin.

"The inhabitants were more demon-like in features. Sunken eyes that were blacker than deep space. Protruding forehead and chin. A gray coloration to their skin. And they were much larger than us in height and girth."

I watch him as he explains the details slowly to me.

I ask before I realize what I am saying, "Have you seen one?"

Ezra stops and looks at me. "Yes. And so have you."

I feel burning in the pit of my stomach, spreading to my brain. "What?"

Ezra says, "Let me correct myself. You have experienced the essence of a Sondian in your nightmares."

I thought back over the past few weeks. Then, a specific event pops into my mind.

The kid that bumped into me on campus at the crosswalk?

Ezra responds without missing a beat. "Yes. That is why I had to get you and your parents out of there. They had made contact with you."

Ezra continues, "They are more advanced than us. Sonde is hundreds of thousands of years older than Earth. However, Dobria is just a baby in comparison to both Earth and Sonde. They are both in the same galaxy, Andromeda, but are very different. The inhabitants' adaptation to Sonde and its environment have spurred them to develop advancements much greater than ours.

"Speech was not necessary. They were able to share thoughts like a natural flow of speech. Balthazar was enamored by the transcendental concepts these beings possessed. He and his team saw these adaptations to the environment and language as gems to take back to our world, Earth. That is why Balthazar needed to have the stationary disc. He had plans that were beyond anything Sebastian would ever consider."

My mouth is dry. I take a sip of my drink. "What did Balthazar's team want to do?"

Ezra stands. "Now we are getting close to your purpose, Jesca.

"Balthazar's team grew over the years, mere months in Sonde time. Time there moved similarly to Dobria's. Cosmologists, astrophysicists, environmentalists, medical staff—Balthazar's team encompassed about forty associates initially. All of the team members were young and eager to be a part of this historical endeavor. The collateral damage that could result was a distant fear that was overlooked by the amazing benefits they perceived for Earth."

I ask, "Collateral damage?"

"Team members believed that they could create a cosmic link between Earth and Sonde indefinitely, allowing constant passage between the worlds. It was common in the 90's for theoretical physicists to consider our universe to be expanding at an accelerated rate. Both Sebastian and Balthazar were neck and neck on their findings and research at this point. Sebastian was trying to halt what he had put into motion with Dobria and now with Sonde. Balthazar was pursuing his obsession with creating an indefinite cosmic link between two worlds. As both worked in two different directions, pulling against each other, another theory was uncovered. Because of Sebastian's and Balthazar's discovery of travel to another galaxy, and Balthazar's obsession with creating a constant cosmic link, something never considered before had been put into motion: a collision of two galaxies."

I add, "A collision? Many scientists believe that type of collision could be destructive to either or both galaxies." I quickly stop and correct myself. "Well, that is so far off in the future. Billions of years, right?"

Ezra sighs. It is painful for me to hear that sigh. Ezra looks at me.

"Jesca. It is upon us."

My nervousness intensifies.

Ezra walks to the window and stretches his arms above his head. "Remember Caleb Onoch? Sebastian's eldest son? He ran with many of the same friends that Balthazar did back in London through university activities. Caleb had been seeing less and less of his brother and his growing group of rogue scientists. Caleb caught on to Balthazar's periodic disappearing act that resembled his father's from years before.

"Well, out of concern for his brother, Caleb called on his father. Caleb told Sebastian about Balthazar and his team's traveling, discovering life forms in uninhabitable atmospheric conditions. Sebastian played along, knowing that Caleb would unknowingly talk with Balthazar about his and Sebastian conversations. Sebastian pretended to be aloof about the outrageous rumors that Caleb had heard about his brother behind closed doors. Sebastian reassured Caleb that Balthazar would never be a part of such an endeavor. That he was smarter than that.

"Sebastian knew that this conversation would only hold Caleb at bay for so long, though.

"Sebastian immediately put two trusted cohorts on a mission to pose as scientists interested in joining Balthazar's team in London. Within days, Sebastian's two associates confirmed the rumors. Sebastian knew that Balthazar's team would speed the universe's imbalance by attempting to create a permanent wormhole between Earth and Sonde. Two worlds open to each other, allowing passage for other beings to mingle in our world and vice versa. It is not like leaving borders to countries unguarded and open. We are talking about other species with different physiological make-ups and physical appearances through adaptation to their atmosphere."

Ezra pauses, realizing he is getting too deep for me again. "Okay. Sebastian sends in infiltrators. Ariel and Alice Sera."

"My adopted grandparents?"

Ezra nods his head, confirming my words. "And they quickly became accepted onto Balthazar's team due to their strong background as astrophysicists. They were granted passage onto Sonde. It took weeks for Ariel and Alice to get the level of trust needed to complete their mission.

"They were to disassemble the stationary disc on Sonde and destroy it along with the station and lab that housed all of Balthazar's team's work. They were then to initiate their Copulas and link directly from Sonde to Earth after the link from Earth to Sonde had been severed. When they succeeded in their mission, Balthazar was incapacitated and unable to recreate and access the copper disc materials. And unable to return to Earth."

I am on edge.

Ezra says, "But Balthazar is his father's son. He and his team rebuilt what was destroyed quickly. The superior Sondians found it to be advantageous to generously provide materials comparable to the ones Balthazar blueprinted for the disc."

I ask cautiously, "Advantageous?"

"I think you know the answer to that, Jesca, passage to our world. Was it to co-exist? Or to take over?"

Ezra comes to sit next to me. "This is where you come in, my dear.

"Sebastian could no longer protect Earth with his team of trusted colleagues since they were dedicating all of their time to discovering vast amounts of information on Dobria. He had to have guards to protect Earth.

"Coincidentally, Balthazar discovered he could not protect the link between the two worlds, Earth and Sonde, without guardians on both planets. They both began to build a following through their colleagues. It became like a fellowship. Sebastian referred to us as Dobrians since we were supporters of humanity for Earth, further discoveries on Dobria, and protectors from the Sondian fellowship bringing about an imbalance to our world, Earth. Balthazar referred to his fellowship as Sondians: supporters of linking the Earth and Sonde and merging co-existence on both worlds."

I think out loud. "So I am a guardian. I am to defend Earth and our universe from merging with another, which could result in pure chaos or possible destruction of everything?"

Ezra puts his head in his hands. He looks up. "Well, it is not just you. There is a battle, and you are undeniably involved."

I slowly rise and begin to pace.

Ezra continues, "Your recent abilities. The vibrations you feel and humming you hear before an attack. How can I know about these things unless I have experienced them myself and know why they happen?"

I look at Ezra as I pace. This can't be real. A guardian? Wormholes? Worlds? Galaxies colliding? I go to grab my coat and purse.

Ezra raises his voice. "The abilities will only intensify, Jes. I am…"

Ezra stops himself and restarts in a more calm manner. "I was sent to train you and prepare you to be what you are, a Dobrian guardian."

I reach for the door. "I can't." I am tongue tied. I can't breathe. "I have to go."

Chapter 17

Ezra steps in front of the doorway, blocking it with his body.

"Jesca, I know this is overwhelming. Just…just know that I will not leave you vulnerable. I will be here to guide you from now until the end."

I am wringing my fingers together. I feel claustrophobic all of a sudden. "Can I go now?" I figure if I can be flippant enough about the download of information I just received, that it would all dissipate into the ethereal.

Ezra moves out of the doorway, leaving it clear for me to escape.

I hardly remember the walk home from campus. I keep replaying the details of the story Ezra just told. It seems like a dream that I have just woken from, unreal like a dream. Who am I to say that dreams aren't real? My track record lately doesn't separate dream from reality too well. I walk more quickly. As I do, my mind works just as quickly. Rapidly all the connections between my life and Ezra's story take hold in my mind, like a puzzle being put together. I start to cry at the undeniable realization that he may be right about it all.

I'm almost home when the humming begins. I sense being followed, a dark and heavy presence. Very familiar. My heart begins to pound in my chest and throat. I run.

Two more blocks and I'm home.

I feel the tracker closing in. It approaches from behind and is soon beside me. I stop dead in my tracks. I am radiating a vibration; humming is reverberating from my body into the atmosphere. I can almost see it, like a wave of visible air. The lamplight above me is dimming and brightening in rhythm with the vibration within me. I can feel the heavy presence immediately halt and retreat far enough away from the barrier I have created for myself. It remains there, waiting.

My life force is my protection.

"Please protect me," I whisper with hope. I remember the reoccurring nightmare, the feeling of empowering energy. That energy finally has relevance in my reality.

I move my hand out slowly toward the dark, heavy entity. The darkness shifts away from my reach, from the electrical current radiating from within me. The vibration continues to pulse energy farther and farther out from my body with every beat of my heart. I take my arms into my chest, and then thrust my hands outward toward the dark force. A wave of pure, bright, white energy rolls from my body into the darkness. The dark predator shrinks away as the wave hits it with force. Within seconds, it is surrounding me again, trying to suffocate the white energy around me. My mood shifts from fear to anger, then determination to escape, to get out of this situation as quickly as I can.

I send one more surge of pure energy into the darkness, attempting to distract the tracker and get away. It works. I turn and run. It is the kind of run I experienced in the woods a few days ago. The speed is fantastical.

I am at my door within seconds. Behind a dead-bolted door within a second more. My pulse is still raised, but I am not winded. I stand staring at the door, then shift my eyes to the windows. I back into the kitchen and lean against the refrigerator. Minutes pass. Nothing. A half hour passes. I close my eyes and let my mind take over. I no longer sense the dark entity. Another half hour passes, I am now sitting on the sofa, legs crossed and eyes shut. I feel warmth on the left side of my face. I open my eyes to see the dawn light coming in through the window. I take my cell phone out of my pocket and dial.

"Hey, Mom, I'm on my way over. We need to talk." I wait for a response; it never comes. I shower quickly, dress, and walk out the door into the morning light.

Chapter 18

I approach my parents' street and begin the turn onto it when I sense someone close by and in my house.

Ezra? What the hell is...

I pull into the driveway, park, and move swiftly with determination to the front door. I don't knock, just let myself in. I am beyond good manners after last night and no sleep. I walk into the family room, and my eyes immediately meet Ezra's, ignoring my parents' welcome.

I jump right in. "What the hell? Coming to my parents' house to worry them. What right do you have to involve them now?"

Dad stops my rampage with an uncharacteristic yell. "Jes, stop it!"

I am taken aback since this is so out of character for my dad.

Mom starts, "We already know, Jesca. We have always known."

Mom's eyes well up with tears. Dad walks over to her and embraces her quickly. Ezra looks at my parents with heartfelt sadness in his eyes. It angers me the way he looks at them. How dare he.

How could he come here, talk to them behind my back, then feel sadness for them? How could my parents keep all this from me?

"Why?"

The rest of my thoughts get caught in my tightening throat. I clear my throat and try again. "Why keep so much from me?"

I look at each of them, now knowing they all have a part in this.

Dad breaks the silence. "Your biological mother wanted it that way. She wanted you to grow up with as normal a childhood as possible. Mom and I honored her wishes and did all we could to keep things normal, the average American life. We knew eventually it would come to this. This day."

Mom and Dad both look at Ezra with worried eyes.

I look at Mom and Dad, then at Ezra.

"What? The secret that my biological mother wanted you to keep?"

"Jesca, your mom and dad are referring to the next step, our training."

I move to the sofa, which is covered in moving plastic.

"I need lots of answers. First, Ezra tells me that my freak-out episodes and hallucinations are normal. Mom and Dad, you tell me you're moving, like, tomorrow! Ezra unloads the Doberman..."

Ezra corrects me, "Dobria."

I continue, "Dobria, Sonde, another galaxy, traveling to other worlds through wormholes, and more sh...stuff that still has my head spinning."

I put my face in my hands. "Now you are telling me my biological mother, who I know very little about, wanted all of these things to be kept from me until I could handle it? Now?"

Ezra says, "Until your mind would no longer allow it to be caged within you. Your abilities are beginning to flood your mind and body. If you keep on like this and don't learn how to control and harness these gifts, you might very well lose your mind. That is why I 'unloaded' all of this stuff on you and…" Ezra sighs. He looks sad all of a sudden. "Look, Jes, God knows you need answers. We are able to give them to you now."

Ezra, Dad, and Mom look at each other, then at me.

I get the cue.

I am at center stage and not prepared. I need to organize my thoughts. All of this is insane, unreal. I can't deny the abnormal things that are happening within me. How can I deny that reality? And I cannot seem to control any of it. Ezra, Mom, and Dad are the only people I can trust to give me answers. The thing that frightens me is, am I ready to hear the truths that could alter the path of my reality for the rest of my life?

Chapter 19

"Who was my biological mother?" I look over at my adopted mom with soft eyes; I don't want to hurt her.

Ezra brushes his hair back with his hand. "Your mother's name was Anna Gershon. She was a Dobrian guardian. You look so much like her, Jesca." Ezra's eyes become tender. "Her eyes were bright green, though, and her skin was fairer. And she was about an inch or two taller than you."

Feelings stir within me just hearing about someone that I am a part of, other than what I have known my whole life. It makes her more real for me.

Ezra continues, "She was one of the best at seeking out the Sondians and specialized in the undercover missions. Anna was so brave. A true mentor to many, including myself." Ezra looks down with a small smile on his mouth.

I can't help but feel a bit in awe of her from his very emotional description of her. I quickly gain my composure. I need answers, not a walk down memory lane. I harden emotionally.

"What happened to her? Why did she leave?"

Ezra looks up at me sharply. His brown eyes narrow with anger behind them. "She did not leave you by choice. She was murdered."

I feel a long breath leave my body, like hope is seeping out. A hope to know this woman someday.

"During her last mission, she became pregnant with you. She immediately wanted to become inactive as a guardian and settle in Georgia. She wanted you to have a normal life. And she succeeded after you were born. She was able to enjoy being a mother for a short time before she passed."

A knot develops in my throat.

Ezra says, "The Sondians had spies as well. She was such an asset to Sebastian and the fellowship. Balthazar sent out head hunters to eliminated her...and you."

Ezra's voice becomes deeper and angrier. "I was sent in as one of Anna's protégés. I was the best choice to protect her and you. One day, Anna sent me to run some errands for her, and when I returned, you were both gone. With Sebastian's and other guardians' help, I was able to track Anna and your location. The Sondian head hunters had you and your mother holed up in an old, run-down cabin on the edge of town, near the first set of hills before the terrain became mountainous.

"We wanted to wait until dusk to attack, but Anna was putting up such as strong fight from the sound of it." Tears begin to well up in Ezra's eyes, turning them a golden color. His voice becomes more intense. "She wasn't the type to back down from a challenge, especially with you in harm's way. I can only imagine the hell she gave him."

Ezra looks up at me, then away quickly. "We knew we had to get in there silently and quickly. As soon as we heard her cry out, we attacked."

I am on the edge of the sofa, tears clouding my eyes. I know this isn't going to end cleanly and peacefully.

"We attacked from every entrance to the small cabin, and you were in safe arms immediately."

Tears finally begin to flow from his eyes. "I was able to talk with Anna briefly before her passing. Her only request was that I find safety for you and give you a normal life. When the time came, I was to mentor and prepare you for your purpose as a guardian."

I wipe furiously at my cheeks now stained with tears. I can't stop them from overflowing. Mom and Dad come to sit next to me.

Mom starts, "And that is when Ezra found us. He was a single man, not an instant family. Sebastian told Ezra about us. We were inactive Dobrian guardians and could provide safety and normalcy for you."

Dad says, "We were so happy to have you, Jesca. We wanted you to know that you were a part of us, but you still had a biological mother. That is why we gave you your mother's maiden name as part of your name, Jesca Gershon-Sera. Your mother, Anna, was a great leader for the fellowship. We were honored to become the parents to you that we knew she would have wanted to be herself." Dad's voice begins to crack. He clears his throat. "Ezra stayed close by. He remained an active Dobrian guardian, now a lead mentor himself, for this very purpose—to train you. Your mother, Ezra, and I knew this was inevitable. You would begin to experience the abilities you inherited from Anna. The need for your mind and body to seek out the purpose it was meant for. All of those discussions about space, the possibility of wormholes that we had so many times as a family…"

Mom adds, "The conversations about God, Heaven, and Hell. The conversations about where and how they could have been created. How Earth may not be the only inhabited world. Those conversations we had over the years all had a purpose. Those conversations were the only influence we could give you that might help you through this very event in your life."

All of the memories of talks under the starry skies as a little girl, dinner table conversations about space, the universe, and God all came flooding in. All the pieces of the puzzle are beginning to take on a grander picture.

Dad says, "You needed to be prepared somehow for this. If we didn't reveal all of this at the right time, the time we prayed about…"

Mom adds, "The time we would have to let you go and find your purpose as a Dobrian guardian." Mom begins to sob loudly. Dad leans in to comfort her.

Dad looks at me as he hugs Mom. "This is you, Jes. No more hiding. You are just like Anna: strong, independent, intelligent, and brave. It is time that you find yourself, your true self."

Ezra speaks after a moment. "We will be meeting with the others on the outskirts of Nevada for debriefing and intense training at the facility…"

All of the added details seemed to melt away as my mind begins to numb. Then I hear nothing more.

I interrupt, "What about my life here? How am I going to explain to my friends, the university, and my boss? I can't just say, 'See ya! Gotta go save the universe.'"

Ezra says, "Jes, all of it has been taken care of."

I challenge him. "How?"

Ezra looks at me. "Within every state, city, town, suburb, company, school, group of friends, there is one of us, a fellow Dobrian. And at least one Sondian, unfortunately. Over the last two decades our numbers have grown exponentially. I only need to make a few phone calls, and you are clear to go. No questions asked."

I push. "What about Elisha? She has been my friend forever, I have to tell her something more. She won't understand. I have to talk with her."

Dad interrupts, "She knows. Her family knows. They are inactive as well. She has been aware of her purpose since she was very young."

Elisha was told about this years before me? Did they think I wasn't mature enough? Did they not trust my judgment or my level of responsibility? I feel betrayed by all of them. My best friend kept such a huge secret from me. How could she?

It really pisses me off now as I think about it.

"Why was she told and not me?"

Ezra says, "Her family and her purpose are different from yours. Elisha and her family are part of a cast of watchers. They monitor the safety of higher-ranking guardians and their families, like yourself. Elisha has been a watcher for you. She was to keep you safe and be close by when I couldn't be. You have to know, Jesca, she was your best friend before anything else. She found out that she was a watcher when you were both in middle school. You have to understand that she was not to tell you anything, for your own safety. She would never intentionally hide anything from you unless it was to protect you."

I reflect on the times Elisha had been by my side. I still feel I owe it to our friendship to say good-bye myself. We shared years of life together. I need to let her know that all of that time still meant the world to me and that I am not as mad as I could be. I know why she did what she did. I look at Ezra. "I have to see her."

Ezra nods, already knowing my intentions.

I walk to Elisha's house from mine. Mom and Dad's good-byes with me were not so bad. Overall, not much would change from the relationship that we've had since I had moved out on my own. Still, my heart feels a little deflated at the absence of them that I would be experiencing. I guess I wasn't prepared for that.

With Elisha, it is going to be really hard. Not physically seeing her every day is definitely going to take a toll on me. We have been inseparable forever.

Elisha comes to the door, and the conversation starts awkwardly. Elisha makes light of it by opening the door a crack and whispering, "Do you come in peace?"

I half-smile. "Yes, Lisha."

Elisha opens the door and lets me pass. We sit at the kitchen table. Her parents are out to the movies for the night.

Elisha says, "So on a scale of one to ten, how pissed are you with the situation?"

I put both of my hands on Elisha's shoulders and respond. "About a five." My voice softens, and I smile at my dear friend. "Ezra told me how you struggled. I know what you had to do. I love you, Lisha."

Elisha's face becomes serious. "Jes, I wanted to tell you. But it wasn't time yet. I had to wait until you started experiencing your abilities. That night at the shop when you passed out and Ezra took you to grab some food, oh man, I was so close to telling you. Ezra said that it wasn't time. You are my best friend, Jes. We have been through all the stereotypical and clichéd best friend stuff. Please know that I did not do all this out of duty first. But out of love for our friendship."

I hug my best friend to get her to hush. And with that, we both stand there, embracing, and everything is forgiven.

Elisha breaks the silence. "It really blows that we won't be able to talk while you are in training."

I playfully punch Elisha in the shoulder. "Yes, it does. But after training, you are the first phone call I will make."

We both smile.

"Are you freaking out? I mean you have gotten some major breaking news within the past twenty-four hours that will change your life and the way you look at reality forever."

I sigh, feeling the anxiety creeping in again. "Yeah, I'm freaked."

Elisha touches my arm. "Hey, you are strong, Jes. You have always been the smart and brave one. I have been so honored to be your best friend all these years. And now, your purpose is here. Embrace it. It is yours!"

Elisha is right. My purpose is right in front of me. It scares the hell out of me, though. I can't walk away from it. Not after all that I have learned in the last twenty-four hours.

Twenty-four hours ago my life was predictable for the most part. Now, my reality is unquestionably altered.

Ezra has arranged for my apartment to be packed up and stored while my training takes place. As I pack up my clothes for the month of training, I reminisce of times with Dad, Mom, Bethany and Elisha. The days working at Benson's Bookstore with Elisha. Talking with Mom on the balcony as we look up at the stars. Walks around campus in the fall as the leaves just start to turn and litter the ground. Jogs with my dad around the lake.

The other memories creep in. The darkness in the nightmares, the hallucinations and contorted, grotesque faces. The voices. My abilities. Those memories keep pushing the happier times farther and farther away from my grasp. There is no way I am going to retreat and cower now. It is time for all of it to be revealed.

Chapter 20

Ezra has no responsibilities for me prior to and on our trip to Nevada. Everything has been taken care of. The packing of the apartment, the dismissal from my job, my withdrawal from the university. *Mr. Ezra Kahn has everything under control.*

Within three days, we are in route to the training facility known simply as "the facility". I am still adjusting to the new direction my life has taken. I keep replaying all the events leading up to today to see if I could have identified any of this earlier on through my father, mother, friends, and Ezra. I am so exhausted, but sleep is the last thing on my mind since I learned about my purpose as a guardian for Dobria. On the plane, I am able to doze, but not a real deep sleep. I think I am afraid to fall too far into sleep, especially with my track record of dreaming lately. My audience might not approve. On the other hand, Ezra does not have a problem sleeping. As soon as we get on the plane, he is out. I look at him, still in awe that my professor had more to do with my life than merely instructing me in a class on a huge university campus. He is more tangible to me now as I look at him peacefully sleeping.

Man, I wish I could do that!

The trip is a mere three hours. By the time we begin our descent, Ezra comes out of his self-induced coma. Ezra looks at me, scratches his head, and rubs his eyes. "Get some sleep?"

I look at him with a heavy-eyed stare of envy. "No such luck."

* * *

We depart from the plane to a waiting car and driver.

As we drive away, Ezra yawns and looks over at me. "Once we get settled, you really need to get some rest."

The drive is long and uneventful as far as the scenery goes.

I ask, "Where is that exactly?"

Ezra says, "At the facility, everything is subterranean. Training rooms, debriefing room, cafeteria, and suite-type rooms. The list goes on."

I am curious. "How massive is this subterranean facility?"

Ezra answers without blinking. "About a ten-mile radius. Decent size for the amount of staff and trainees and mentors we have on the property."

I question, "How often do you train new guardians?"

Ezra responds, "Once every year. We usually have four or five in each class and one mentor for each. Unless there are casualties."

Ezra eyes me, waiting for the next concern on my mind.

"Jesca, the casualty ratio is significantly low. Our training is rigorous, and we make sure the new guardians are confident in their abilities before being sent to their territories. It is when they are in their territories and are 'influenced' that their judgment can be clouded."

Ezra growls at the fact that he probably has said too much and has opened up a whole swarm of questioning for me.

I hear his fear.

"Ezra, I'm not going to hit you with a swarm of questions. Just don't hold back anymore when you do tell me things. Okay?"

Ezra exhales and nods. He smiles at me. "Try to get some rest, Jes."

I smile back and turn on my side to face my window. I shut my eyes, but not to sleep. I wonder what to expect at the facility. Is it like a huge cave underground with a bunch of connecting caverns that span out like spider legs? Is it going to look primitive and dungeon like? I feel so lost and vulnerable all of a sudden. Like a student attending a new school.

Who am I kidding? This is nothing like school. I have no idea what I am getting myself into. I am leaving all my trust in my adoptive parents and my professor. It makes me livid, edgy, and ready to burst at the seams. I don't like not knowing my surroundings and my next step. It makes me extra defensive, too. Defensive enough to mentally block anyone from getting into my head, particularly Ezra. I had plenty of time to practice, imagining a huge wall around me blocking Ezra from getting in. I think he knows I have done this, which has added to his frustration.

The monotonous speed of the car is hypnotic. When the sound of the speed shifts down, my eyes pop open, and I sit up to look around. Ezra is already poised and turning his iPod off.

I look out my window to see a small, run-down gas station in the middle of nowhere. It looks vacant. The metallic sign shifts in the dry wind, Willy's Gas and Repair. I lean over to look out Ezra's window. All I can see is miles of dry, orange and brown desert. My anxiety spikes briefly.

Ezra feels it and puts his hand on my shoulder. "Jesca, it's all right. We are fine. This is the safest place in the world for you right now."

Instantly I feel peace and ease from his simple touch and gesture.

I take a deep breath in and release the small bit of anxiety.

The driver exits the car and walks briskly into the gas station. Within seconds, the garage door begins to rise. The driver moves swiftly back to the car, gets in, and pulls us into the garage. As soon as the car is in the darkness of the building, the driver gets out and walks to what looks like a security system panel. He punches a few buttons, and the garage door begins to close, snuffing out the little bit of light that remains in the building. The driver is back in the car in seconds. The car jolts downward. I grab for the door handle, and Ezra grabs my other arm. "It's all right."

I let go of the handle and stare out the window in observance. We are descending. It is like an elevator, but quick and smooth. One more jolt of the car and we are on solid ground and moving forward. The sides of the underground tunnel seem to be lined with metal. I guess that is to reinforce the structure of the tunnel. It reminds me of a tunnel you would travel in when passing through mountains, just narrower. It is very well lit with street-like lamps along the tunnel. The tunnel opens to a parking lot area. Not huge, but big enough for about six or seven cars. There are four other cars parked. Four black Ford Tauruses. Our black Taurus joins the rest.

Ezra says, "All right. Home sweet home. Let's go."

I open my door and take a deep breath, wondering how the air would feel, smell, and taste down here. The air is cold and crisp, nothing stagnant about it. Winter in Vegas can get cold. We are more than 100 feet below ground, I imagine, so it is bound to be colder than the surface. I am taking in my surroundings when I realize Ezra is already walking to a set of metal doors with our bags.

He yells back, "You coming?"

I jog over to help him with the bags. Ezra stops at the doors and waits.

I look at him curiously. "What are we doing? Are we going to ring a doorbell, or is there a secret knock or something?"

He points up at the camera to our right. "Just waiting for them to answer."

A loud click, then Ezra reaches for the handle and opens one of the metal doors. He holds the door for me. I reluctantly enter and wait inside of the doorway for him. Ezra starts down a long, brightly lit hallway. White walls with nothing on them all around us. No doors, just the long passageway. The passage goes on for a while. Our steps become synchronized as our shoes touch the ground, and then squeak. Our bags shift in unison with the sound of our feet.

We come to an elevator. Without pressing a button, the door slides open. Ezra enters, and I quickly follow. We drop slowly in an even further descent.

How deep into the earth were we going?

Ezra says, "The farther off the grid and hidden by Earth's natural electromagnetic field core, the better off we are when it comes to Sondian trackers. Remember, they are after us as much as we are after them."

I look at him with surprise.

Did he just answer my thought directly? So he can read my thoughts. I'm glad I practiced putting up my wall in the car. I'm going to need it.

Ezra says, "Yes, I did read your thoughts, Jesca. What? You thought you were the only one with cool abilities?" He smiles and keeps walking.

I snort. "I wouldn't say cool abilities."

"Believe me. You'll have a different opinion after a few sessions in the field."

"The field?"

Ezra says, "Mock missions. Can't wait to see what you can do."

This brings on some anxiety and pressure. "Great, I'm glad I fascinate you!"

We come to a stop. The door slides open, and Ezra leads the way into the entry. A very nice entry, I might add. Ezra puts his bags down and walks toward one of the three corridors, where quite a bit of talking is taking place.

Ezra is ahead of me, entering the corridor. "We're here. Sorry, we were delayed. Is everyone else here? Hey, Luke."

My curiosity moves me to the corridor Ezra just entered. I stand in the doorway, taking in the atmosphere before entering. It is amazingly warm and comforting. There is a burning fire in the hearth, three oversized leather chairs, and two leather sofas, all facing each other. It is a huge contrast to the sterile tunnel, hallways, and elevator we just left behind.

Ezra moves towards a group of people. "Jake, Siobhan, Luke."

I assume these are the other mentors. And I'm guessing their guardian in training is the person sitting next to each of them. The people that Ezra did not address look just as vulnerable as me. This brings me some much needed comfort, knowing that I am not alone.

Siobhan looks at me, then Ezra. "So this is Anna's girl."

Ezra replies, "Yes, this is Jesca Gershon."

He left off the Sera? I don't mind, but make a mental note to ask him why later.

Everyone is looking at me like I might have some magical response.

"Hi," is all I can muster.

Jake jumps in. "Well, this is a perfect time for introductions from the green peas!"

I can tell that Jake is going to be the lively one of the bunch. He is just a tad shorter than Ezra's tall six feet. Jake is built bigger than Ezra, though, more muscular. He has dark hair and dark brown eyes. He wears a sweatshirt and jeans with combat boots.

"I'm Jake, as you already know. I am Nicholas' mentor."

Nicholas looks up at us with a head nod acknowledging us. "Hey, I'm Nick."

He looks like he could be Jake's twin with his similar features and build. Only difference is the color of his eyes—blue.

Siobhan stands; she's very tall, slender, and has auburn hair. She is dressed in a black tank and black combat pants. She looks very Lara Croft Tomb Raider. She pulls up the girl to her right from a seated position and holds her up as if she were a ragdoll. "This is Angela. She is just a bit nervous, so she won't talk very much."

Immediately, Angela spews a chain of unintelligible sounds that must be words, but are clustered so continuously I can't decipher them.

Siobhan immediately reaches over and covers her mouth with her hand. She looks into Angela's eyes. "Angela. Slow down."

Siobhan looks at us. "Just nerves."

Siobhan uncovers Angela's mouth cautiously, fearful of what she might say I'm sure.

Angela sighs. "Hi."

Angela has straight, light blond hair, is very thin, and has these big blue eyes that look too large for her face. Angela seems to be unlike what I would consider a "guardian", but who am I to judge.

The third mentor stands.

"I'm Luke. I am Nathaniel's mentor. I look forward to learning more about each of you." He seems so pleasant and welcoming. I really feel like he is looking forward to getting to know us. Luke has a tan complexion and black hair. His eyes contrast his skin; they are a light honey color.

Nathaniel stands up; he is taller than Ezra. He is slender, but muscular. He brushes his wavy, brown hair back with his hand as he looks at each of us. His eyes are a light green color. They remind me of the forest back home.

He says, "Hi. You all can call just call me Nate. Nate Sera." He smiles and sits back down.

That smile.

My trancelike stare is broken when I hear the last name. I look at Ezra. So this is why he didn't give my adoptive name. I wonder how Nate is related to my adopted parents. *Is he a nephew?*

Ezra leans over to me. "Yes, a nephew. Don't feel awkward about staring; you aren't related."

He winks at me. I feel my cheeks flush, and I turn away from Ezra quickly with frustration and a hint of embarrassment.

Damn it.

I keep forgetting to put up that big mental wall when I don't want him to hear my thoughts.

I look around the room and wonder if they feel like me. Trying to keep the skewed reality straight in our heads.

I guard my thoughts now. I can't home in on which of them, if not more than one, is telepathic. Then it occurs to me. They are probably just as guarded with their thoughts as I am.

Enough with the introductions. I am ready to get this show on the road.

I jump in with an all-business attitude. "When can we start the debriefing?"

The mentors look at each other.

Siobhan starts, "We can start now. We thought we would wait until after lunch originally. Give you all a bit to settle in."

Nate speaks up. "I agree with Jesca. I think it is safe to say that we all want answers. I mean, we can't get around the elephant in the room. You're just prolonging it."

Angela and Nick both nod in agreement.

Ezra claps his hands together. "All right, let's head to the debriefing room. Follow me."

We all file out following Ezra down a hallway across from the living room with the fireplace we initially met in. The walls in the hallway look muted, with no decorations or wall hangings. We pass one door on the left and one on the right. We come to a T in the hallway. Ezra turns right, and we all follow. I glance down a hallway to the left and notice a handful of doors.

It must be our rooms.

Ezra speaks up as we walk. "We will give you a complete tour of the facility after the debriefing."

I mumble, "Thanks, Ezra."

He yells back in a singsong way. "You're welcome, Jes."

Nate catches up to me. He is wearing a pair of jeans and a white T-shirt. "Why is he talking that way?"

Quickly I put my mental wall up.

I look up at him. *He is so good looking.*

Nate smiles down at me.

He has a really great smile.

I quickly look straight ahead and give a half smile. "It is his special way of addressing me."

Nick walks directly in front of us and pipes in. "When did you all start figuring out you were different?"

I answer, "Um, well. I always felt a little different, but I just started having more intense experiences recently. I guess about three weeks ago now."

Nick questions Nate. "How about you?"

Nate thinks for a moment then answers, "I guess it has been about three or four weeks for me, too. But I agree with Jesca, I have always felt things were a bit 'off' for me. All of a sudden, those crazy, bizarre, realistic dreams and nightmares I had for years were crossing over into my reality."

Angela sneaks up behind us to listen in and whispers excitedly, "Me too! At one point, I couldn't separate the dreams from reality. And the feeling of something tracking me was becoming so frightening."

I ask her, "When did you start experiencing all of this?"

"Same scenario. About a month ago things short-circuited in me. I mean, that's what it felt like. My parents and Siobhan intervened as soon as things started getting really unbearable for me. I thought I was losing my mind."

It isn't just me. We all experienced similar events.

We enter a room. It reminds me of a conference room back on the university campus in the library—one huge table and

121

lots of chairs around it. Once again, the décor is sterile: gray walls and fluorescent lighting. There is an expansive projector screen at the front of the room. Each of us takes a seat.

Ezra remains standing. "All right. Why you? Why now? How can all of this be possible? Those are just a few of the questions that replay in your minds on a frequent basis now that you know what you will be—a guardian."

Ezra must be the first link in the chain of command since he is the spokesperson of this debriefing.

"I am aware that each of you has been personally informed about what we are up against. It is no mistake you have been chosen to fight this battle, so get that out of your head. You have been through many events recently. All of these events on your map of life have occurred for a greater purpose beyond anything you have ever known. For one, you have been gifted with abilities. Second, you have been told that you are a part of a fellowship of guardians. You are to protect humanity."

Angela speaks up. "You have to admit, those are some pretty big shoes to fill. Not just for us, but for you. I mean, what are you going to do to prepare us? What makes you mentors?"

Jake speaks. "We have created a training program customized for each of your abilities. You each are gifted with variations of specific metaphysical abilities. Yes, they have been inherited. These gifts are worthless without practice. Right now, your abilities are inconsistent and hazardous to your health. We need to train you to use them.

We will be working to make these gifts valuable assets to both you and to others. Each of us possesses dominant abilities: superhuman strength and intense physical speed. We each have more unique abilities.

"Nate, your unique gifts are Ushering, which is controlling others through Compulsion, and Latrosis, which is healing with your mind using your inner energy, your life force."

Siobhan speaks. "Nick, you can shift into anything with a life force, any animal or person. This ability is called Transfiguration. You also have the gift of Pyrokinesis, producing and controlling fire with your mind."

Ezra jumps in. "Angela, your highly tuned combat skills and your ability to levitate are your unique gifts."

Luke continues with me, "Jesca, your gifts are Telepathy, Ushering, and Qi, the use of your life force from within. But that is only what we have gathered so far."

The "so far" makes me a little concerned and anxious.

I wonder if the humming and vibrations are the unknown? Is that what Qi is?

Luke continues to speak, "Bottom line, each of you will be able to control, defend, and protect yourselves and others with your abilities.

"Until now, you have each thought you were going insane with the abnormal things going on in your lives. I have been there. We all have."

Luke gestures to the other mentors. "We have each been through variations of what you are experiencing right now. We successfully gained control of our abilities and have used them to protect ourselves and humanity. Now that we have

123

spent years defending humanity, we have been chosen to teach you, guide you, so that one day you can continue the training for future guardians. Once we have trained you and you are sent to guard your territory, Sebastian will be in direct communication with you."

Nick asks, "And how does that happen? How does Sebastian communicate from Dobria? Cell phone?"

Nick scoffs and elbows Nate. Nate smiles and rolls his eyes.

Ezra laughs as well, then answers, "Through sleep, visions actually. In your dreams and nightmares. Since he has been in Dobria, Sebastian has adapted to many properties of that planet in that galaxy. Communication is different on Dobria. It is unlike the way we communicate here on Earth through auditory words. In Dobria, simply thinking is enough communication."

The four of us, the newbies, look at each other.

I raise a question. "What about when you aren't sleeping and he needs to communicate with you?"

Ezra replies, "As your abilities become second nature to you, you will begin to harness additional abilities that are interlinked. It's like opening a door to your mind you never knew was there. Once you open the door, it's like you have opened the floodgates. Telepathic communication is one of these gifts that you will grow into if it is not your dominant ability. For now, your mentor is your first line of communication between you and Sebastian. Once your telepathic gift has grown, Sebastian will communicate directly with you."

Jake adds, "Training will last for four weeks. It will be both physically and mentally intense. After your training is complete, you and your mentor will be assigned a territory in the US to actively monitor and guard. You will be prepared to infiltrate Sondian sleeper cells as well as perform combat missions to shut down Sonde guardian activity. Balthazar and his guardians are still trying relentlessly to follow through with the plan of opening a passage between our world and Sonde."

Nate says, "Can't he see what imminently will happen? It could be the demise of both galaxies."

Ezra says, "See, that is the thing. Balthazar has been playing the role of a god in Sonde. The power that he has, the adaptation of his abilities and his strength—he has been gone from Earth for so long, he has lost his humanity. Now, all he sees is the ability to bend and push the nature of science. And our world is just that, another world to collect. Yes, it is beneficial to pursue sciences and their possibilities. But there must also be respect for nature and humanity. Balthazar has been blinded with greed and power. He has lost himself in it."

Chapter 21

Ezra tells me just after debriefing that these four weeks will be extremely exhausting, but revealing. Ezra says that the feeling at the end of every day of training could easily be compared to the unleashing of an inner part of me that otherwise would have never been uncovered.

The rest of the first day is busy with touring the facility, lunch, and settling into our individual units. The facility is enormous. Not anything like I expect. The cafeteria is like a dining hall. Four round wooden tables with four chairs at each table. That would allow for staff in the cafeteria, security, and the maintenance crews of the facility. It is not at all like a sterile hospital or like the entry of the facility. Once you enter the units, the hearth room, the cafeteria, and the gymnasium are warm and welcoming with wall hangings and canned lighting.

The smell of food from the cafeteria is overwhelmingly welcomed. I have not eaten much in the past 72 hours. As I walk along the cafeteria assembly line, I notice nothing is pre-made. And the staff is standing along the other side of the counter waiting for requests. Cooking supplies, fresh produce, meats, and seafood, the spread is impressive. There are three chefs and two servers. One of the chefs reminds me of Jack Black. He has this animated voice and personality that shows through as soon as Angela speaks to him with her order.

"Grilled cheese and portabella mushroom, uh, sir."

He responds, "Please call me Patrick, Angela. So you want the best grilled cheese and portabella you have ever tasted, my dear? Not a problem." Patrick proceeds in startling us with a huge howl.

The chef next to Pat is Charisma. She is African American. She has the biggest smile on her face when she asks Nick what he would like. "Nick! How are you, sweetness? You a New York boy, right?"

Nick responds with caution, "Uh, yes, ma'am, that is right."

Charisma snickers. "Ma'am? Ah, please. Call me Ms. Char. Now, what will you have?" Char bats her eyes. "I make a wicked Rueben sandwich, if I do say so myself."

Nate and I look at each other and smile.

I step up in front of the third chef. He is very tall and has blond hair. He has soft, honest, blue eyes. He greets me in a very proper English accent.

"Hello, Jesca. My name is Fenton. What would you care to eat, my lady?"

Lady? I'm pretty sure I am drooling at the sight of food. To be honest, anything would have been great. I choose a club sandwich with sweet potato fries on the side.

All of the mentors snatch up one table. I wait to see where Angela and Nick plan to sit.

Nate stands next to me with his tray of food and nudges me with his elbow in a friendly manner. "Let's go sit with the others."

We walk over together.

Nick looks up first. "Hey, guys."

I respond to break the ice. "So, what do you guys think? Pretty heavy, huh?"

"Yeah, pretty crazy," Angela says.

"Yep. The galactic godlings, Sebastian and Balthazar, were simply mythical when I first learned of all this a few weeks ago." Nick gestures with his hands. "Now, with all of this," he points toward the mentors, "and them," he points to us, "and you guys and the validation of your testimonies. It is starting to sink in that I am not in a nightmare. It's surreal, and I could totally use a support group right about now."

We all smile at his candidness.

We decide we need to learn more about each other, our abilities, and dealing with all of this baggage. We are up for meeting after our first full day of training in the rec room.

After lunch Ezra gives us free rein of the facility. My immediate thought is to go for a run and explore the numerous trails through the caves that had been cut out and maintained over the past four decades of the facility's existence.

Jake told us on the tour that Sebastian created this facility right after his first few teleports to Dobria. Jake said Sebastian had a very strong influence on the creation of the compound. It needed to be conducive to the type of training the future guardians would endure.

The facility started as an area the size of a standard high school gymnasium. As the numbers of guardians grew, the facility expanded and now the facility spans miles underground in all directions. Construction is still occurring, further expansion. There are multiple facilities scattered all over the world from what Ezra has said.

The trails are gravel, and the cutouts are very large, about six feet wide and ten feet tall. I head down the first cutout, which takes me deeper underground. The twists and switchbacks are like back home in the woods, minus the smell of trees. I feel a chill.

How? Where is it coming from?

I wonder if they have created massive central air units and air duct systems in order to keep the oxygen levels stable for us to survive down here for an extended period of time. I breathe in the smell of the earth, rich with minerals. Then, I smell water; it smells like the moments before it rains.

I come up quickly on an open area. The height of the area's ceiling takes my breath away, and I stumble back to take in its grandness.

The stalactites are a soft, chalky white. They are dripping water into a pool of the lightest blue-green water I have ever seen. The pool looks fairly deep. I scan the open space around me. There are four more openings, cutouts, wrapped around the pool of water.

This place is massive.

Siobhan told us that our tour would only cover the basic facility rooms that we would be using on a daily basis. The rest was for us to explore.

I cross my legs and sit at the edge of the glowing pool. All that is audible is the trickle of water from the fingerlike calcifications above into the water below. The best part is

129

there is no humming, or vibrations, or whispering. No looming, heavy, dark feelings.

I hear a crunching of gravel coming closer from a distance. I turn to see Nate exiting one of the cutouts. He takes his earbuds off. He must have had the same idea.

He sees me from across the pool and walks over. "Hey, Jesca."

Without a second thought, he pulls his shirt off as he tries to catch his breath. I shyly divert my eyes back to the pool.

"Hi there, Nate."

Nervously, I pick around in the gravel for a small pebble to toss into the pool. A thoughtless distraction to replace the really attractive one.

"You noticed it too, huh?"

Is he talking about my nervousness? I feel my cheeks redden and my heart race from embarrassment. "Noticed what?"

Nate dips his shirt in the spring and looks at me from the corner of his eye. "The silence. No humming. No whispers. You noticed it just now, didn't you?"

I lie a little, "Yep. Yes, I did." Then I wonder if he is lying a little, too. *He could be telepathic.* "How did you know?"

Nate wrings the excess water out of his shirt. He slides down and sits next to me. Then he looks into my eyes, really looks at me. It takes my breath away.

Nate blinks. "I feel it, too. It feels so peaceful and safe."

Nate pulls his shirt back over his head.

I look away and start breathing again.

Nate continues to talk. "I noticed the silence when I got away from everyone and started my run. When I saw you sitting there, you looked so…" Nate looks down quickly.

Okay, how could this gorgeous guy be embarrassed in front of me?

Nate continues, "It just feels so serene. I knew you had to have been experiencing it too."

There is a long silence.

"Yeah, you're right. I was enjoying the experience." Oh God, please don't let him think I am referring to him as the experience! *Change the subject, Jes.* "So you hear the humming and whispers around you, too?"

Nate shifts, and his leg brushes against mine. "Yeah, ever since kindergarten. That is the farthest back I remember, anyway."

We are looking at each other again.

Those green-blue eyes match the pool of water in front of us perfectly.

Nate continues, "I remember the nightmares that Mom and Dad would comfort me after." He scratches the tip of his nose. "The whispers were real, too. I was hearing actual conversations. I was linking my mind with people around me. It was like I had a really awesome hearing device on."

Nate grins, and I can't resist smiling; it is contagious.

He is contagious.

"What am I saying? I don't have to tell you. You know exactly what I'm talking about."

131

I grin. "Actually, you explain it so much better than I can. I never thought of it as my mind linking with theirs. I just thought of it as my mind intercepting everything around it."

Nate's expression becomes serious. "Well, then there is the dark energy. The heavy, oppressive force. When I was little, it was so frightening. I was afraid that it was going to gobble me up and I would never see my family again. But Mom and Dad got me through it every time. They always have. I can see how a person could easily lose their mind."

I nod. "Mom and Dad got me through so much also. They kept me from losing it many times. Finally, it was becoming too much, an overload. I thought I was so weak and helpless. Now, I see that what I thought was weakness was strength just below the surface of the fear. I just needed to grab hold of it."

We keep looking at each other.

Nate breaks the silence. "So you're a runner as well."

"Yes. Back home we have amazing trails in the woods. They are so beautiful."

"You're from Georgia, right?"

I didn't drop my hometown during introductions.

I look down, feeling a little apprehensive.

I look back up at him with a half-smile. "Are you checking up on me?"

Nate smiles and wipes his brow with his forearm.

Adorable.

His smile softens as he looks at me again. "No, I just like to know the company I am keeping."

132

The energy in the room is becoming so intense, I have to lean back on my arms to relieve the tension we are exchanging.

As soon as Nate's gaze turns back to the pool and away from me, I feel the tension dissipate.

Nate says, "Well, I'm going to head back and shower up before dinner." He stands and extends his hand to me and helps me stand.

"Thanks."

The help up extends a second longer than necessary. I pull my hand away. "Um. I'm going to finish my run."

Still watching me, Nate puts his earbuds back in and smiles. "Okay. Be careful, it is a little rocky. It was nice talking with you, Jes."

Did he just call me Jes? How does he know my nickname? How did he...

I decide to let it go for now.

I reply with a dazed smile. "It was nice talking with you too, Nate."

Nate turns and jogs back through the entrance cutout. Quickly the loud crunching of gravel becomes silence.

I take in a deep breath. I'm savoring this peace, this moment, because only God knows what chaos is beyond this facility in four weeks.

Chapter 22

Our rooms are very spacious, about 700 square feet, give or take. I have my own commode, shower, mini fridge mainly for leftovers, a nice queen-size bed, an oversized chair with ottoman, desk, and chair. The lighting in the room is canned, not the yellowish fluorescent I hate. I have wall hangings to compensate for the lack of windows.

The first night I slept hard. I'm sure the silence had a lot to do with that. No dreams. No nightmares. I can't remember the last time I slept so deeply.

At 5:00 a.m. a knock on my door wakes me. Well, it is more like a pounding on my door.

With the initial pound, I sit straight up in bed. The second pound has me falling back onto my pillow and covering my ears. Then, the continuous pounding with Ezra's voice behind it.

"Jesca! Rise and shine. See you in the cafeteria in twenty minutes! Oh, and wear something lightweight, like running gear!"

He starts pounding again.

I crawl and scurry to the door to give him a mouthful. By the time I have the door open, he is gone.

Damn it, Ezra!

Not the ideal way to wake up on day one of training.

I crawl back to the bed. I think about what I have ahead of me, today, tomorrow, and from now on. With that simple thought, feelings of fear start to flood into my mind. I rise and get into the shower to wash away the thoughts, quickly.

Fifteen minutes later, I am in the cafeteria with a tray full of breakfast comfort foods! Angela, Nick, and Nate file in and sit at the table with me. They look like zombies.

Nick mumbles in a sarcastic tone, "Good morning, ladies and gentleman."

Angela and I simultaneously let out a low grunt.

Patrick, the chef, delivers a huge carafe of coffee.

Nick shows his appreciation by grasping Patrick's forearm. Then he stands and embraces him. Patrick looks at us and slowly, but cautiously completes the embrace with Nick.

Nick releases him finally. "Thanks, man. I love you, Patrick."

Nate laughs at Nick.

I look over at the mentors. They look like they have been awake for hours.

Nick calls after Patrick as he walks away. "Hey, can you just, like, hook me up with a java drip?"

Patrick snickers, waves his arm at Nick, and keeps walking back to the kitchen.

"What? I'm just joking, man!" Nick returns to his chair and laughs.

Siobhan comes over and stands next to Angela and I. "Morning, little ones! Ahh, day one." A big smile spreads across her face. She looks back at Luke, Jake, and Ezra. They look down at their food and cover their growing smiles with their folded hands. Siobhan turns back to us. "I'm not gonna lie. Your asses are going to get kicked today. Tomorrow will be painful, too. But you will condition quickly at the rate we will be training."

The four of us lowly trainees look at each other briefly, sensing the mutual feeling of intimidation.

"Just keep up and endure, kids. That is the only way you will get through today." Siobhan sighs and smiles. "All right! Fifteen minutes, then meet up with your mentor. Training will run from 6 to 11:30 a.m. Then you will shower and meet back in here for lunch at noon."

Luke interrupts, "Yeah, we don't want to smell your five and half hours of sweat over lunch!"

Jake and Ezra laugh and then stand.

Ezra wipes his mouth with his napkin. "You heard Siobhan. Get a move on. We'll be waiting for you in the gym. Remember, exit the cafeteria, take a left, and then pass three corridors and take a right at the hallway. Go straight ahead into the gym."

Angela whispers, "Don't worry, guys, I have this place memorized like the back of my hand."

Apparently, Angela's abilities encompass a perfect memory and the ability to store loads of information accurately. Having already read her thoughts this morning, I didn't doubt she had already mapped out the entire facility.

* * *

The gym is about the size of a football field.

Luke steps up to us. "Jesca, Ezra wants you on the circuit for an hour. Angela, you and Siobhan are going to hit the trails. Nick, Jake is in the pool waiting for you."

Nick nods. He salutes us and heads on in a jog.

Luke continues, "Nate, you and I are going to do some endurance training."

I see Ezra on the left side of the gym in a glass-windowed room. I walk over to the room. I see free weights, benches, and all types of contraptions. I assume this is my circuit training area. Ezra puts some upbeat music on loud enough to make his yelling voice barely audible.

"Have you stretched?"

I yell back, "Huh? No, not yet! I just got here!"

Ezra yells, "Well, get moving, Jes! You're burning training time, girl!" He winks and smiles.

That was the last smile I saw for the next hour. I must have lifted, pushed, pulled, and stretched every piece of equipment about thirty times each. The rotation did move quickly with Ezra in command, but that also cut out breaks between sets. Ezra laughs at me when I ask for a water break.

Halfway through the training session, I start to see stars and feel like I am going to pass out. I give Ezra my most pitiful look.

He yells, "Stop!"

He walks over to me and puts his hands on both my shoulders. "Jes? Do I look like I'm that much of a pushover? Keep going!" He walks over to the music dock and cranks the music up louder.

What a jerk!

137

That, of course, has the effect he is looking for. His comment pisses me off enough to spur me on through the second half of the session.

When the hour is up, I look like my clothes have been soaked by a fire hose. My skin is crusted with layers of sweat. I smell horrible.

"Can I get a shower?"

Ezra says, "Shower? It's not even 8:30, Jes! We still have hours of training before lunch."

"C'mon! You don't want to have to smell me for the next few hours, do you? I mean, I really stink!"

"I've smelled worse, love! Let's hit the trails."

* * *

Ezra runs with me on the trails.

"You keep up pretty well for an old man!"

Ezra responds, "Yeah. Well, you don't do so bad yourself, little girl!"

We run through the cutouts onto the switchbacks. We pass the cavern with the beautiful pool of water. God, I want to jump in so badly.

Ezra breaks away and heads toward a cutout to the left, and I follow. I have not been on this path yet. It is like a rollercoaster. The turns are sharp. The dips are unexpected. The ground is rockier than the gravel I experienced yesterday.

This must have been the trail Nate was on.

The gap between Ezra and I begins to widen because of the terrain.

138

Ezra hollers back at me, "Don't slow down on me now, Jes! We are almost to the turnaround!"

This gives me hope, and I pick up speed again. My right foot starts to slip on something. I look down and see a drop-off to nowhere! I see a rock wall to my right just in time to keep my footing clear of it. I slow to look over the sharp ledge.

I holler after Ezra, "Thanks for the warning!"

The canyon drop-off must go a long way down, since I hear a void of sound to my right. I slow to a stop to listen closer. No sound reverberating or echoing off the canyon at all.

Ezra appears in my peripheral vision and yells, "What are you doing?!"

It scares the hell out of me.

Even though he is standing a few feet away from me, I yell back mostly out of frustration. "I was checking out the cliff where I almost met my death, thank you very much!"

Ezra elbows me casually. "Oh, don't be so melodramatic. C'mon, it's time to head back."

I stop him from moving by grasping his arm. "Wait! What is this, this hole, this canyon?"

Ezra says, "It's a sinkhole. We found it about two years ago when we made this cutout. This is the most recent cutout, as you can tell by the rugged, unmanaged terrain. Siobhan and the gang decided to leave this cutout trail rugged for more rigorous training."

I respond in a sarcastically sweet tone. "Aw! Thanks, Siobhan!"

Ezra pats me on the top of my head. "You're welcome, green pea." He winks and starts running back in the direction from which we came.

I quickly follow him, not knowing the way on my own. My mind starts to wonder about all the uncharted territory this facility still has, just waiting to be discovered.

The rest of the morning, I am in the pool. I thought that it would be heaven compared to what we had been doing.

But I am so wrong.

Ezra smirks. "You ready?"

I grit my teeth and force a smile. "Yes."

Ezra looks me up and down, examining me. "No."

"No! Why? What now?"

Ezra jogs over to this huge storage closet, opens it, enters, and begins digging around.

"Need help in there?"

Ezra yells back, "Nope, I've got it!"

I see him appear in the doorway with a pile of black, plastic, air duct tubing. It looks like a gigantic, black anaconda suffocating a little man.

It is partially wrapped around Ezra and partially dragging on the floor as he walks back toward me. When he gets to me, he drops the entire pile, letting out a heavy breath.

"Now you are ready!"

I am drawing a blank. *What the hell is he going to have me do?*

Ezra stands in front of me with his arms crossed. "When you get into a water-related situation, one of two things will happen. You will either be fighting against someone…" Ezra looks me up and down again, "...most likely much bigger than you. Or you will be trying to save someone that could also be much bigger than you."

Ezra kicks the black tubing. "This is going to prepare you for those two situations. Now, get into the water."

If he does what I think he is going to do, that tubing will drown me.

Ezra becomes irritated by my internal commentary. "Jes, it will not! Now get in!"

I snap at him. "Stop that! Stop reading me!"

He shoots back with a coy smile, "In training, it is imperative I read your thoughts. So don't put up your magic wall, Jesca! Get into the water, please, with a cherry on top!"

He is so getting under my skin.

"Fine!" I jump in.

He throws the first part of the tubing toward me. Like an unwinding garden hose, he keeps letting out more and more of the tubing, slowly at first.

"Start wrapping it around you from your waist up. Just like that. Push it down around your waist."

I am treading water and simultaneously trying to wrap tubing around me as quickly as I can. At first I am fine. Then the weight begins to pull me under. My treading becomes increasingly labored. Ezra starts to toss the endless tubing faster. My head starts to bob in and out of the water. The tubing is inching up my torso, now wrapping around my shoulders and neck.

Before I go under, Ezra yells, "Sink! Then when you touch bottom, begin unwrapping yourself, and break to the surface!"

I can't hold myself above any longer. I watch the hanging fluorescent lanterns with metal wiring around them move further away, getting smaller, then blurrier. The drop to the bottom of the pool feels endless. The sensation to release some air out of my mouth starts.

Wait! Wait until I touch bottom. I won't last if I release air now!

My ears are popping from the pressure as I continue to sink.

Then I feel my feet touch. I try to look down, but I can't because the tubing is constricting my ability to move my neck. I try to unwrap methodically at first, thinking it will make the job easier. My hands are testing any loose areas. I find a spot. I am rotating to the left and unwrapping the tube to the right. I have to unwrap under one arm, then the other. I feel the urge to let out air again. I speed up the unwrapping, knowing that I can't hold it in very much longer. With all the twisting and turning, I wind up reversing the unraveling.

No! Damn it!

I finally release some air. I feel my body react to the brief release of air and its craving for more, the inhalation of oxygen that I couldn't give it. I feel my body begin to tremble—adrenaline. My hands, arms, and muscles work with more power, unnatural power. The tangled tubing is coming off at greater speed now, and I feel the weight of it releasing me briefly.

142

Ezra is thinking, *C'mon, Jes. Just hold on! You can do this!*

I release more air, and I look up, feeling myself levitate a fraction after every sweep of unravel. When I look up, I notice the light from the lanterns above the pool are less blurry and closer now.

Maybe ten feet away from the surface. God, I hope so.

I look down at my fumbling hands. The tube is taut around my waist.

Just my waist.

I start to feel the urge to inhale again. My body is starting to revolt. It's starving for air. Unable to stop it now, I release more air. I close my eyes to focus on removing the tubing. I try to propel myself upward, but it is pointless. The weight of the tubing is still too heavy.

So far away. I'm running out of time.

Suddenly the tubing shifts downward from my waist.

Yes.

My excitement is short-lived. The tubing has moved down over my thighs, making it harder to tread.

I'm sinking again.

My heart is pounding in my throat. I start seeing shards of light streaking in front of my eyes. It's like hundreds of shooting stars.

Stars? No, not again.

I feel my body begin to go limp. I am no longer in control. Darkness starts to absorb me. I'm passing out.

I feel arms around me.

Ezra thinks, *Hold on, Jes. Don't breathe in yet.*

143

A second later, I am out of the water and on the deck.

Ezra is commanding me, "Breathe, Jes! Now, damn it! Breathe! Open your eyes, Jes!"

My mouth and eyes aren't listening, even though I want them to.

Then, my eyes shoot open and focus on Ezra's. My mouth opens and responds with the sound of starvation for oxygen.

Ezra's hard face softens when he sees me gasping for air. He runs his hands through his hair. "Jes! That was amazing for your first time! You are going to be unbelievable!"

I am panting with wide eyes. I finally catch my breath. "Are you freaking kidding me? I could have drowned and you are congratulating me?"

I use the little bit of energy I have to push him away. Ezra barely shifts under my hand. He sits back on one foot and one knee. He looks like he might explode with anger.

"Look, Jesca, this is real! This is not summer camp. You are going to be put in death's grip with situations way worse than this!"

Ezra lifts a portion of the tubing and throws it down with a thud. "This! This is nothing compared to what you will see, experience, fight for, save, and protect. In under four weeks, you will be out in the open. No safety net. You are the only defense for yourself! You will be ready! If I have to almost kill you myself, damn it, you will be ready!"

Ezra gets up and paces. He is obviously frustrated with his momentary loss of control. After a few minutes, his sarcasm comes back with a vengeance. "Pardon me for thinking your endurance and strength was impressive for a green pea."

Ahh! He pulled the guilt card.

It is true. I am being an ungrateful green pea. I am being the jerk now. And this is not a game.

This is happening. It is not a game. No game over, please insert another coin. This is the only practice I will have before I'm out there. In here, I'm safe. Out there, I'm vulnerable.

I look up at Ezra with thought-filled eyes. "Thank you, Ezra."

Ezra's wrinkled forehead relaxes a bit. He shakes his head back and forth. "Well, there it is. It's hitting you now."

We both welcome the silence to digest what is happening at this very moment. I am submitting to my purpose.

Ezra claps his hands loudly and breaks the moment. "Good! Now get your ass back in the pool, and let's go again!"

Chapter 23

Lunch is moments away. But the shower first is what my body needs more than anything. The water down here is piping hot...perfect for exhausted muscles. After another ten times in the pool with the artificial anaconda, standing in a steaming, hot shower of relief is all I want. I feel my body melt a little. I lean my body against the shower's wall and let the water wash over me. I think I might have dozed for a minute. Ezra's infamous pounding knock snaps me out of my brief Zen.

I answer him with a mumble. "Be right out!" I lean my head back against the wall again. The water hits my face now.

Ezra speaks again in a singsong voice. "I will come in there."

More obsessive pounding.

"All right! Fine!"

* * *

Lunch is superior to any other I have had in months! Chicken picatta with angel hair pasta in a creamy lemon sauce and capers. I am the last to arrive at the cafeteria. I must look exhausted from this morning's training session.

Angela smiles a little. "Are you all right? You look like you have been through hell!" Her smile quickly fades as she realizes her fate of pool training in this afternoon's session. She begins to shred her dinner roll nervously.

I muster a smile and shrug. "Nah. I'm all right. Just starving." I start to eat quietly.

Nick snickers. "Yo! Look at Jesca! She can really pack it in. It is an awesome sight to see a woman with an appetite!"

Nate smiles in my direction and puts his head down as he continues to eat. I roll my eyes and laugh, grateful for the little bit of humor I have brought to the table.

Lunch hour is not enough. As soon as I shovel in the last bite of my carbohydrate-loaded lunch, Siobhan is giving us our afternoon training locations.

* * *

The rest of the day is just as rigorous as this morning. The remainder of my day requires less physical work and more mental work. Ezra took inventory of my abilities while I was showering and eating lunch. The telepathy, mind reading. The humming and vibrations I am feeling, Qi. The Telekinesis, the Ushering, and the visions. Ezra looks down at his notes now and blows out his lower lip. "I have a lot to work with here."

"Thanks, Ezra. I'm glad I could oblige."

Ezra scoffs, "You haven't obliged me yet, Jes. I can't wait to watch you develop your gifts. To watch you realize who you are and what you are capable of. How you can change the path of anything and everything."

Chapter 24

The rest of the first week is filled with sore, achy limbs and a tired body. I am drained by 7 p.m. every night, and not ready to rise daily at 5:45 a.m.

The second week is much easier since our bodies are becoming more accustomed to the physical and mental training. Nate, Angela, Nick and I are able to hang out a bit in the rec room after dinner now that our bodies aren't so exhausted. A couple of hours of normal conversation with people that we could relate to is exactly what we needed.

We wasted no time finding an activity, foosball. Nick, being the uber sporty that he is, suggested this downtime activity.

Nick lies across the pool table, rolling the eight ball between his hands. "Ugh! We need to unwind a bit, guys. Between the physical and mental demands, we need a mindless release."

He holds the eight ball in one hand. "I got it! Foosball! It's perfect. Ang, c'mon. You and I, babe!"

Angela's eyes widen. Her cheeks turn bright red. "Ang! It's Angela. And it's on, BABE!"

So begins our foosball tournament.

* * *

Week three, the body aches and sore muscles stop altogether. The abilities that each of us possess are getting so much stronger. Now well into our training routine, our delusions of being kingpins in the facility become too reckless for our mentors to accept.

One morning we enter the main gym after breakfast, pushing each other's buttons about the resulting win from last night's foosball game. All the mentors make it obvious that they have been waiting on us.

Jake is sitting on the bleachers and looks up. "You guys are late!

Ezra looks at me with his arms crossed. Disappointment is on his face.

We all stop laughing.

Jake, anticipating Nick's quick wit, walks up to Nick. "Don't you start now!"

"Start what? All I was going to say was that Jesca schooled Nate last night in the tournament."

Nick reaches over and elbows Nate's arm playfully. Nate smiles and punches Nick on his arm less playfully. They both look at each other. Their smiles turn to mischief. Nate and Nick begin wrestling to the ground. Angela and I cover our mouths to hold back our laughter.

Ezra yells, "Enough!"

This gets Nate's and Nick's attention. They both wrestling immediately.

Nate sighs. "C'mon, Ezra. We have been working so hard. Being ten minutes late isn't the end of the world."

"On the contrary, Nate, that is the very thing on the line here. And you are going to be on THAT front line in under two weeks!"

Siobhan starts in. "You really don't comprehend this, do you?" She slowly walks over to Nate, then me, looking each of us up and down with her steel blue eyes. She stops at Angela and stares at her with anger.

Angela looks at me, then Ezra; fear is in her eyes. I can hear her thinking about Siobhan.

What?

Why are you looking at me like that?

She looks like she is going to attack me.

Siobhan steps closer to Angela; they're nose and nose. I can't read Siobhan's thoughts. She has blocked me. Angela knows that I am reading her.

Angela thinks, *No, I won't. I'm not. That is absurd. Stop. I do take this seriously. I will prove it in two weeks. The hell you will!*

I can't help Angela without being able to hear both sides of the conversation. I can feel the tension between the two of them, though. I think we all can feel the tension by the looks I see around the room. All of a sudden, I feel a small vibration within me. It feels strange at first since I haven't experienced it in weeks. The hair on my arms stands on end as a result.

Why am I feeling this here, in the facility?

I look at Nate. Then at Ezra. Siobhan pulls out a dagger from her belt. Angela pushes past Siobhan and is in a combat stance quicker than I can blink.

What the hell is going on?

150

Ezra? Luke? Jake?

They hear me. They look at me with stoic faces.

They've blocked me. They're testing us.

Nate takes my arm. *Back up, Jes. Don't get involved.*

I have my wall up. *How did you get into my head?*

It wasn't easy, Jesca.

Nate pulls me close to him a second before Siobhan swings her blade at Angela.

Angela flips backwards, landing in a hunched stance ready to attack. Her movements look like a quick dance; it is crazy fast.

Siobhan shifts her body to stand normally. She places her dagger back in her belt and begins to stretch her arms. Angela doesn't let her guard down. Siobhan fastens her belt.

"Ezra, Jake, Luke, and I think it is about time for us to put all of the training to practice."

Luke starts in. "Siobhan, if I didn't know you better, I would say that this is your favorite part of the training."

Siobhan finishes her stretch. "Well, yeah! This is the closest to real these green peas will get. Then they will be plummeted into their territory and scared to death."

Ezra has his arms crossed the whole time, watching the interaction. Jake pulls off his sweatshirt. "Well, I've been ready for about a week now!"

Jake walks over to Nick. Nick pulls off his wind pants, leaving shorts in their place.

Nick says, "Hell yeah, baby! I'm ready! This is awesome! Mock combat."

Luke and Jake give each other a sideways glance and mouth, "Mock combat?"

Ezra pipes in, "All right, take it down a notch. We are going to wait 'til mid-week to begin that phase of the training. However…" Ezra pauses.

He is obviously trying to ease us into the back-story.

Luke doesn't hesitate. "…something catastrophic has happened in Japan that is very relevant to our purpose as guardians."

Nate releases my arms, but is still standing close behind me. Nate asks Luke, "What is it?"

All of us become very serious. Angela stands next to Nate, Nick and I now.

Ezra says, "Many years ago, it was theorized that wormholes could occur in close proximity to areas of high electromagnetic fields, EMFs. The EMF made the opening of the wormhole much easier to maintain since strong electric energy was naturally in the atmosphere. There is said to be a handful of locations that emit such EMFs. Two locations on two different continents have been publicized more than the others in recent years."

Angela breaks in. "I read about this. The Bermuda Triangle and the Dragon's Triangle."

Ezra nods. "Yes, those are the two areas: the Devil's Sea near western Japan, north of Tokyo, and the Bermuda Triangle near Florida. Einstein spent some time in Bermuda back in the 1930's. It was said that Einstein lived there in order to qualify for US citizenship. Albert was then employed by the US government to investigate the Bermuda Triangle, and its justification involved his infamous Einstein-Rosen Bridge theory."

I ask, "The government paid him to try to find the other end of the wormhole?"

Ezra replies, "It was only a theory with very little justification. Einstein spent over 15 years being commissioned by the government to make the wormhole theory plausible and true. His research continued until his death. He never finished resolving the theory."

Nate asks, "Do you think he knew? Do you think he discovered that it was real and didn't publically disclose the results, like Sebastian and Balthazar?"

Ezra shakes his finger and smiles. "Ahh, Nate. I believe that Einstein's purpose was very significant. I believe he chose to protect the world until his death. Unfortunately, others were not so insightful and cautious."

I realize what Ezra is saying. "So you think he knew, but kept it to himself to protect us from ourselves."

Ezra says, "Potential misuse of the discovery. To be tempted by the power and control this truth could produce. To reveal a treasure that should be protected and regulated, not exploited and abused."

Nick brings us back to the pressing issue. "So what happened? What catastrophic event has increased our need to be ready sooner than later?"

Ezra replies, "Three days ago Japan suffered the worst earthquake in its history. The quake's initial destruction was significant and horrific. Aftershocks are still being felt in Japan as strong as 7.7 on the Richter scale."

Angela says, "That is terrible. But I fail to see how this links to us, though." Angela's face changes. "Unless you think the quake had something to do with the Dragon's Triangle. Did a wormhole opening cause this?"

The four mentors look at each other.

Luke begins, "The guardians we have in Japan were sabotaged last night. We sent five guardians in to shut down the unit of Sondians that were opening the wormhole there. The wormhole had been open for more than thirty minutes from what our surveillance showed. That type of length could create a gravitational instability in our world, like a quake of great magnitude.

"Unknown to us, three of our five guardians were deep cover Sondian guardians. Once our guardians were in the warehouse, the three deep covers eliminated Jonathan Hatton, one of our two true guardians. Joan Leal, the other guardian, was the one that single-handedly wired the explosives, then terminated the Sondian unit's warehouse, closing the wormhole."

I ask, "Where is she now?" I was intrigued by her strength and selflessness.

Luke says, "In order to shut down the unit, she had to choose: try to escape, surrender, or save humanity by destroying everything including herself." Luke pauses and looks down. "She saved humanity for one more day."

Everyone is silent. Partly for such a brave and selfless act. Also, partly because of what we have become—guardians. We can feel the fear shoot through each of us. Soon, one of us may be expected to make that same choice.

154

Siobhan says, "She sacrificed herself. Needless to say, somewhere along the chain of command, someone let their guard down. The momentary lapse could have been a temptation, or pride, anything. And now we have to replace the guardians we lost."

Jake breaks in, "And no, Nick. You are not going to Tokyo."

Nick looks slightly disappointed.

Jake continues, "We have mentors and guardians scattered throughout the world. The hot spots for now are in the US and Japan, for obvious reasons."

Ezra says, "There are guardians already in position to take over in Japan along with their mentors. And the sleeper cell has cleaned up the aftermath and covered up any reason for police investigation."

This is a well-oiled machine. Systems are in place to replace those that perish without missing a beat.

Luke regains his frustration. "So when you guys strolled in ten minutes late, like you owned the place, it was hard for us to handle."

We all feel the pangs of guilt.

I speak up. "We are very sorry. It was irresponsible of us."

Siobhan says, "This is why we are changing training a bit today." She looks at Ezra for confirmation.

Ezra adds, "The remainder of your time in the facility will focus on three core activities: abilities training, mission combat, and intelligence training. You all need to know the back-story and most recent accounts of enemy attacks on our guardians. The more you know about Dobrian and Sondian guardian warfare in the past, the better guardian you will become for the future."

"How is the combat going to work?" Nate asks.

Siobhan walks up to Angela. "First, we will combat mentor against trainee for a solid two days. Then you will team up together and combat the mentors. You need to have team experience as well. Using your abilities together makes you stronger than using your abilities individually. Energy attracts energy. The buildup of the energy infuses with your abilities and can be exchanged through you both like magnets drawn together. Your abilities will work in unison."

Siobhan walks over to stand in front of Jake. Siobhan closes her eyes and clasps one of Jake's hands. Jake closes his eyes and smiles. At first, I thought the ground was lifting under them. Then the slow rise becomes sudden and they are about twelve feet off the ground.

Nick whispers excitedly, "Aw, sweet!"

Siobhan and Jake open their eyes.

Jake speaks to Siobhan. "You ready?"

Siobhan looks over and smiles at him. Jake opens the palm of his other hand. A vapor stirs from it. Then fire from his palm turns orange, then blue. They both simultaneously turn their bodies toward each other. Siobhan voluntarily raises her open palm to Jake's palm. The blue flame dances from Jake's palm to Siobhan's.

Ezra explains, "Siobhan and Jake are able to share their abilities, like Siobhan was describing to you. What you don't see is the metaphysical aspect. The mind of one being evolved and permitted these abilities to infuse and manifest in another's open mind. It's harder than it looks, kids."

Siobhan and Jake return to the ground, and the flame dissipates. Siobhan leans against the wall for a minute. Concerned, Angela walks over to Siobhan.

Angela asks, "Are you all right, Siobhan?"

Siobhan tilts her head upward and then pushes off the wall. "Yeah. Yeah. We haven't teamed up in a while. It's been about a month, month and half now. Right, Jake?"

Jake is squatting on the floor, taking a few long gulps of Gatorade. He ruffles his hair a bit and looks up at Siobhan and winks. "Yeah, it's been a while. But it's like riding a bike. You don't forget."

Seeing the way they are looking at each other makes me a little embarrassed for having spied such a personal exchange between them. I block my thoughts for a moment.

Are they romantically involved?

I shift my eyes to Nate. He must have seen it too since he looks away from them then at me also.

I wonder how they became more than just friends, if that is what is going on. My mind starts to create its own story for them.

Nate elbows me and whispers, "Oh, this is so sweet it's giving me a toothache."

I elbow him back and feel my cheeks turn red. *How did he get through my mental block, again?* I growl, "Will you stop that, damn it."

I retaliate by listening in on him as he rolls his eyes at me and thinks, *What?! It was sweet though, right?*

157

We both are looking at each other now, fire in my eyes and Nate with his boyish playfulness.

I roll my eyes and mumble, "Whatever."

Ezra claps his hands, bringing us back. "All right, kids, now it is time to see you in action! First, we split up with our mentors. We will combat, and then work on exchanging energy between each other. Then we will do the same between the four of you only. We will divide you up into a pair, and you will combat each other. Then you will exchange energy with your partner. If you don't mind, we will save the ultimate combat of mentors vs. trainees until after lunch. I never like to whip up on green peas on an empty stomach."

Luke laughs. "Touché, Ezra!"

Luke and Ezra exchange a high five. The four of us "green peas" look at each other with competitive zeal and huge grins on our faces. Nobody needs to say anything. We all simultaneously feel the same way. This is what we have been waiting for.

Chapter 27

Each of us partner with our mentor and go to our own part of the facility. Angela and Siobhan take the open gym area. They need space with the very acrobatic combat style they both possess. Jake and Nick head to the pool. They need to be in close proximity to water just in case Nick's fire-starting gets out of control. The shifting for Nick can be done anywhere, but they are going to try to incorporate that under water as well. Since being in the facility, Nick has graced us with a German shepherd shift, a camel shift, a Zach Efron shift, and a Kristen Stewart shift. He took requests also. It was awesome. But Nick needed to work on shifts that helped him blend into the environment, not draw attention to him.

Luke and Nate target his Latrosis, Nate's ability to physically heal others with his mind and inner energy, his Qi. This ability is very valuable, but very difficult to balance and master. Luke thinks it would be best to start small. Scrapes, blisters, nose bleeds, headaches, and vertigo from the energy drain we experience after using our abilities. All of these are bound to happen with us using our abilities rigorously today.

Nate moves from Angela, to Nick, to me in rotation. He observes and takes inventory of our wounds and heals us with Luke's monitoring. One slip-up on Nate's part can leave any of us in really bad shape. Luke told us that Nate could be attempting to heal a blister on a finger and send a surge of energy too strong that could burn the finger to a crisp.

I can see Nate is very apprehensive to say the least. He knows that he could lose control and balance and hurt one of us. Luke reassures him that he is right there to step in if he senses an imbalance or surge coming. Luke developed a bit of Clairvoyance, being able to tell the future, over his years as a guardian.

Then there is Ezra and I. Ezra plans to work on the abilities that have been hidden, that I have not experimented with yet. I have already had plenty of practice with Telepathy and blocking my mind from others. Nate's recent break-in still has me wondering about my strength. The other three abilities are still weak. I tell Ezra that they really don't appear to be abilities at all.

Ezra says, "Oh, I assure you, Jes. You don't realize what you have stored up inside of you."

Ezra is as giddy about my gifts as a child would be waiting to open a birthday present.

Ezra and I head to the trails.

The trailhead?

I understood why the others are in the designated areas that the mentors chose. Jake for the fire stuff. Angela for the space. But which of my abilities qualifies the trails as my training area? I stand apprehensively thinking of all the possibilities.

Ezra says, "Jes. Take a leap of faith. You have spent most of your life calculating and organizing a bulletproof plan. It's time to let go. Here you are safe. This is the time and place to practice your faith, your gut, and your intuition. All of those abilities within you have been weakened by having every little detail planned and accounted for in your life. You will need these skills as soon as you set foot above ground. Embrace them. They are within you, waiting to be awakened."

Ezra walks ahead of me. I stand there, like I am physically stuck in setting quicksand. The longer I stand and think, the more indecisive I become. My ears follow Ezra's footsteps leaving the gym. I put my head down and close my eyes.

Go, Jes. Leap. Don't wait. Don't hesitate.

I open my eyes and jog to catch up with Ezra.

* * *

Ezra and I stop at the mouth of the trail.

"All right, let's go!" Ezra smiles and disappears right before my eyes.

What the hell?

I feel a warm presence near the back of my right shoulder. I turn, instantly in combat stance, and ready myself.

Ezra says, "Just jumping! Don't tell me you've never tried it." Ezra is standing there with his arms crossed over his chest now. "We aren't going to fight yet, Jes. Just going to work on finding you."

I roll my eyes and relax. "Okay. So what am I trying to find within me? And this jumping thing? I have only done that in my dreams."

Ezra points at me. "Exactly. Lucid dreaming. It is like physical jumping, but in the ethereal sense. Astral projection can be lucid dreaming as well. Quantum jumping is the use of your inner life force and energy in waking hours. Lucid dreams are jumping using your life force and energy in your sleep."

Again, I had the blank look on my face. "Uh. Okay?"

Ezra sighs. "Tell me about your dreams. Like the most vivid ones that you have had lately."

I respond, "The most vivid one is the one where I am running to Mom and Dad's house and I am confronted by a dark being."

Ezra interrupts, "That is a life force that you experience. A Sondian guardian trying to enter your mind with his or her well-tuned abilities. The dark aura you see is the form your mind has given this life force. It is a person. Has it happened to you in waking hours?"

I reply more anxiously now, having heard this dream experience was becoming reality, "Yes. I had one on a daily basis until we came here."

Ezra rubs the stubble on his chin.

I wait for a few moments. "Ezra? What? You are making me worry?"

Ezra says, "Sorry. I'm really glad we got out of Georgia when we did. Someone was onto you and your purpose. I can only imagine what could have happened."

I interrupt him. "Well, let's not, all right. I'm here now. Let's not dwell on what could have happened." I sound awfully brave for someone who is so full of fear right now. I listen to my own words and refocus. "Like I was saying, I am face to face with this aura, and I begin to use some inner force or energy to defend myself and my mom and dad. It feels like I'm using every single muscle in my body. When I wake, I am drained physically. I feel like I have just run a marathon. My brain is exhausted, too. The drain only lasts for half an hour or so, sleep paralysis. Then I'm able to get out of bed."

Ezra says, "That is the Qi I was telling you about, your inner energy. The drain is not sleep paralysis. It is the exhaustion of your inner energy. You deplete your energy levels every time you use your Qi. We need to shorten your drain time, though. We don't want you to get caught with your defenses down out in the field.

"When I first started using my Qi, it took me and hour or more to replenish. It took time to learn how to control the amount of energy I expended. I needed to pace myself. We will work on that. Something you may not realize is that Qi also helps you to Astral Project, jump, from place to place like I just did. The distance you can jump is gained with practice. Obviously, the shorter the jump the less drain on your Qi. At first, your projection will be weak. You will need to practice to get more accurate with where you jump."

I have a question. "So you are saying I jumped in my dreams from my house to my parents' house?"

Ezra reads this spark in my mind and my growing confidence. "There! Hold on to that fuel. That fuel protected you and your family when you jumped in your last nightmare while we were in Georgia. Yeah, it sucked that you were violated. Believe me when I tell you that I got you and your parents out as soon as I knew things were getting too close for comfort."

I thought for a minute. So Ezra was really there, in my last jump.

Ezra is aware of my thought. "It was only guidance, Jes. You did all of the work. You had the grit, the strength to jump to your home from your apartment and fight back. You were able to project and fight without much drain. Keep that fire in you, Jes. Don't let that fire die."

* * *

Part of the morning, Ezra models and I follow. I have full control over the Ushering. I use it tactfully to render the enemy submissive to my command. I practice on the chefs in the dining hall. It is quite humorous to have Miss Char, Patrick, and Fenton creating awesome confections and home-style comfort food upon my request. Fenton is making homemade macaroni and cheese. Miss Char is baking peach and raspberry cobblers, as well as yummy snicker-doodle cookies. Patrick is working on a beef stew and White Lightning Chicken Chili. The southern dishes would have given our chefs a heart attack if they were in their normal state of mind.

Ezra and I are sitting at one of the tables.

I take advantage of the moment. I have wanted to ask Ezra this question for a while. It is just not something you can blurt out in between training sessions. My contact with Ezra outside of the training realm since we got here was nonexistent. I want to know more about the man that knows so very much about me. The man who seems to know every detail about my life, the events in it, and the people involved in it.

Ezra is snacking on homemade potato chips while he tells me about the afternoon training he has planned. I am having a protein shake and banana, training food in all its glory.

I tread cautiously as I try to find out more about Ezra Kahn.

"So how old were you when you were called to become a guardian?"

Ezra pauses mid-crunch. He wipes his hands with a napkin while he thinks. He clears his throat. "I was about your age. Maybe a couple of years younger. I had just graduated high school and was set to attend MIT in the fall."

I am waiting for more, but nothing comes. "Well, where did you grow up?"

With this question, he is sipping his Pepsi. It is torture watching him drink the dark, carbonated bubbly in the frosty tumbler.

"I was raised in Cambridge, Massachusetts." Ezra continues to eat his deep-fried snack as I pull at the stringy part of the banana peel.

I try to keep the conversation alive. "Well, that is convenient being that you grew up and were attending college in the same city. I have never been to Massachusetts. What was your family like as a child?"

With that question, he takes a long drink. "Mom and Dad were very faithful Christians and raised me to know my faith and spiritual connection with God. They also raised me to know that science and metaphysics could be the tools that

God had given to us to make sense of the things that would otherwise be nonsensical or impossible. Very similar to your parents when it came to upbringing." Ezra got a long crease in the middle of his forehead. "But I was defiant with the life my parents were guiding me through. I was a bullheaded and a rebellious kid.

"It took a slap in the face by the hand of God to make me realize it, since my parents had done everything in their power to turn things around with me. I was cocky, impulsive, and arrogant. I was always in trouble at school. In middle school I was labeled a troublemaker by teachers and classmates alike. I pretended that it didn't bother me. I hung out with the other 'bad kids' and did some pretty unsavory things. No, I'm not telling you, Jes!" He smiles with that last comment.

"My parents were guardians. At the time, I was not aware. It was kept from me. My mother was a professor at MIT in the geophysics department. My father a professor at MIT in the biology department. They were always traveling for work. I never knew where they would go. But they were always home when I got home." Ezra seems to daydream for a moment.

I interrupt, "Did they meet there? At MIT?" I continue to savor my French Vanilla flavored protein shake.

Ezra says, "They met while attending as students."

"When did they become guardians?"

"When they entered university is what Sebastian told me." Ezra looks down.

"Why was Sebastian the one to tell you?"

Ezra snaps, "Mom and Dad were murdered when I was in seventh grade."

I lower my eyes to my banana skin and soften my voice. "I'm very sorry, Ezra."

"I was at school. As I was walking out of the building, there he was standing across the street: Sebastian. He was dressed in a suit, tie, and tan trench coat to ward off the cold. He had salt-and-pepper hair and was shorter than me. He took his round sunglasses off when he saw me and walked across the street toward me. That was the first time I met the man that was an instrument in catapulting my life into chaos. He informed me of my parents passing, that I was a target and needed to go with him quickly. I wasn't about to go with someone I didn't know, let alone someone who just told me my parents had died.

"I took off running as hard as I could, but didn't get far. Sebastian could jump. He blocked my every attempt at escape. It did not take many jumps to subdue me. I was in shock and more frightened than I had ever been in my life. I mean, I just saw a man disappear and reappear right in front of me. I fought and clawed and tried to scream. He grabbed my face and forced me to look at him. He stared at me, an odd stare, like he was burning a thought into my mind. I continued to fight him. Finally, he released me. He told me that I could already build walls. That was all he said."

On the edge of my seat, I ask, "What did that mean?"

Ezra says, "It meant that he couldn't Usher me. I was blocking his Compulsion. I could block him from reading me, too. All I remember after that was a cloth going over my face and the world slowing down until everything was dark. I remembered waking up in a very brightly lit, quiet room. I was lying on a couch, looking at the rotating ceiling fan, hoping that my parents' death, this mysterious man, was all just a nightmare. I shot up off the couch with my heart racing, thinking that might jolt me from the nightmare. But it did not."

* * *

"Hello, Ezra. I am Sebastian Onoch." He is sitting in a chair in a dark corner of the room.

"Where are my parents? Where am I?"

"You are in a safe place. The facility. We started this safe place in this very room." He pauses to look around the room and breathes in deeply. "You are here because your parents have been murdered."

I growl, "You are a liar."

Sebastian replies with genuine care. "No. I'm not, Ezra. This is real. God knows, this is real."

I begin to cry with anger first, then sadness and sorrow. All of the terrible things I had done, been doing, all come flooding over me. I had so much regret built up inside me. I start to bang on the walls. I throw the only lamp in the room. I drop to the floor and yell until my voice is hoarse and exhausted. And Sebastian lets me. He let me be and go through the motions of my grief. When I finally slow my sobs to sniffles and hiccups, I look up at him. He has tears welling up in his own eyes. He looks like he is breaking inside for me. I stare at him.

Sebastian speaks in a shaken voice. "Ezra. I am so very sorry that this tragedy has happened to you. My sons went through the same pain when they were young. They lost their mother just like you, to a terrible and violent death."

He stands, walks over to me, and kneels. "Just now, watching you go through the emotions. I see now what I didn't see my own sons go through years ago. When they needed me."

Sebastian watches over me as I continue to sob. When I am exhausted and have no more tears, I whisper, "I don't have any other family. Where am I going to go? I have no one. I'm alone."

Sebastian places his hand on my shoulder. "Yes, you do, Ezra. You have us."

* * *

Ezra wipes his hands on a napkin after eating another chip.

"Sebastian told me that my parents became guardians when they entered college. They were majoring in the sciences, ideal for guardians. Sebastian sought them out with invitations to go on a scientific expedition during their junior year. Intrigued and adventurous, with nothing holding them back, they both accepted eagerly. Unknown to them, they were invited based on their academic prowess. And the scientific expedition turned out to be a quantum leap from Earth to Dobria."

"They traveled to Dobria?"

"They were part of the first colony to Dobria. They were originally going to stay there and research, develop, and study the environment. They were the analysts that studied the space-time differential between Dobria and Earth. They helped construct the subterranean living quarters for the colony. They stayed for about two Dobrian years, eight Earth years. They were part of the initial colony dedicated to absorbing as much of the planet and its potential as possible. The planet had its own unique properties for life to flourish, life-forms unlike Earth's. Unique organisms with duplicate organs and multifunctional appendages for defense and for protection."

"Why did they leave?"

"Mom became pregnant with me. They talked with Sebastian. They were all unsure of how a pregnancy would withstand the altered properties of Dobria as the fetus developed. The gestation could vary because of the space-time factor. They were also concerned about the adaptations the fetus might experience with being in the Dobrian environment.

"Mom and Dad had firsthand experience with both physical and metaphysical changes that they had adapted to while in Dobria. Sebastian and my parents agreed that they needed to return to Earth for my sake. Sebastian found my parents to be a perfect match to form a sleeper cell stationed in Massachusetts."

Ezra takes another gulp of Pepsi then speaks. "My parents agreed with this and returned to Earth."

"How did everything turn out? Did everything go normally with your development?"

"Everything was in the right places physically. Some of the metaphysical properties carried over through my mother due to her adapting to Dobria."

An enormous explosion startles us from our conversation.

Ezra looks up at me. "What the hell was that?"

It wasn't from the kitchen. I look out the window holes in the café entry doors behind us. Smoke is billowing down the hall from the direction of the pool and gym. Ezra jumps up, and I quickly follow. Just before we get to the doors to the cafeteria, Jake and Nick open the door. Nick has a look of shock on his soot-covered face. Jake is coughing from the smoke. The rest of the team files in behind them.

Jake is smirking. "That's what you get, show off! Damn it, Nick!"

Nick's look of embarrassment is priceless.

Nick says, "Oh, c'mon. I was in complete control. I just wanted to give you deadbeats a little surprise."

Angela says, "Yeah, right, hot stuff." She gives him a light pat on the shoulder.

Nick rolls his eyes and straightens up. "Hot stuff, huh? I like that." He struts past, the laughter echoing behind him at his expense.

Nick quickly changes the subject. "Let's eat, ladies and gents."

Nate looks at me. "It smells amazing in here."

"Thank you. I thought some southern comfort food was due."

Angela says, "Thanks, girly. Ushering?"

"Yep."

The chefs have set up a buffet at the main table and places are set on a long table brought in by the maintenance staff.

We watch as the food is wheeled out on carts: one, two, three carts worth.

Chef Fenton announces, "Lunch is served."

All of us applaud as we get in line to indulge in the delicious spread of southern-style goodness.

Chapter 28

The afternoon is very physical with jumping while in combat. Ezra does not speak any further about his life or parents' lives. I don't push the topic. He opened up quite a bit today, and I don't want him to clam up on me.

Ezra is all business this afternoon and for good and obvious reasons. We are one week out from leaving the facility.

Ezra doesn't hold back. I scramble to my feet after the first blow to my midsection. We dance around each other for a moment.

I ask breathlessly, "Aren't you going to give me any clues on how to jump during the day, or are you going to continue beating the crap out of me. Seems a little unfair."

I jab and miss, but follow with a leg sweep that takes him down to the floor.

Ezra disappears from the ground and reappears standing behind me. Ezra is breathing evenly, not fazed the slightest physically.

"It's just like jumping in your dreams. Your Qi needs to be released. You have it, Jes. It is in there." Ezra points to my head.

He points to my heart. "And in there."

He puts his hands on his hips. "Remember this morning. Fuel the fire."

He slaps me across the face. My head snaps back at him.

Oh no, he didn't.

I zone in on Ezra. I feel the vibration and hear the humming. Everything around Ezra becomes blurry. He is in sharp focus, though. I imagine myself behind Ezra. I feel vertigo and weightless suddenly. All the blurriness shifts into sharp view; I am looking at the back of Ezra's form.

I feel Ezra smile when he speaks. "Perfect."

This feels like the feeling I got at the bookstore before I found out everything.

Ezra nods at my thought. "You didn't know what it was then. Your body was trying to defend itself without your knowledge of it. Your body was trying to jump."

He turns quickly, poised for another round of attacks. For the next two hours, we battle throughout the facility. We spar in the trails, in the rec room, in the gym. Jumping is nauseating at first. The feeling of vertigo just before each jump is sending my stomach upside down. By 4 p.m. I am heaving.

"Are you okay?" Ezra is out of breath and bends over with his hands on his knees.

I smile a little at the thought of my making Ezra Kahn exhausted. "Yeah. Yeah. I'm just feeling a little light-headed. I think I need to throw up."

Ezra disappears and is back with cold washcloths in seconds. He places one on the back of my neck and one on my face. "Keep this on your head and neck. Sit down."

I walk over to the bleachers on the far side of the gym.

Ezra yells, "Nate? We need you in here!"

He enters the gym just after Ezra yells.

"I know. I was heading your way as soon as I heard her thoughts. I was deep in the trails so it took me a little longer."

I did not want to be vulnerable around Nate. Ezra shouldn't have called him; he is overreacting. "I'll be fine. Really, I can handle this."

"C'mon, Jes. Let him heal you. That is part of Nate's purpose here. Let him help with the vertigo."

I try to stand up and walk away from them. I start to see flashing shards of light before my eyes as soon as I stand. I'm getting hot and clammy. Everything begins to race inside of me. I can feel the blood pumping through my veins. I can't see anything all of a sudden.

Nate hisses, "Ezra, she is crashing!"

My body wants to lie down, while my mind wants to escape from here.

"God, Jes. You're burning up! Help her, Nate!"

I feel them both pulling off my shirt. Someone grabs me and picks me up. I lean against the person carrying me.

"It's me, *Nate*. I'm getting you into the pool."

I think Ezra jumps in after us.

I feel Nate's hands, arms, and chest infusing me with warmth. Then, I feel cooling course through my body. I put my arm around his neck. Nate holds me tighter.

He puts his mouth close to my ear. "Shh! Stay still. Just breathe. I've got you, Jes."

He sounds breathless.

Ezra asks, "You got her? Is she responding?"

I feel the soothing coolness calm my racing heart. My pulse is slowing, becoming regulated. I open my eyes and can see the rise and fall of Nate's chest. I move my hand down from his shoulder to where his heart is. His heart is pounding so hard.

Nate answers Ezra after a few moments. I think he is taking inventory of what is going on inside of my body. "Yes, she is." He is still breathless.

I lift my head slowly to look at him. Then I look at Ezra. My head still feels heavy.

Ezra says, "Jes? Hey, you all right?"

I nod and look back at Nate. He is staring down at me.

Ezra yells and claps his hands together. "Jes!"

"I…I'm better."

I realize that Nate and I are still in an intimate embrace. I slowly try to wiggle out of it. Nate is slow to let go, but does. His hands linger on mine. I pretend that he is just making sure I am steady on my feet. I know otherwise.

I whisper, "Thank you." I slowly pull my hand away and turn from Nate to Ezra. "I'm all right. A bit wobbly, but all right."

As I climb out of the pool, I hear Nate's thoughts, and I blush.

Ezra decides to call it a day and sends me to shower. He and Nate give me some privacy. Ezra asks me to meet in the main hearth room after I finish.

As I dry and dress, I can't help recounting the meltdown I had moments ago. Nate's arms holding me, healing me, calming me. Feeling so safe and protected, like I was the only thing in the world he had to focus on. And his thoughts.

Those thoughts.

176

I begin to blush again. I don't let on that I read him. He has to know, though. He read mine so easily before. He obviously had practiced his gift more than I.

Why didn't he block his thoughts?

The thoughts that his feelings may be stronger for me than he first anticipated? That I made him breathless. Did he want me to know?

Ugh, this isn't the time or place to have these feelings. Romance needs to be the farthest thing from my mind. This is a perfect reminder that I need to learn how to block my mind better than I have been. I don't want to allow just anyone crawling around in my head, deducting information that can put the team and others in jeopardy.

I head to the hearth room. I hear Ezra and Nate talking, so I quiet my approach not to interrupt. I use the opportunity to block my thoughts as well, so they can't detect my approach. Nate is speaking.

"When I was holding her, it was different. I mean, I could hear her pulse inside my own body. I didn't feel that when I was healing Angela's broken arm after her combat with Siobhan. I didn't feel that with Nick after healing his burns. With them, it was straightforward and simple, two people. But with Jes, it's different. It was like we were connected, linked."

Ezra releases a long, tense breath. Ezra looks at Nate. "You are linked."

It was silent for a while.

Linked?

I hear Ezra growl. "Who would have thought out of all the guardians in the world that it would be you? Usually, it is someone more...experienced with their abilities. Not to say that you aren't learning quickly. If it was going to be anyone in our group, I would have thought it would be Luke."

Nate responds with irritation. "Well, it isn't. It's me. Now, what the hell does it mean?"

"This means that you are bonded to Jesca. No matter where she is, you will know what she is thinking, feeling, and doing. And vice versa. She will know everything you are thinking, feeling, and doing. You and Jes are linked, forever."

Chapter 29

I wait until there is a break in the conversation and round the corner.

They both have their arms crossed and are looking at me like I have just committed a crime.

Damn it. I must really be bad at blocking my thoughts.

"I guess there is no reason to say that I didn't hear anything, since both of you can read me so easily."

Ezra says, "Well, that isn't entirely true. It isn't easy. But when you are linked, it is less difficult than trying to get into a person's mind that you are not linked to. And you can force a block between two linked people, but I don't recommend it."

Nate's eyes shift to Ezra, looking a little guilty. "Why is that?"

"Blocking your partner can weaken your ability to share energy. It's like a stream of electricity. When the current is interrupted, the conductivity is weakened and it takes more energy to link mentally. The last thing you need to do is interrupt that energy flow. It could leave you vulnerable during a battle."

I repeat the question just to make sure. "So we can block our thoughts with everyone else, except each other?"

Ezra says, "You can block each other. It is just not recommended for both of your safety."

I ask, "How is this possible? How can a link between us be possible?" I think I know the answer, but I want Ezra to confirm it. My heart starts to pound in my throat as I anticipate the answer.

"It is possible because you both have abilities that permit it. These abilities are not shared by everyone. That is why you are here. Those that share abilities can link because they are..." Ezra is visibly looking for the right words. "...wired differently from the general public. You know, the majority of human beings use only 10% of their minds."

I look down, a bit disappointed. I thought maybe it had something to do with the Copula that Sebastian had developed.

I look at Nate. "Are we going to agree to not block each other for our safety and the safety of everyone that we care about? I don't want to end up dead because you are keeping something from me."

It sounded so cruel, I was going to do all I could to keep feelings out of this. If I need to sound like a selfish brat, then so be it. Too many things depend on us now.

Nate looks at me. "I agree. Do you agree you won't get me killed by withholding how you feel?"

I feel my cheeks redden. I answer sharply. "Yes."

I quickly look at Ezra to shift the focus from my expression. "I think I need more work on blocking others from reading me. I mean, Sondians."

Nate adds, "I could use some practice as well."

So, Nate is willing to put these romantic feelings aside as well. I have to admit it is a relief. I can't deny that I feel a small burning in my heart, though.

Ezra explains blocking to be like a virtual wall built by your inner energy life force. With the use of imagery, you build your wall around your thoughts when in the presence of an unwelcomed reader. Safe idea, block anyone that you don't know. This practice is easy since there wasn't any physical expenditure of energy. It is all ethereal, which makes it detrimental to the bond between Nate and I. Within an hour, Nate and I fully understand the ins and outs of blocking others' thoughts.

The rest of the week we spar, infiltrate, share abilities, and pump up each other's egos, especially when we're teamed against the mentors. Jake and Ezra are definitely a force to be reckoned with when they pair up; the energy force between them is so strong. Siobhan is a force all on her own. A "spitfire" is what Jake calls her. Her flexibility, speed, and grace are unreal. No one can see her coming, except Angela. We are all being trained by the best. Nick is in complete control of his fire wielding by mid-week. And with a few minor incidents added to the explosion earlier in the week, he has become more humble with what he refers to as his bag of tricks. Nick's sense of humor is not affected by the humbling experiences, which we are all thankful for. His comic relief gets us through many grueling afternoons.

* * *

The final week comes. I wake up Monday morning earlier than necessary. It is 5:30 a.m. I lie there thinking about the week ahead. The territory I will be assigned to is a constant thought in the front of my mind. Mostly I am eager to get on with it. I have never been one to keep still for long. And even though the facility and training are physically demanding, I miss the atmosphere the outside world above ground offers. The woods, the sky, the sun, the wind, and constant movement of life around me.

I can't help but think that the tension between Nate and I will be gone since we will be in two different territories.

The bickering between us has become unbearable. Daily there are exchanges of crass thoughts back and forth. And yesterday was the last straw.

I am running the trails after dinner. I got a wild hair to venture deeper into the caverns. Ezra said that there are many caves that have not been developed or maintained, only cut out. The manpower needed to develop the trails took months per trail. The number of maintenance staff permitted in the facility at a given time is limited. The number of anyone in the facility during training sessions is limited and monitored for safety from too many people being transported in and out and the possibility of Sondian spies.

The cutout I choose is very rocky and narrow. The lighting is poor compared to the charted paths. As I struggle to maintain my jog and footing, I feel a lot like the ants in Ezra's office on campus back home. I think back to that night Ezra told me who I was. It seems so long ago. I am creating my uncharted destiny in more ways than just climbing this uncharted trail.

Up ahead I see a steeper climb with very low lighting. The passage is about five feet wide and seven feet tall. My jog slows to a walking climb, using every bit of strength from my limbs at this point. Then the sharp steepness levels out to a smooth shelf. The shelf is short-lived; there is a huge drop. No switchback. Just a landslide drop right onto my butt. The rocks crumble under me. I try to regain my footing, but continue to slide down. Hindsight, it is probably good my backside is taking the brunt of the abuse. My slide turns to a stumble forward. I stretch my hands out to either side of the narrow passage trying to slow my forward motion. The rock continues to crumble around my stretched and clawing hands and fingers. A light to my left gives me a glimpse of my potential future—a ledge and a straight drop into nothing.

I dig my hands into the rock walls on either side, trying to catch hold of anything. I turn away from the drop-off and dig my feet upward and away. The rocks are sliding all around me now. There is a cracking sound and flash of light before everything goes dark. A sharp pain pulsates in my head. I smell and taste something metallic before everything disappears.

When you are knocked out, there is a spot in your life that is void. Then, one event, sound, feeling, or sensation brings you out of the void. It brings you back to reality. When I was young, I had a bad case of influenza. In the middle of the night, I needed to use the commode. I got out of bed, and then the void occurred. I passed out once at the edge of the bed. Then woke long enough only to pass out once again at the top of the staircase. A void. I woke again to pass out again on the bathroom floor. It was hard to believe that I was alert enough to make it down the stairs before passing out. God was definitely watching over me.

He has bigger plans for you, Jes.

As I lay there on the tile floor of the bathroom, I remember the distinct sound that woke me from that void. It was a click of something turning on. The sound of something heating up, a mechanism. When I was able to sit up, I saw that it was a simple space heater that we kept in the bathroom in winter.

I feel a warm hand on my head. Then the sound of a heartbeat in my ear. Then a separate heartbeat out of synchrony from the first. In the instant I hear the distinct beats, they come into rhythm with each other.

I begin to shift my sore body. I try to lift my head; it's too heavy. My eyes do not want to open yet. I hear gravel shift under me, and arms tighten around me in an embrace. "Shh, Jes. You're hurt pretty bad."

Nate.

"I'm going to help you heal. Be still."

Nate touches the back of my head and my lower back. He lifts my head and body to a sitting position. I don't want to let myself fall into him, but I have no energy of my own to pull away without causing a sharp pain in my head and ribs.

Nate whispers, "Lean against me, Jes. Don't try and sit up. I've got you."

His words are the permission my body needs to give in. Nate lifts me onto his lap and leans me against his chest. I rest my cheek on his chest. One of his arms surrounds my torso to keep me from crumpling. He softly brushes the hair from my face. I feel him place his lips to my forehead. A calmness washes over me. His other hand moves to my abdomen. Again, warmth and a feeling of my body melting rushes through me.

The pulsating energy radiates throughout my body, dulling the pain. My eyes are still closed.

"Jes. How are you feeling?" As he speaks, his breath brushes against my forehead.

I open my eyes slowly. My eyes immediately gravitate to the lamp sitting on a boulder directly in front of me. Things are a little blurry for a moment. I feel Nate brush his lips against my forehead again and place a brief, almost undetectable kiss there. *Almost.*

I realize what he just did, and I sit upright too quickly and feel myself start to crash down again. I catch myself against his chest and grab hold of his shoulder to steady myself. I look at his dim profile in the dimly lit cavern.

Change the subject, Jes. Quick, change the subject.

I speak in a thick voice. "How did you find me?"

I can feel his smile on me even though I can't see it.

The answer comes to me before he can answer. "Oh, yeah. The link thing."

I smile a little and immediately regret the feelings I am having right now.

I pull away from Nate and sit against the wall behind me. I tuck my knees up and encircle my arms around them. I try and make my voice sound cold. "Thank you for healing me. It was...noble of you."

Nate looks down. I know he realizes the moment we were having is over.

"Well. I couldn't very well ignore my conscience and leave you down here to die and rot. It would be immoral, even if you are a pain in the ass."

With that, he grabs my hands and pulls me up. I fall against his chest. I feel his breath on my face.

Nate asks, "Are you all right?"

My voice shakes. "I-I'm all right. Just a little light-headed."

Good cover.

Nate says, "I am too."

I could feel his energy closing in around me, drawing me closer to him. *Or is it me drawing him in?* I am breathless at the thought.

His hands encircle my waist and pull me into him. I don't resist. His gaze is so intense, it makes me a little self-conscious.

I am breathing rapidly now. "What?"

Nate snaps out of the gaze. "Uh. The linking and healing thing..." He pulls back and looks away from me. Nate is stumbling over his words. "Uh, it can drain me and make things a little loopy for me as well. Luke said that it could happen." He lets go of me and picks up the lantern. "C'mon. We should head back."

The talk up the narrow cavern is filled with grunts and curses. I am not sure if it is aimed at the platonic relationship we are trying so hard to maintain, or the awkward, intimate, nonplatonic encounter we just experienced.

Just one week left. We would go our separate ways.

* * *

Mid-week, our mentors knock on each of our doors at 5:30 a.m. Ezra, in Ezra form, bangs on my door. I almost fall out of bed. I pick my head up briefly. "What?"

Ezra says, "Aw, Jes. Now is that a way to greet your mentor when he comes bearing news that you have been anxiously awaiting for almost four weeks now."

This gets my attention. I scramble hands first out of bed with a light thump as the rest of my body follows. I crawl to the door and open it wide enough for my eyes to catch his. Ezra is holding a glass with a little purple umbrella in it, wearing sunglasses, and an obnoxiously pink Hawaiian shirt.

"Going somewhere tropical?"

Ezra is mid-sip when he pauses to answer. "Just starting early, my dear. C'mon. Get up. Your future awaits." Whistling the Hukilau, Ezra saunters back down the hall toward the cafeteria.

Chapter 28

I open the cafeteria door, prepared to hear my fate. My eyes find Nate, Nick, and Angela huddled at a table eating and talking in low voices. I grab some coffee, a bagel, and a peach. Food is not the main thing on my mind right now. I sit next to Angela.

"Have you heard anything yet?"

Angela says, "No, you?"

"No."

Nate shifts his eyes to the mentors' table. "What's up with the wardrobe on Ezra?"

Nick says, "I think it's awesome."

Nate leans toward me. "So where do you think you will be going?"

"The way Ezra's dressed, I'm guessing Hawaii."

Angela says, "I hope I am going somewhere exciting, fast moving. Like New York!"

Nick says, "I hear you. I'm a Big Apple boy myself."

Nate says, "I'm hoping West Coast. The beach, the mountains, and the city. A little bit of everything."

Siobhan comes up to our table. "Okay, wee ones. Time to divvy up your sentences." Smirking, she walks toward the cafeteria exit along with the other mentors.

Luke says, "Heading to the conference room now. Who wants to know their assignment?"

All four of us simultaneously push our chairs out loudly, toss the rest of our food in the trash, and rush the door. Nick and Nate are wrestling each other down the hall. We speed into the conference room wide eyed and eager.

It is torture. Ezra is slurping his fruity, umbrella drink, looking from me, to Angela, to Nick, then Nate.

My patience is thin. "C'mon, Ezra!"

Ezra stops drinking and slowly puts it down. "All right, All right." He looks to Siobhan to do the honors. "My lady?"

Siobhan says, "Well, thank you, kind sir."

Ezra smiles. "Oh, well, you're welcome, my lady. Thank you for thanking me."

Siobhan smiles. "Of course, kind sir. Thank you for welcoming me. I so apprec—"

Nick growls, "Ah, damn it! I need to know now! I can't stand it anymore! Please!"

Siobhan laughs. "All right. All right." She pulls out a paper from her pocket and unfolds it. "Angela. You are going back home, girl. Dallas, Texas."

"Really? I get to go to my hometown?"

Siobhan smiles. "Yep."

Luke is next to open his envelope. "Nate. Santa Barbara, California."

Nate gets this huge smile on his face.

Nick elbows Nate. "Nice! Surfin' and babes. Huh? Huh?"

Nate lowers his head, then looks up at me. I quickly turn to Angela, giving her extra tissue for her tears of joy after her good news.

"Congratulations, Angela. You're going to be on familiar territory. And seeing your family is going to be awesome for you."

Angela looks at me with tears of joy in her eyes. "Thanks, Jes."

I shift my gaze back to Ezra. I know that it won't be that easy for me. I can't go home like Angela. Home isn't safe anymore. Plus, it feels like my life there happened so long ago.

Jake takes a folded piece of paper out of his back pocket. "Nick. New York City."

Nick jumps out of his seat. "Whoo hoo, baby! Yeah! Yeah!" He runs over to Jake and picks him up off the floor in a huge embrace. Nick puts Jake down and starts dancing with him. Nick starts singing Alicia Keys' song. "...Concrete jungle where dreams are made of..."

Jake looks like a rag doll being pulled here and there by Nick. He rolls his eyes and laughs.

Ezra says, "All right, Nick. We still have one more."

Nick lets go of Jake. "Jake. I love you, man! We are gonna be NYC roomies!" Nick clears his throat and changes his composure instantly. "All right. I'm done. Sorry, Jes."

"Jes. Miami, Florida." Ezra lifts his drink in the gesture of congratulations. "Cheers, Jes."

Beaches, sand, and warm weather. Hawaii was just a hope. I have never been there. To be honest, I really don't feel like I belong anywhere in particular after my life transformed without my control. I guess this is my opportunity for my life to begin again. The new beginning of me.

Chapter 29

The rest of Thursday is spent with our mentors. We are debriefed on the city we are each about to claim as our territory. All that is left of our time at the facility is Friday and Saturday, really. Those two days are our time to research our territory, who the other guardians are in the city, how to contact them, make arrangements for living, job interviews as our cover, and make sure our realm of daily activities are in close proximity to the Sondians we are keeping an eye on.

The files left behind by the Dobrian guardians that had our territory before us are a huge benefit to Ezra and I. Well, that is what Ezra said, anyway. All day Friday we scour file after file. Ezra and I are sitting in the rec room. He is sitting on the recliner, and I am on the floor propped against the sofa. We have stacks of records spread into piles by year on the coffee table between us.

I break the silence. "So, the big player is this guy."

The picture shows a very distinguished slender man. Salt-and-pepper hair, suited, and exiting a very nice sports car.

"It says he is an investor and entrepreneur in the Miami club scene."

Ezra is studying his own stack. Looks at me. "What? Oh. Yeah. He is a real jack-of-all-trades."

There is a brief tone of loathing in his voice.

Much of the research is what I would consider private investigative:

8:30 p.m.: S. C. enters main building of executive suite, downtown Miami. Awaiting next move.

9:30 p.m.: S. C. exits main building with young unknown associate.

9:45 p.m.: S. C. leaves unknown associate at entrance of Club Helion.

9:46 p.m.: S. C. heads south along coastline to Club Meridian.

10:00 p.m.: S. C. enters Club Meridian.

3:00 a.m.: S. C. leaves Club Meridian and heads north along coastline to Club Helion.

3:15 a.m.: S. C. enters Club Helion and remains there until 4:00 a.m.

4:05 a.m.: S. C. leaves the club with young, unknown associate and unidentifiable female. Associate takes own car, 2010 Porsche Panamera (espresso).

S. C. takes unidentifiable female in his car, 2010 Porsche Carrera S (black).

Both drive west toward residential area.

4:25 a.m.: S. C. unknown associate, and unidentifiable female enter gated residential community. Not accessible. 24/7 security guard.

4:30 a.m.: surveillance terminated for the night.

My eyes are crossing at this point. "Is this it? Three years of this?" I fiddle with the other files.

Ezra flips from one file to the next, not looking up at me. "Yep."

This is pointless to me. "Well, what is so intriguing over there because this is not giving me any information."

"I'm trying to find the name of this young unknown associate that seems to be Sam's right-hand man. He is a very well-kept secret for some reason."

I am not getting all of this research. I have a compromise for Ezra. "So how about this? You be the brains, and I will be the brawn."

Ezra looks up at me. "Excuse me?"

I hold up the files. "This means nothing to me. I mean, I learn more about things, people, places, by being there. Living it. So, you can be the captain, and I will be the soldier." I smile my biggest cheesy smile.

Ezra smiles back. "Well, my dear, that was my intention the whole time. I'm glad we see eye to eye on that. I was giving you an opportunity, though. I know how much you like to have control of the situation and…"

I roll my eyes. "Point taken. I know I am a little bit of a control freak. But I also know when I am in over my head. And this stuff, words, time frames, means more to you than me right now."

I pass the files back to Ezra. "It's all yours, El Capitan. So, tomorrow is our last day here."

Ezra looks over his file at me. "Yes, that is correct." He goes back to organizing the files.

I desperately want to ask Ezra to finish the story that he started days ago in the cafeteria about his past.

"So. You never quite finished your story about your years as a trainee and guardian."

Ezra stops organizing and looks up again. "Yes. You are correct."

"And I suppose you aren't going to tell me the rest?"

Ezra takes off his reading glasses. "Jesca, it would be of no benefit to you now to know my experience as a guardian. I am not you. And you are not me. Our experiences, our beginnings, our purposes are not meant to be mimicked. So I will tell you."

I am surprised. "You will?"

Ezra puts his hand up to stop my excitement before it can start. "I will tell you as we progress in your experience if the situation you are in at the moment can benefit from my story. I will not cloud your perceptions and decisions with my story."

He looks at me, anticipating a reply.

"I get it."

I did get it. I mean, how can I truly experience life and my purpose if I am influenced by Ezra's. He is looking out for me. I am overwhelmed with emotion all of a sudden. "Ezra. This may seem awkward to say, but thank you for saving me."

Ezra's face softens for a moment. Then he quickly looks down at his files again.

I stand and start to leave the room.

"Jes?"

I turn to look back at him. "Yeah."

Ezra smiles at me. "Thank you for letting me save you."

I leave the room knowing that I am blessed to have a very strong person watching over me.

Back in my room, I grab my headphones and iPod and head for the trails. I am feeling nostalgic, so I choose the path

I ran the first day I was here in the facility. As my run is underway, I can't help but recall what happened on that first run, running into Nate.

A brief smile crosses my face. I remember how it felt to see Nate in the open cavern next to the pool. All the emotions start to flood back into my mind.

Stop thinking about Nate.

Tomorrow we leave for our territory. Nate and I will not be an issue anymore. I look up for a split second and see a hooded figure in front of me. I don't have time to dodge out of its way, and its massive swing catches me on the shoulder.

I yell out, "Hey!"

The figure quickly stops and pushes its hood off.

Nate.

"Oh, sorry. I was so focused, I didn't even see you, Jes."

I see that he is genuinely apologetic and feel bad about lashing out. "No. I should have been more alert, too. I was just thinking and got wrapped up in…my thoughts."

Nate is breathing heavily with his hands on his hips. His eyes are burning deep into mine. "What thoughts?"

Don't think about it.

Nate moves toward me. "Too late."

He cups both of his hands around my face so delicately. I can't take my eyes off his face, his eyes, his lips. I could have easily slipped away, but didn't. He brushes a few hairs off of my face that had fallen loose on my run. I feel myself breathing faster, not from running. I put my hands over his.

I think, *I have wanted to touch you like this for weeks. I know it is too late. I just want you to know that I don't hate you. That it is just the opposite. I can't get enough of you.*

He teasingly leans closer. I can feel his breath on my lips.

Nate slides his hand down my neck, onto my shoulder, down to my waist, and pulls me into him. Our energy instantly links. We both simultaneously respond to the breathless feeling. It feels like there is electricity all around us, a warm charge in the air. A continual surge of energy rolling between us, holding us together.

Nate whispers, "Just right now, Jes. Just let us be for right now."

My lips respond and graze his so gently; that is all it takes. His lips take mine. The heat radiates from my mouth to my face, neck, chest, and heart. My body feels like it is melting into Nate's.

My hands go to his chest. Not to push him away, but to accept him.

Our kiss slows. We start to pull apart, but I find myself moving back in to touch his lips again.

Just once more.

I pull away slowly. Still tempted to revisit those lips again, but settling for his warm lips against my forehead. I feel his lips form a smile on my right temple as he begins to trace his lips along my face, returning closer to my lips again. I put my fingers to his mouth just as his lips moved to mine.

We need to stop, Nate.

Nate's arms pull me tighter. *I know. Damn, I know.*

My arms wrap around his neck, and we both pull each other into an embrace, burying our faces into each other's shoulders.

We both slowly pull apart, thinking how unexplainable it would be if one of the others came up on us. Nate moves his hands up my back slowly to my arms. His breath pauses at my neck. My hands move to his forearms. I shift my face purposefully to graze his cheek. Our hands find each other's, not wanting to let go. Nate pulls my hands into his chest and shifts his gaze so that we are looking at each other.

I whisper, "We better get back."

Nate is still focused on me. "Yeah, we should get back." Nate doesn't budge.

"I'm going to, uh, finish my run."

Nate smiles and breaks our gaze. "I'm going to take a shower."

Our hands are still linked and are slow to unravel, lingering for as long as possible. I put my headphones back on and move past Nate, putting the necessary separation between us.

I feel Nate leave. Not just physically. I mentally feel a void. The void is so strong it stops me in my tracks.

The link. It's gone. Can that happen?

For weeks now I have felt a constant link with him. But now, I don't sense the link. I feel empty inside where it was once full. I am pacing in a circle. How can that be possible. Ezra didn't say anything about this.

What did you do, Nate?

I yell for him. "Nate!"

The moment I say his name, I already know. It is his way of putting a permanent separation between us. He is trying to make this as easy as possible for me.

I walk to where the cavern opens up, and I shift to turn back, but stop myself.

He broke our bond. It had to be done. It is the only way for him to focus. For me to focus on my purpose. We can't spend any more time thinking about what happened between us here. We can't be linked. I guess I think telling myself will make me feel better or stronger.

I start running again, pumping hard now. I am kicking myself for not being careful of what I wished for.

Chapter 30

Saturday is packing day. There isn't much for us individually to do since we packed light when we got here. We have to do some shut-down protocol in the facility. It would be weeks before the facility would be in use again.

Angela is on tech duty with Siobhan to properly shut down the systems to hibernation and heighten the level of security to automatic termination if breeched by infiltrators. Jake and Nick are cleaning the pool and locking up the gym equipment. Luke and Nate are on cafeteria duty and shutdown. Ezra and I are on trail cleanup, evaluation of trail maintenance, communication of maintenance, and construction of the existing and future trails. It is kind of cool to know that we are creating trails that future trainees will be running and hiking on. In my opinion, we have the most hands-on and creative duty of all of the facility shutdown.

Mapping and recommendations are the most tedious, but so interesting. It sparks a memory. "You know, Ezra, this mapping stuff reminds me of your ant farm back in Georgia."

Ezra is taken aback by this. "You think so?"

"Yeah. But you already knew that, right?"

I can see Ezra's smile from the corner of my eye.

"Touché, Jesca."

We finish shutdown around 5:30 p.m.

I am curious. "So, if the kitchen is shut down, what is our plan for dinner?" I can't help it. I have a huge appetite at times.

Ezra says, "Come with me. We are meeting in the rec room."

Ezra opens the door to the rec room. It is dark. This makes me a little confused and a lot apprehensive. All of a sudden, the lights come on.

"Surprise! Happy birthday, Jes!"

Everyone is in the room, including the staff and chefs.

My breath gets caught in my throat where a lump instantly forms. I feel tears forming as well. I look from face to face. I'm trembling. "Thank you, guys."

Angela rushes up to me and gives me the biggest hug ever and discreetly tucks a tissue into my palm. "We love you, Jes."

Nick walks over and puts his arm around me. "Yeah, *chica*, we love you. How old are you? Like thirty?"

I elbow Nick. "Nineteen, dork."

One at a time, everyone comes over to give me a hug. When it is Nate's turn, we both look at each other. I test the waters by trying to read him. Nothing. The link really is gone. I drop my eyes.

"Happy birthday, Jes."

He moves in first. In the brief embrace, Nate whispers into my hair, "I will miss you."

I whisper back, "Me too."

Ezra breaks the moment with his announcement. "Jesca, we couldn't let your birthday pass without a celebration."

Nate falls back with the others in the small crowd. Nick turns on some music. "Aw, yeah baby!"

Apparently, the chefs had prepared this early prior to shutdown. Luke tells us that Fenton had started the cake last night after dinner and worked all night on preparations. The buffet looks like a feast that would test every single taste bud on my tongue.

I walk over to Fenton before indulging in the feast. "Thank you, Fenton. It is truly amazing."

Chef Fenton bows before me. "You're welcome, Ms. Jesca. Enjoy your day."

Ezra is holding the line for me. I walk over.

"How did you remember? I even forgot. I guess being so focused on training and all, I lost track of time down here."

Ezra looks down. "Jes, you mean so much…so much to us. We have become a family in a way. Not just a team. These past four weeks have created bonds, friendships, love, that will be with you forever, no matter what may happen."

I change my expression to match his, knowing that Ezra is very serious about his words all of a sudden. He looks away, but I can see something stirring behind those eyes before he looks away.

Nick chimes in behind Ezra, "Jes! Birthday girl! I'm starving!"

Ezra smiles at me. "Yeah! C'mon, birthday girl, move along!"

I smile hesitantly at first. Ezra winks at me. "Happy birthday, Jes."

With that, I give myself permission to enjoy the feast and celebration for the last night at the facility with my family!

* * *

My eyes open.

Sunday. It's here. Finally.

Then the anxiety starts.

Sunday. It's here. Already.

It is bittersweet. I am going to miss so many moments with my new family. So many moments. Especially one moment I can't tear away from my mind.

Nate and I.

I roll over quickly, hoping it will dislodge the thought from my mind. No such luck. *Damn.*

I look at the clock. It is 5:30 a.m.

Get in the zone, low emotion, high energy. We leave in three and a half hours.

9 a.m. Ezra and I will be out, in the sunlight, driving to the airport, and getting on a plane to Miami. That is the focus for the next three plus hours.

I am not the only one giving myself the pep talk. When I wheel my bag into the hearth room, everyone is there, focused on our inevitable departures.

No one speaks, just acknowledges each other's presence. The tension is thick, and everyone has their guard up. This is the one time, if any, that blocking our thoughts is understandable and acceptable.

We have been out of touch for four weeks. Luke told us last night that sometimes the first few days are tough. Day and night confusion, headaches from the sunlight, anxiety, and panic attacks due to sensory overload from the world around us. The mentors have warned us to take everything slowly. They said to ease back into the world.

Luke says, "It's like you are being born again. You are like a dragonfly in a way."

Nick scoffs. "A dragonfly. What?"

Luke rolls his eyes. "A metaphoric dragonfly, Nick. Dragonflies start in larval stage, newbies, green peas. They burrow in the ground to develop, grow, change, transform. When they transition, they come up from the earth as a dragonfly."

Siobhan comes in last. She looks at each of us. "All right, guardians. You have achieved your transformation from trainee. Now, you need to put to work all that you have learned, absorbed, and experienced. Bow your heads."

We look at each other with confused looks. I guess a bit surprised at how spiritual Siobhan sounds.

Siobhan is irritated by our looks, rolls her eyes, and growls. "Bow your heads!"

That's the Siobhan I know and love.

Siobhan closes her eyes. "Dear loving God. We are your servants first and foremost. Please give each of the guardians the wisdom and knowledge only You can to make decisions and choices for the salvation of humanity. Amen."

There is a pause. Then Siobhan raises her head. "Now. You know in your heart what you need to do. Don't lose your focus out there. There will be distractions, temptations, and illusions to try to trip you up. Know that God will be there. Call to Him. He will have your back."

Siobhan walks over to Angela and Nick, who are standing next to each other, and pull them toward her. Ezra grabs Nate's and my hand and pulls us into this growing huddle. Once all of us are included, we just hold each other arm on arm in silence.

As we leave the facility one by one, I can feel that we all have an unspoken understanding to not say goodbye, not look at each other. Just know that we may meet again sometime, somewhere.

Ezra and I are the first to ascend. The elevator seems larger than before, even though logically I know that it can't be. My pulse quickens while in the elevator. I am anxious about leaving the safety of the facility. We reach the parking lot.

"Jesca. Breathe. You are fine. Put on your sunglasses. Your eyes will need protection from the sun when we ascend. You will need to wear them for a few days."

The glasses are huge and covered most of my face. Hideous really, but necessary. Siobhan gave everyone a pair before leaving.

We swiftly walk to the car and put our bags in the trunk. Ezra starts the ignition and begins driving. It feels like we are driving forever.

It didn't take us this long in the descent, did it? Surely we are almost out.

"When are we going to be out?"

Ezra replies, "Just a few more minutes."

I take a deep breath in and sigh. I start to fidget with my hands.

Ezra hands me a stick of gum. "Here chew on this. It might help distract you a bit."

The grey, greenish tint of the dashboard begins to change, lightens to a soft rose color.

My eyes are drawn up to my side window.

The first thing I see is reddish, brown dirt. Then a cactus. Another one. Then hills in the horizon. Then sky with soft, thin, stratus clouds. The colors of everything around us are dull, because of the extra coating on the lenses of the sunglasses. I want to feel the air. I hesitate as my hand reaches for the button to put down the window.

Ezra sees my movement. "Go ahead."

I look over at him. He smiles at me and winks. That small gesture relieves me enough to venture to open the window.

I slide the glass down slowly. I feel a small, warm breeze that whips a few hairs across my face. It feels amazing on my skin. Like it is breathing life back into it after being kept from fresh air for so long. I roll down the window further. My hair begins to whip more quickly around my face. I pull it back with one hand and hold it to the side. It must have grown at least three inches since I was in the facility. I put my other hand out the window to feel the breeze, the sunlight.

"You all right, Jes?"

"Yeah. It's going to be fine."

Chapter 31

Samson Crest wakes to a whispering in the courtyard outside of his suite.

Sam mumbles and stumbles out of bed as he makes his way toward the voices. *I work too hard for the paid help to disrupt me. Now which one am I going to fire today. Gardener, pool guy?*

He creeps to the window in an attempt to catch the idiot that woke him at ten in the morning.

"They know I work late."

He rubs his grey eyes and scratches his head with annoyance, shifting the shutters to get a glimpse. He sees Xander in his pajama pants and no shirt and a disheveled young lady in a sundress. She is playing coy and giggling, while Xander is holding her hand between his. He is holding her gaze with his hazel eyes.

Sam whispers to himself, "Xander. Of course!" Sam shifts his gaze to the girl. "Oh, c'mon, hon. The morning after is a little late to be playing coy." Sam flips the shutters closed and puts his tan robe and slippers on.

Xander kisses her hand and waves her off. Sam watches the rest unfold from the porch off of his suite. Xander runs his hands through his dark brown hair. A wide smile develops, then it's quickly replaced with tight lips and a deep wrinkle in his forehead.

Sam interrupts Xander by knocking on the wood decking he is leaning against.

"There's my boy. I take it you had a good night and a good morning?"

Xander is caught off guard and spins around with a hint of a smile. "Yeah, it was a good night. The club did well! We had some heavy hitters come in around 10:30, and they kept the flow of traffic running all night."

Sam laughs and pulls his robe taut across his lean chest. "Xander, I was talking about the beauty that was exiting the building just now." Sam points toward the departing young lady carrying her sandals through the side garden gate.

There is a waiting car Xander had arranged for. "Oh, yeah. She was truly unbearable. Blah, blah, blah is all she did from the moment we left the club until the moment I crashed from her ranting."

Sam's look becomes confused. "You mean you didn't..." Sam walks down to the stairway to the deck.

Xander scoffs, "Between the blah, blah, blah, and getting in at 5 a.m. No, not interested!"

Sam smirks. "Okay, stud? Then why so charming this morning?"

Sam heads to a lounger next to the pool and lies out.

Xander joins him. "Well, being the stud that I am, you should know that she was one of our heavy hitters' best friend's niece, and she needed a place to crash. I wasn't about to leave a piece of future revenue out in the streets of Miami at 4:30 in the morning, Dad."

Sam laughs softly with his eyes closed, letting the warm morning sun touch his face. His graying light brown hair ruffles in the breeze. "Xander. Always thinking one step ahead. You are one awesome young man. You remind me so much of me when I was in my twenties."

Xander closes his eyes and reclines back on the lounger next to Sam. He jokes, "How could you possibly remember, that was so long ago."

A very tall butler walks over to them. "Good morning, Mr. Crest."

Sam and Xander both look up at the butler and address him in unison. "Good morning, Daniel."

Sam and Xander drink their coffee and take in the exotic landscape around them, the saltwater pool with numerous waterfalls and a grotto. The multiple palms throughout the garden, peppered with bright bougainvilleas and fragrant gardenia.

"So, Xander, what are your plans for today?"

"I have some low-level errands to run. I wanted to catch up with my boys. Grab some lunch with Christian and Zach. You remember them from the fraternity." Xander had attended the University of Miami.

Sam nods. "Yes. Chris and Zach. Didn't they go to Pendleton Preparatory with you as well?"

"Yep. Anyway, real low key. Tonight I will be getting in to the club around 9:30, 10." Xander is about to explain why, but Sam waves him off.

"Xander, I appreciate your checking in with me. But I know you take care of business. When you became general

208

manager of Club Helion two years ago, you earned it. You have proven to be not only a great son, but an exceptionally talented leader in our corporation. Will you need a ride to Helion before I head to Meridian?"

Xander squints at a passing plane above. "No. I'm taking the Panamera in for an oil change and wash while I'm out today."

"How are you liking it?"

"The car? It's awesome, Dad! Remember the first time we met?" A wide smile spreads across Xander's face as he looks over to Sam.

Sam is lying there with a big smile across his face. "That was the beginning of my life. I could never forget that day, man." Sam opens his eyes and looks at Xander. "You were checking out my silver '99 Porsche 911."

"And now I'm cruising in my very own Porsche. I never imagined—"

Sam interrupts him. "You deserve it, Xan. You work damn hard." Sam's face becomes serious then. "You have turned your life around since…since we met."

"You had a lot to do with that, Sam."

"Yeah, but your leap of faith, that had a lot to do with it also. You chose to get into my car. You chose to change your life in that instant."

Xander nods and puts his head down.

Sam yawns and stretches. "Daniel! I'm going to retire to my room for a few more hours. Can I expect lunch around noon?"

Daniel immediately appears behind the men. "Of course, Mr. Crest. Lunch will be prepared and on the veranda at noon."

Sam looks at Xander and puts a hand on his shoulder. "I will see you tomorrow, then. We have a 1:30 meeting with a few of my associates about a venture we are trying to pull into Miami from overseas."

Xander's attention becomes heightened. Curiosity creeps into his mind since this wasn't the first overseas associate meeting. The past four months have encompassed at least three, each with a different group of associates. Xander was only allowed to make a brief appearance as general manager of Club Helion.

Xander takes this opportunity to test the waters of the meeting's significance. "Do you want to have a pre-meeting conference over an early lunch tomorrow?"

Sam pats Xander's shoulder. "That's my Xander. Always one step ahead. Catch you later, my boy."

Sam's response was predictably vague. When it came to these meetings, Sam always dodged Xander's requests to be involved.

Xander leans back, feeling a little deflated as Sam walks back to his suite. Xander closes his eyes again and sighs.

I sure have come a long way. He is thinking back to the time before he met Sam. The numerous shelters he stayed in night after night. He would put them on a rotation so the staff wouldn't report him to foster care. They caught on eventually. He thought back to the foster families he lived with. The yelling, the anxiety, and the fear of beatings.

Xander's peaceful, content face becomes hard and serious.

Chapter 32

I put my hands over my face and groan. I shake my head as I try to shed all of the baggage I just brought back up to the surface. I open my eyes and feel the swollen feeling of tears. I don't dare let them spill.

I distinctly remember being taken from Grandmother's home when I was five years old. Her name was Nina. Nina Fosston. She had passed in the middle of the night. It was sudden, her heart. I can still remember her smell. The mixture of flowers and cocoa butter.

I was always safe in her arms.

I close my eyes again and lean back against the lounger, remembering her hands over mine at night as she prayed over me.

I am continually amazed at how long I made it with the abuse. Something, someone kept me alive and safe. I prefer to think it was my grandmother watching over me.

Then I met Samson Crest.

I was walking up Sunset Drive, and this guy pulled up in a car and offered me a ride. He said that he had something important to talk with me about. He looked nervous. He kept looking around, like he was searching for someone. He freaked me out, so I kept walking and tried to ignore him. SW 80th street, then Kendall Drive and he still followed about twenty feet behind me.

He didn't look grungy; he was clean cut and shaven. That is the very thing that shot up a red flag for me, though. He looked like a cop or an officer of the court. No way in hell was I going back into the system. I had two more years until I was legally an adult. I picked up my pace. He got stuck behind a bus. I started to run. As I crossed Old Cutler Road, I dodged into a shop and watched from the window until he passed. I left the shop quickly and headed south on Old Cutler to Arvida Parkway and entered the Gables Estates. It was a private, exclusive, and gated neighborhood. It had a sidewalk gate for residents to enter. I pretended that I was supposed to be there and entered the gate after a woman walking her dog came through. I pulled my hood tighter over my head as I strolled more slowly.

I heard a car pull up slowly next to me. My eyes rose and gravitated to the sound of the engine. A '99 silver Porsche 911 Carrera. A distinguished-looking man in his 40s, black slacks, and a deep blue, long-sleeve shirt was driving parallel to me. I kept walking, but kept the car and the man in my peripheral vision.

I heard car tires screech. I turned back toward the main gates. The guy following earlier hopped out of his car, passed through the sidewalk gate, and was walking quickly in my direction. I stopped and looked at Mr. Porsche. He stopped the car and rolled down his window.

"Looks like you could use a ride."

I looked behind me again. The stalker guy was about 100 feet out and was pulling something from his side pocket and waving at me.

"You better come with me."

Those simple words seemed to be filled with trust and honesty to me.

"Hop in, kid. Let's get you out of here."

I was in his car and we were driving away in less than five seconds. The side mirror reflected a man putting his hands on his head in frustration.

"My name is Samson Crest. Call me Sam."

"My name is Alexander Fosston. You can call me Xander."

I gave him my grandmother's surname, not mine. After my parents died, Nina Fosston was my parent.

From that day forward, Sam and I were inseparable.

He took me into his home, no questions asked. He accepted me. He taught me everything he knew about life and business. He gave me confidence. Sam nurtured me. And that was something I hadn't experienced in years. I trusted him.

Sam's first mission was to talk me into enrolling at Pendleton Preparatory High School. His confidence in me was intoxicating and addicting, I agreed.

As the days turned into weeks, then months, the past started vanishing from existence. Sam wouldn't let me forget, though. Sam reminded me that my past was going to develop my character and inner strength.

It was my senior year when Sam asked to be a permanent part of my life as my father. He explained that the adoption process would be conveniently accessible due to his 'connections'.

"I have always wanted to be a father. To be able to watch my child grow, blossom, and succeed. I want to commit to be your father, your guardian."

I was blown away by Sam's evident unconditional love for me.

I attended the University of Miami with many of my buddies from high school prep. Sam was well off, if it wasn't evident enough. He did not hide his wealth. And he taught me to not hide it, but to wield it as a tool of power and entitlement that gains respect.

Popularity was never a strength of mine, until I met Sam. The confidence I developed made friendships and romantic relationships come easy. I was on the fast track to graduate college in three years, plus two years for my masters in business administration. By the time I was twenty-three years old, I had my masters and was introduced to Sam's business. When I was younger, I would repeatedly ask Sam what he did.

"I am an investor and entrepreneur."

That was it; that was all he gave me. Never anything more no matter how much I asked.

"What does the corporation invest in? The clubs around town?"

Sam would look at me softly. "You will have many years to focus on our business. Right now, enjoy life a little. You have had many years of sorrow. Savor now, while the universe has given you an opportunity to have some fun and be a kid."

I did. Every moment of every day was for my enjoyment, my success, my entitlements. And here I am with so much to live for. So much ahead of me. It's all mine.

* * *

Xander's cell phone rings. He must have dozed off. He opens his eyes and pulls the phone out of his pajama pocket to see who it is. *Zach.* Xander picks up with a smile, while looking out over the deep blue pool and the lush landscape.

"Zach. We still on?"

"Yeah. Chris and I are on our way. Be there in about thirty minutes."

"Great, man. Some hoops then lunch still good?"

"You got it!"

"Sweet, man. See ya."

Xander puts the phone back in his pocket. He sits for a little while longer, just taking in the fresh air and the tangible beauty all around him. He slowly closes his eyes again and sighs.

Behind those eyes, just under the surface, something grabs his curiosity again. It is regularly festering in his mind lately. A few weeks ago, Sam had approached Xander with a proposition after the departure of one set of the overseas investor meetings. Sam wanted Xander's involvement in the business to become more 'hands on'.

Xander remembers.

"Hands on? You mean like opening another club?"

Sam paced back and forth like a lion all pumped up with adrenaline before a kill. "No, Xander, it has nothing to do with the clubs. This is a separate endeavor altogether. A key investor in our company has asked for my most trusted advisor to carry out some research."

Xander looked a little perplexed at the vagueness. "Okay?"

Sam slowed his pace and turned to Xander. "You need to travel to Georgia. And you need to keep tabs on a couple of people."

"Why?"

Sam raised his hand toward Xander to stop any further questioning. "There can be no questions asked, yet. The less you know right now, the better. If you were to...to be intercepted, it would unleash a hornets' nest of chaos on our family and corporation." Sam's eyes were blood shot and dead set on Xander's agreeable response.

Xander carefully studied his father. Sam was never this serious about a duty from Xander; it was intimidating.

Sam softened, seemingly knowing the turmoil Xander was dealing with inside. He ran his hand through his hair. "Look. All I can tell you right now is that you were specifically called for this duty. You are the future of this project, Xander. You have a purpose in the big picture. Can you understand that I can't reveal too much to you right now?" Sam looked at Xander with pleading eyes and a wrinkled forehead. In that moment, he showed his age.

Xander folded his arms over his chest. "Yeah. Yes. I understand. When do I leave?"

217

When Xander returned from Georgia, Sam was all business with respect to Xander and the clubs. The only conversation about the project was if Xander had done what was asked. Xander did his research in Georgia and reported the findings on the two people. Every time Xander thought about asking why he was sent to Georgia to find two seemingly ordinary people, he was curtailed by marketing and advertising projects to bring in more revenue for the clubs. Nothing more had been said about his duty in Georgia, and it had already been a few weeks since his return.

Daniel calls from the balcony, "Mr. Crest. Your guests have arrived."

Xander snaps out of his deep thought to acknowledge the announcement. "Thanks, Daniel. Send them down to the basketball court, please."

Having a few minutes to himself before putting business out of his mind, he thinks. *Who were these people in Georgia? What did they have to do with our corporation? What is this secretive project Sam can't give details on? Everything is so elusive.*

He can't deny that his curiosity has been piqued again.

Chapter 33

Back in his suite, Sam is lying in bed with his eyes wide open and breathing deeply. He slowly closes his grey eyes. His eyelids begin to move from the movement of his eyes beneath. The ethereal realm begins to seep into Sam's mind as his lucid dream becomes vivid.

* * *

A dimly lit lounge and soft music playing in the background, Sam walks into the room toward Balthazar.

"Everything is in motion."

Sam continues toward the two chairs facing the elaborate mantle and fireplace; one is already occupied by Balthazar. "Thank you, Balthazar. Alexander is unaware of the details, but he is loyal and trustworthy. He will do as I ask."

Balthazar turns his ageless face to Sam. "Are you certain he is not going to pursue learning any more than you have given him?"

Sam sits for a moment and looks at his hands. "I can hold him off."

"Good. Telling him about his purpose, his influence, and the gifts he can wield can backfire and turn against all of us."

Sam looks up at Balthazar. "Yes, I am aware of that."

Balthazar speaks more aggressively. "Telling him of his lineage as a guardian will need to be revealed soon. It is inevitable obviously."

Balthazar pauses and looks at the fire embers in the hearth. "They are in route. It could affect what we are doing here in Miami."

That gets Sam's attention. "When will they be here? How do you know they have found us?"

Balthazar looks at Sam and raises his voice. "I know!"

Sam shifts his gaze back to the fire. "Ezra?"

"Yes. And her."

There is silence between the two.

"Alexander will inquire of his parents, Sam. It is undeniable that as his purpose unfolds, he will learn of their tragedy."

Sam scoffs and begins the tragic story. "Yes. The two Dobrian guardians. Paul and Rebekah Sera. Murdered by the Sondian guardians and survived by a child. A boy, Alexander."

Balthazar takes his half-smoked cigar and plants it into Sam's arm. Sam winces and tries to shift his arm away, but Balthazar grabs him and holds him still.

"Don't mock the situation. You may have the assurance of our golden boy right now. But your upper hand can easily be replaced. You can be replaced. Don't undermine me, Samson. Your salvation, the power that you so desperately desire and hold dear, can be gone in an instant."

Sam is hyperventilating from the pain. He answers through gritted teeth, keeping his eyes on Balthazar's. "Yes. Yes, I understand."

Balthazar releases his arm and stares back into the glowing orange flames of the fireplace.

Sam holds his injured arm close to his body as he quiets his rapid breathing.

Balthazar seethes through gritted teeth. "Feed him the story we discussed."

Sam turns to him, perplexed by Balthazar's words. "What? You just said—"

"I know what I just said!" Balthazar turns his eyes to Sam. "Plans have changed. Tell him that he has been chosen as a guardian for Sonde. Tell him of Sonde and the guardians involved in its protection and progress. But as I said before, do not reveal his parents' lineage."

Sam becomes angered. "Why now? He could hardly be ready to handle the weight of all of it."

"Don't underestimate your boy, Sam. You may know him now. He may seem pliable now. It will not always be so. He will learn certain things along the way, and he will choose what to believe. Then, will you have his unfaltering loyalty? His trust? Will you be allies or enemies fighting a battle?"

Sam focuses on Balthazar's words and answers flatly with no emotion. "I will tell him. And I will have his unconditional loyalty, Balthazar. If he chooses wrong, then he will be eliminated. The same way I eliminated his parents."

Sam stands up with his eyes on Balthazar. "Don't underestimate my loyalty."

Chapter 34

I am running in the facility. It is so much like the first run I had there. The sound of treading on dirt and rock echoing through the caverns. Then there is a second set of feet. Dense in sound and out of sync with mine. I want to turn and look, but I can't. My body won't let me. My pace picks up; that is the only thing I can control. The heavy weight of humidity whirls around me. Then my speed begins to slow, like I am running through snow. I press on with fear being the stem of my adrenaline.

A tall, muscular man in a hood comes alongside me. He does not look at me, just keeps the pace. The hooded sweatshirt he wears is familiar. I can see the steam from his quick exhaled breath.

Where have I seen that sweater? Then, it clicks. *The sweatshirt. On campus in Georgia.*

The memory floods back into my mind like a dam being released.

Those addicting green eyes.

The concern about me. "Are you okay?"

Even though I am in a dream state, I somehow control my body enough to grab his arm and turn him toward me. It was him. The guy from campus.

Breathlessly I ask, "What are you doing here? Why are you following me?"

He smiles, then flips his hood off. His face shifts and contorts into someone inhuman and unrecognizable. He grabs both of my arms. I push him away from me, but he holds on to me tightly. I am standing close to a very steep drop off. He is trying to push me off. My footing starts to fail; he is too strong. I look up at his face. He looks terrifying. The bone structure around his eyes is protruding. His mouth has widened like a jack-o-lantern.

As quick as his face contorted, it shifts back to the comforting, human form. Then he shifts again. His smile is sinister, like the sides of his mouth are being stretched beyond normalcy. The color of his skin is lifeless. His appearance takes my breath away, and I feel my body weaken from fear. In the midst of my shock and trying to hold my ground from his strong pushing arms, he throws me back like a ragdoll into a free-fall over the ledge.

I feel myself trying to yell and scream, but only a whimper comes.

I feel my body pull out of the dream with force in the passenger's seat next to Ezra.

Ezra hastily pulls off the road, obviously taken aback by my response. I am crouched with my feet on the seat, hands on the ceiling, and my back against the passenger's window.

Putting the car into park, Ezra turns to me and begins yelling. "Jes! Jes! You are okay! You're in the car! Here, roll down your window and get some fresh air!"

I am breathing rapidly and staring at him, catatonic and frozen. I don't move my body.

He looks at me strangely.

223

I whisper, "I…I can't move, Ezra."

Ezra looks both frustrated and confused. "What?"

I am trying to slow my breathing and produce saliva. My mouth is so dry. I close my eyes, feeling irritated by his response and whisper again, "I can't move. Damn it!"

He realizes why I can't move. "Oh."

He runs his hand through his dark brown and silver peppered hair. He sighs nervously. "Your mind is trying to get back to your body right now. Either you initiated the separation or someone else did. Most likely the latter. Someone is targeting you, us, again."

Ezra begins to mumble to himself. I am able to move my hands off the ceiling. He is gripping the steering wheel so tight his knuckles are white.

We just left the facility.

I shift my body, and Ezra's eyes shoot over to me.

I reassure him, "It's fine. The practice has made it easier. See?" I am able enough to sit back down in the seat.

Ezra speaks, "It didn't take them long to find us." Ezra becomes angry and wells up.

I put my hand on his shoulder. "Did you just hear what I said, Ezra? The practice is being used. I am fine." I put my hands up to either side of my head and made moose ears at him. "See? Look!"

I smile at Ezra trying desperately not to let my own fear come through. "I just didn't realize I was going to experience that right out of the facility. Now that I'm aware, my guard is up. You have prepared me, Ezra."

Ezra's wrinkle in the middle of his forehead starts to subside. A half smile surfaces on his face.

Just that half smile sets me at ease.

Instantly Ezra calms his expression. For his or my sake, I wasn't completely sure.

He blocked me.

He shifts into drive, and we pull off the shoulder of the road.

"More practice, Jes. You need to put yourself into the meditative state and begin controlling the lucid dreams regularly. Now is the perfect time to practice jumping, while we drive."

I think for a minute. Not sure of what he means. Then I sense his thoughts.

The lucid dreams. The humming. The vibration. "Jump" while we are driving.

"You're right. I can feel everything that was gone at the facility coming back, like a slow leak at first. The sound of the humming is barely audible. The vibration is streaming in now that I'm aware of it."

Ezra says, "If it makes you feel better, my demons have been attacking too."

I wonder what demons those would be for Ezra. He starts in quick to dodge my approaching question.

"Let's get started, then. I don't need my guardian being out less than a week and dying on me. That would really tarnish my reputation." Ezra winks at me.

I give him a small smile. "All right. I'm ready."

The next two days of travel are filled with more self-induced lucid dreaming and jumping. I become a pro at putting myself in the dream state through deep meditation within a couple of minutes. Taking myself out of the lucid dream state is tedious. Every so often, I feel a presence break in and shift the path of the dream state. The more this happens, the faster I develop getting out and giving the presence 'the slip'.

The dreams become a game. Talk about bizarre road-trip games; this one topped them all.

As we passed landmarks, I would set the lucid dream into motion, targeting the landmark. Then I would project there, separating my mind from my body. Interaction with objects in the dream is easy. Knocking over a salt and pepper shaker at a roadside diner. Opening a front porch door. Public interaction, not so much. I can't interact with beings that don't have the mental capacity and open mind.

For instance, I can interact with one or two, maybe three people out of a crowded restaurant. I wonder if this is what it is like to be a ghost. Maybe lucid dreaming is equivalent to a spirit's state of mind. Actually, it is equivalent to a spirit without a body. Death is only material and irrelevant to the presence a strong spirit can maintain here on earth.

It seems the longer or deeper I am involved in the setting of the dream, the jump, the more accessible I am to the presence attacking me.

Ezra reminds me to be cautious. The Sondian guardian may be more experienced than I am, easily over taking my control of the jump and creating a diversion and keeping me from getting back to my body. I am a little intimidated by that. Maybe that is what the dark aura in my dreams in Georgia was meant to do, be a diversion of fear to catch me off guard. Having me use my life force to protect myself, while the real attack was looming. It was waiting for the perfect moment to strike.

Chapter 35

The sun seems so much brighter here. The special sunglasses from Siobhan came off a day ago. It really is stunning. We arrive around five in the evening. The sun is casting shadows on the sidewalks that are lined with palm trees and beautiful brightly colored hibiscus flowers. We have the windows down.

The term "sea breeze" is something I never understood until I actually experienced it driving alongside the ocean. I look over at Ezra with a smile on my face. He gives me a conservative smile and winks at me.

Ezra's mood had changed immediately upon crossing the Florida state line. He is more reserved and quiet than usual. He keeps checking his side and rearview mirrors for anyone that could be trailing us.

I keep quiet, knowing that he has his way of being a guardian. And if I didn't respect that and let him be, then how could I expect the same from him.

"So, did you get in touch with the connection in the file about our digs?"

This distracts Ezra enough to break his stare.

"We are staying near Coral Gables at Coconut Grove."

Ezra is scrolling through his iPhone and quickly changes the subject. "This car will not suit us any longer. We are set to stop at a dealership and swap cars. My connection there has everything prepared for us."

"Us. Wait. I'm getting a car?"

"Miami is not like Marietta, Jesca. You are not in Georgia anymore."

Ezra saying that is intended to strike a chord of seriousness.

No, I'm not in Marietta anymore. I am in an unfamiliar environment both in the physical and metaphysical sense. I have an intimidating purpose ahead of me. Why me? Why ask? It just is. All I know is that I am a puzzle and the pieces of me have been disconnected. For the life of me, I am hastily doing all I can to reconnect the pieces before I enter the lion's den.

* * *

We pull up to a BMW dealership. I give Ezra a sideways glance.

"Yes, Jesca. You and I are getting BMWs, a superior automobile."

Thirty minutes later, I am in my fully equipped 5 series BMW following Ezra. He is in his fully equipped 7 series. We are heading to our villa. I hear a phone ring. It sounds like it is coming from all around me. I look in the center console, nothing. It keeps ringing, then stops. The ringing starts up again.

Who would be calling?

Ezra.

Damn it, Ezra! Where is the phone?

I move my right hand hastily under the front car seat, no. In the glove compartment, no. The ringing stops again. I refocus on the road.

Once again, the ringing starts.

Ah! Ezra. Enough! Why don't you just tell me where it is!

I pound the steering wheel, and a loud chime sounds in the car just then. "Phone. Answer or Ignore call."

I cautiously respond to the soft female voice. "Answer."

Ezra speaks over the car speakers. "Well, it's about time!"

"Sorry, you could have used your abilities you know!"

"Check under the passenger seat. You should find what you've been looking for."

I reach under and pick up a white iPhone.

"I have taken the liberty of programming in some numbers for you. Jim, from the dealership programmed everything in your car."

I scroll through the contacts. Sera, Roan (Delilah). Sera, Bethany. *How did he do this so quickly?*

"Thank you, Ezra."

"You should give them a call. Let them know that you are safe."

"Is there anything I shouldn't tell them?"

"No. They are your parents."

There is a long pause.

He continues, "Talk to them. If you are worried that it might put them in danger, don't worry. Sebastian has sleepers in place around your family, as well as us for that matter. We will be to the house in fifteen minutes or so. Enjoy some time talking with them before we get there."

I push the button on my steering wheel that has a picture of a phone on it.

(Chime.) "Phone."

I smile. "Dial Roan Sera."

(Chime.) "Dialing Roan and Delilah Sera."

On the third ring, Dad picks up. "Hello?"

A knot forms in my throat instantly. "Dad. It's me, Jes."

It is wonderful to hear their voices. They say they are settled into a beautiful cottage-like home in Boulder, Colorado. Bethany will be attending the University of Colorado in the fall. I am so tempted to tell them I miss them. I know that I can't, though. They would worry, especially Mom. She cries the entire time we are on the call as it is.

"Can we visit you soon? Can you come visit us?"

I stumble over Mom's questions. "Uh. I'm not sure when that will happen."

I really hadn't talked with Ezra about all that. I didn't want to make any false promises to Mom, Dad, or myself for that matter.

"Lilah. She is a guardian now. It wasn't that long ago for you and I, remember. Jes, sweetheart, you have a duty ahead of you no matter how much I want to protect you. We won't see you for a while. I'm sure Ezra and you will discuss these things as they come up. That's Ezra's way."

Dad is right.

"Yeah. Mom, you know that we can talk on the phone. It will be just like back home in Marietta. I have always been independent, Mom. It's just you are a little further away now. That's all."

"Yes, Jes. You have always been brave, strong and confident. I love you, baby."

My voice cracks a little. "Me too. Uh, I gotta go. We are at the villa. I love you."

"Love you, sweetheart."

They hang up first.

* * *

We pull up to the gate at The Cloisters in Coconut Grove. Ezra reaches out of his window and punches in a code, and we both drive through. The entrance of the property is park-like. The cobblestone road is lined with a canopy of saluting palm trees with smaller azalea bushes peppered along the path. It seems like the colors of objects and details have been heightened since leaving the facility. Everything appears so vivid and new to my eyes.

We pull up to a white stucco villa with dark brown tile roofing. The drive is lined with small lantern landscape lights. The garage door is made of bamboo, stained to a dark brown to match the roof. A huge, sago palm is near the front porch. A lantern, table, and two chairs are tucked into a perfect welcoming corner on the front porch.

Ezra is already out of the car, unloading the luggage. He works quickly. Within minutes, he has the door open and our luggage inside with all the lights on. I get out of my car and walk up the drive to the front porch. The flowers that line the walkway are so lush and full of life. Even at dusk, the colors are so vibrant. I can hear rolling waves from the ocean.

"Do we live close to the ocean?"

"Oh, we live very close to the ocean."

I walk into the house with two of my smaller bags. I am amazed at the furnishings in the living room. It reminds me of the hearth room in the facility. Ezra is fumbling around in the kitchen.

I turn to look at what he is doing.

He is eyeing food in the most amazing refrigerator I had ever seen. The doors are clear glass. You can see everything in it. It is very well stocked. My stomach instantly growls, giving me its opinion.

Ezra calls to me, "Hungry?"

I tour the rest of the house, taking in the surroundings.

"Yes. Starving."

Ezra starts listing off a plethora of foods he has discovered. I claim one of the smaller rooms of the three.

The master is huge and beautiful, spa-like really. *It would be nice, but I should give it to my superior.*

This got Ezra's attention. He calls from the kitchen, "Superior? Really?"

I round the corner back to the kitchen. "Stop that! I mean I respect your thoughts. Can you please respect mine? I was raised to respect my elders, you know." I smile at Ezra, prideful of my witty sarcasm.

Ezra rolls his eyes and walks off. "Well. I am grateful. My bad back and achy tattered old feet will thank you as well."

A gigantic television is in the center of our living room. I roll my eyes. "Was this your idea, Ezra?"

"What? Oh, don't start on me."

I mumble, "Such a guy thing."

I spot the back door and open it. A moist breeze immediately touches my face and blows my hair back. I feel the moonlight on my skin. The moon is climbing slowly over the sparkling ocean, only feet from the back porch. The beach is white until it touches the crawling, dark water.

"Wow. That is ocean front." *How could we afford this?*

Ezra comes up behind me and joins me on the porch. "Connections, my dear. Byron Haynes is out of the country, Japan actually. He is a biologist working closely with our foundation."

I walk back into the house, and Ezra follows.

"Of course. Connections."

I sense some apprehension in Ezra.

"There wouldn't be any Ushering at work here, would there?"

Ezra is walking to the kitchen. He stops and turns to me. "Touché. He is a founding father. He wasn't planning a long trip abroad. But Sebastian made him an offer that he couldn't refuse. It is advantageous for us and a long time deserved for Mr. and Mrs. Haynes. It's a win-win situation."

Ezra pops a cherry into his mouth. "You should start practicing. Like, now. You are going on an interview in the morning." Ezra turns and starts to prepare two meals.

I sit down at a bar stool. "A what?"

Ezra finishes preparing the food and is placing it on each plate. "An interview at a bookstore near the University of Miami. Oh, c'mon. You are the adaptive soul that does well in the field, and I'm the brains, remember? Plus, you need to be involved in the community. Take in the environment and the people."

I realize the logic. "Yeah, you're right. I need to feel around a bit. Get a hold of my surroundings. That's the only way I can really function."

I yawn a little. I try to hide it.

Ezra quickly takes note. "You should hit the sack after dinner. I have some research to do, but I won't be far behind you."

Ezra puts on the local news while we eat. It was a typical news report. Recent environmental violations and resolutions, robberies and domestic tragedies, upcoming events, road closures, and weather.

Rarely does a robbery or murder occur in Marietta. Not a whole lot of anything happens in Marietta, and that isn't a bad thing.

Ezra shakes his head.

I am a little apprehensive about going to bed. I haven't slept in a bed out of the facility in weeks. I know how to defend myself, so I'm not physically or mentally vulnerable in that respect. Still, I am bombarded by the images of fear that have terrorized me after leaving the facility.

Ezra thinks, *You are stronger, Jes. I wouldn't lie to you about that. Stronger than you know. You are safe.*

With that, I clear my plate and straighten the kitchen for us both; a mindless distraction helped.

Ezra begins looking through files at the table. I look over.

"Anything I can help with?"

"No. I have this side project I'm working on. It has to do with the Bermuda Triangle and the active team of physicists that have been researching in the field. The project is peppered with Sondian and Dobrian scientists for obvious reasons, theories of possible portals and vortexes through space-time."

I am astounded. "I had no idea Dobrians and Sondians were working together."

"They aren't. They are undercover. As would I, upon joining the team. We would know who is a Dobrian and who is a Sondian. But we wouldn't let the enemy know we knew. It's a little complicated."

I walk over to the files and sit next to him. Ezra quickly picks up the files and proceeds in carrying them to the master bedroom.

"Good night, Jes. Please get some rest."

"Night, Ezra."

Chapter 36

The first night in the house is not so bad. No lucid dreaming. I might have kept it at bay since I am so anxious and unable to fully relax during sleep. At some point in the middle of the night, I feel a presence. Can't tell if it is in my dream or in my actual room looking over me. I am so exhausted by that point; I don't spend much time analyzing it. Plus, it doesn't feel threatening. It feels warm, comforting, and familiar.

Nate?

By the time my mind connects with my body to open my eyes, the presence is gone.

I go back to sleep quickly after clearing my mind. After I am down, though, the thoughts of him come creeping back. That kiss. The feeling of powerful energy drawing us into each other. I slowly open my eyes again. I am restless and missing Nate's and my connection.

* * *

Ezra and I are out the door at the same time in the morning. He is heading to a meeting with the field team researching the Bermuda Triangle. I am heading out to the interview at the bookstore about three miles from the house near the university. I drive. Ezra thinks I should drive as much as possible to get a better lay of the land. I am a bit nervous, even though I plan to use Ushering to assist in being hired.

237

The bookstore is a few blocks away from the beach. It is on a very busy street with quite a bit of foot traffic due to the proximity of the university. Ezra and I both agreed that it would be a perfect fit for me, not just because of my past experience, but because the likelihood of an attack on me in a crowded public area would be slim. He doesn't want to leave me unprotected.

I feel a bit nostalgic for the bookstore back home when I open the door and hear an old-fashioned door chime. I take a deep breath and push all of those memories back within me. I can't help but smile because of the coincidence, though.

An older woman with long, salt-and-pepper hair peeks out from behind a stack near the middle of the store. She is small, petite. She walks out toward me and looks me up and down, dissecting me with her light honey-colored eyes. Then she looks into my eyes and stares at me.

Usher her, Jes.

I stare back into her eyes. Everything around her blurs. "Hi. My name is Jesca Gershon-Sera."

Still staring at me, she seems to ignore my words. The woman then circles me and speaks. "So you are here for the job, my dear."

Her voice is soft, but not weak. It is a determined and confident soft voice.

Good. Now hire me.

I reply, "Yes, I am, ma'am."

She comes to face me quickly and hushes me with her olive-toned hand, demanding silence. She clicks her tongue

238

in a somewhat disapproving manner. "My name is Olivia Walker."

I have heard that name before.

Luke Walker? Nate's mentor?

I hear her in my head. *Yes, that is right. My son is Luke Walker.*

She looks at me apologetically for the intrusion in my thoughts. *My apologies, but it's best if we don't discuss specifics of our relationship in the open. Oh, and nice try with the Ushering.*

Olivia gives me a wink and a brief, soft smile. She touches my hand. A familiar current of energy passes between us. She puts her other hand on top of the one already holding mine. She gives a light, reassuring squeeze. A squeeze that tells me I am safe.

Still holding them, she closes her eyes. I watch her as her eyelids maintain a rapid movement. I wonder what those eyes are seeing behind her curtained eyelids.

She smiles and lets out a little giggle. She slowly opens her eyes and sets them on mine. Still holding my hand with hers, Olivia takes one of her hands and places it on top of my head. I instantly feel a wave of energy pass from my head to my toes. I am not sure, but it feels like she washed all of my fear and negative thoughts away.

I can only do that if you believe that God works divinely through me to allow me to do that.

I nod in understanding. She is a healer, just like her son.

"You are hired."

239

Ms. Olivia, as she prefers to be called, spends the first day showing me around the shop. We need to look like the real deal to any spying eyes. The back room is large enough to be a small apartment. It expands to its own kitchen and an upstairs loft. I soon discover that Ms. Olivia lived in this house all of her life, since she was a little girl. Her parents added on to the house, which was a convenience store for years. As she grew into a teen, the store became a restaurant for a while. When her parents passed, Ms. Olivia inherited the shop. When she married, her husband converted it into a bookstore.

* * *

Looking at the store from the street, it did stand out a bit from the rest of the upscale shops and boutiques that lined the strip. Don't get me wrong, it didn't stick out like a sore thumb. More like an eclectic, aged boutique that resembled a house.

The first few days of work with Ms. Olivia are not work at all. Ms. Olivia gives me homework.

So this is all making sense now. Ezra and you had this planned all along.

Ms. Olivia smiles, turns, and greets a new customer. She leaves me with a stack of books: Physics, Deepak Chopra, Cosmology, Metaphysics.

Apparently, the bookstore is the cover for the real purpose of Ms. Olivia's store. Most of my days at the store are spent in the back room studying, reading, learning, and applying.

240

Other days, I am permitted to witness Ms. Olivia's experiences with her customers. They are amazing stories of everyday people that on the outside look collected and at peace. You wouldn't think that they would step foot into a bookstore and entrust a woman to reveal the weight of their life. Physically and mentally unbearable pain, poverty, abuse, guilt, addiction, vanity, and hatred; it ran the gamut.

Day by day, I watch her use her gifts, her life force, to heal lives as they enter her store. They are drawn to her like a magnet as soon as they enter that door. Throughout each encounter, I can hear her thoughts, prayers to God. She is giving thanks and accepting His divine grace to share with each person she heals.

"Praying to God cleanses me and prepares me for the healing of others. My meditation with Him rejuvenates my life force."

I am continuously in awe of this woman. She is old enough to be my grandmother, yet she has endless energy and stamina; she is unwavering. And she attributes it all to God's amazing grace bestowed upon her. I am humbled to watch Him at work through her.

I was meant to see this woman and God at work in unison. Meant to witness the harmonious symphony of it all.

It is quiet in the store one afternoon. I am reading *The Cosmos* by Carl Sagan.

Ms. Olivia clears her throat to get my attention. "Jesca. I am going to visit a friend. Would you watch the store for about an hour? Will you be fine?"

"Sure, Ms. Olivia."

241

"All right, dear. How about you close the store in about an hour; it has been slow today. You have been studying so hard. A little break, huh?" Olivia winks and smiles at me.

I smile back. "I don't mind. I'm really interested in this book. I can stick around if you would like?"

"If you would like. It's up to you. I will be late. I plan to have dinner out tonight. Please don't wait for me to lock up, all right?"

I nod in agreement.

After Ms. Olivia leaves, I quickly become absorbed again in the endless possibilities of our universe through Sagan's eyes. I am so involved in my thoughts as I read, I must have missed the chime at the door.

Was there a chime?

A tall, dark-haired man is standing at the first set of stacks whistling a familiar tune. His back is to me as I watch him. His silhouette is familiar. He reminds me of Nate. His shoulders are broad and muscular.

Oh, Jesca, stop it.

He has on black jeans and a white T-shirt, very casual. From the brief glimpse of his profile, his hair is a bit longer in the front than Nate's but the same shade of dark brown. *Stop it already.*

He looks a little taller than him too...and more muscular definitely. *Enough Jes!*

The guy must feel me watching him. He cocks his head in my direction, not revealing his face yet. "Hi there. I'm looking for something full of suspense and mystery. Can you recommend anything?"

Oh. My. God. Did he really just say that? I drop my book getting up off the stool. I bend to retrieve it. "Uh. Yes, I...um...just put one of Dan Brown's latest novels in the stacks today." I quickly walk around him, trying not making eye contact.

I can feel him look at me, though. His eyes are a heavy weight of intensity. It makes me nervous and anxious all at once.

* * *

Xander

I shift my eyes to the bookstore clerk, catching a glimpse of her profile. *She is breath-taking.* I ask her about a book to distract her from my staring and stumbling to my aid. After that, I could only focus on her as she fumbled through a nearby rack. She is magnetic in every sense of the word. Her presence is suffocating and intoxicating at the same time. The movement of her hand over the books as they glide along the bindings is so intimate, it makes me consider moving closer to her. *Mesmerizing and magnetic, that is what she is.* Finding the book she wants, she gently pulls it from the stacks and turns to me.

***

243

Jesca

With book in hand, I turn toward mystery guy. Our eyes meet for the first time since he walked in.

"Oh." The sound I utter is both a combination of 'I have seen you before' and 'wow'. He is absolutely gorgeous. Deep, tan, radiant skin. *His eyes.* They are light hazel, resembling a deep, spring-fed quarry. It reminds me of a place.

Home. Georgia.

The guy looks just as lost in me as I am in him, but only for a minute. He collects himself more quickly than I do and extends his hand to receive the book I'm holding out to him. His hand brushes mine. Just that small brush radiates warmth that shoots straight through me. I have seen him before. *Where? Think, Jes.*

Like he is responding to my thoughts, the guy extends his other hand to me. "I'm Alexander Crest. Xander."

He couldn't have heard my thoughts. Could he? Put the block up just in case Jes. My response is slow. "Oh, sorry. I'm Jesca Gershon-Sera. Jes." I place hand in his. The familiarity becomes more pressing. "I think I have met you before."

A smile spreads slowly over Xander's lips and he looks down briefly, almost shyly. "I get that a lot. I must have one of those familiar faces."

***

Xander

I think I know this girl. The distraction of her presence keeps me from focusing too much on where I know her from. She looks at me awkwardly, then down at her hand that I am still holding. I pull my hand away and clasp the book she has given me with both hands.

She fidgets with her small hands. I have the urge to reach for them, still them. I look away and scratch my temple. *What the hell are you doing Xander?*

I look back at her just as she shifts her stance. "Um. Is there any other type of book you are looking for?"

"No. I think you took care of what I'm looking for."

Do I know her from the club? If I could just stay with her longer, I would remember. I look to the back of the store, where she appeared from earlier. "What are you reading back there?"

Jesca replies, "Oh. Um. I'm taking a few classes at the nearby community college, and it's pretty slow today. So I just set myself up in the back."

"Well, it sounds extraordinarily boring."

She smiles and God I feel my heart pound, instantly gratified having brought happiness to this amazing woman in front of me with my well-placed sarcasm. I needed to buy me more time with her and if sarcasm and whit was the way, I was going to use it.

It had to have been recent. She is too familiar to be someone I met a long time ago.

Jesca continues, "Well, in the subject matter's defense, I find a lot of it fascinating. At times the content of physics can spiral into an overwhelming monstrosity. But if I stay close to the surface, I think I'm safe from drowning in catatonia."

I must be looking too hard at her, because she looks away and takes a deep, nervous breath. I look away quickly and feel the need to explain myself. *I never feel the need to explain myself!* "Sorry, you just look really familiar also and I am trying to place where I have seen you before."

She is so going to think I'm a stalker.

"And since you said it first, that can't qualify as a cheap pick-up line."

Jesca smiles and moves quickly to the cash register, but not before I see the blush developing on her cheeks. She stutters, "So, will that be all?"

"Actually, would you, um, have coffee with me?"

She stops mid-stride and I feel nervous all of a sudden. You must know that I don't do nervous. Never have. But with her, I am. "You know what. I'm sorry. You must think I'm some weird stalker. Never mind. I'm sorry if I offended you."

Sorry if I offended you? C'mon, Xander, you're dying here.

***

Jesca

His words are so sincere, I find myself wanting to be with him longer. "Wait. I'm pretty new to town. It would be nice

246

to get out and about. Coffee sounds great." *If he was a threat, I would feel it, right? He is safe.* "You've been the only customer in the past two hours. I can meet you out front in a couple of minutes. I just need to lock up."

I can't help wanting to be near him. He makes me feel a rush of emotions that I haven't felt in weeks. Since...since...*Don't go there Jes.*

He hands me the cash for the book and I hand him his change and receipt quickly. His eyes remaining focused only on me. "Great. I'll meet you out front, Jesca."

Just the way he says my name makes my heart react and I want to smile. I bite my lip instead. "Great."

Xander walks backwards a few steps, eyes fastened on mine, then turns and strides out the front door. As soon as the door shuts behind him, I dash around the cash register and to the back room to collect all of the books Ms. Olivia had given me to read. I hit the lights and heads to the door hastily. When I reach the door and touch the handle. I stop and breathe.

Slow down, Jes. And don't let your guard down. He may not be as safe as you think.

I can't help but think of the connection I am feeling with this guy. How his presence and the feelings he is stirring in me reminds me of Nate in the facility. How is that even possible? Frustrated with my thoughts on Nate, I yank the door open.

He is the perfect distraction to get Nate out of my head for a little while.

Chapter 37

Jesca

I close the door behind me, lock it, and take in a deep breath. When I turn, Xander is leaning against a palm tree with his hands in his pockets. I feel a brief rush of energy.

Xander asks, "Do you mind walking a little?"

"No. Not at all."

I know he wants to talk, I can feel it. I keep my senses front and center, even though there is no nervousness with him. Being around a very good-looking guy would normally leave me flushed, stuttering, and unconfident. Right now, with Xander, I feel the complete opposite. I feel confident, strong even. The way he is studying me as we walk right now, I know he is attracted to me. God help me, I am definitely drawn to him.

Xander gives me the short version of Miami's history on the way to the coffee shop. After we order, we claim a booth in the back of the shop by a large framed window. I settle in, wanting to know more about him.

"So, what's your story, Xander? How long have you been in Miami?"

Xander looks out the window. "My whole life. I'm not sure where I was born, but I know my grandmother was from here. My mother and father disappeared when I was two. My grandmother raised me until I was five, when she passed.

Then, foster homes and shelters." Xander pauses and looks up at me, checking for my reaction. I can sense he is embarrassed by his history and is hoping it won't scare me off. He shouldn't feel that way. His history is just that.

"Well. The past is what shapes you to handle your future. It doesn't matter where you were. What matters is where you are right now, right?"

Xander's eyes light up and he smiles, looking back down at his coffee cup. I can't help but feel a joy knowing that I put that smile on his face just now after all he has told me.

He looks up slowly, "Yes. And I am very content with where I am right now." His sultry stare is anchored to my reaction. And, oh boy, do I want to react to those words. Like melt into my chair, react!

I try really hard not to blush, but I feel the heat crawling up my neck and into my cheeks. An involuntary giggle escapes me and I cover it quickly with the sweater sleeves covering my hands. *God woman, get a hold of yourself!*

Xander's smile widens at my reaction. He brings his coffee to his lips and takes a long sip. I look out the window, trying to distract myself from looking too long at those lips.

When I feel the giddy emotions subside again, I take the rubber band from my wrist and pull my long, dark hair into a high, sloppy bun. I rest my hands on either side of my coffee mug now. "So, Xander, how is life for you now?"

Xander is tapping the side of his coffee cup, looking at me. "It's great! After I met Sam, everything changed. He took me in and raised me as his own flesh and blood. He loved me when no one else wanted anything to do with me." Xander's face quirks and his brows knit together. "I don't know why I am telling you all of this."

"He must be a pretty amazing man. I hope to meet him some day." *Woah! Way to make future plans with a guy you just met!* I am not in a position to start making long-term plans with anyone. I have to remember that anyone I get involved with, I am putting them in danger.

Xander eyebrows shoot upward and his lip twitches into a lazy smile. "Maybe you will."

I try and change the subject. "I am adopted." *Jesca! What the hell are you doing? Under cover? Hello!* "My parents died in a car accident. I...I don't know much about them. My adopted parents have raised me since I was young. I know what you mean about having someone take you in and think of you as flesh and blood." *Good cover, Jes. Now keep it light! Ugh!*

Coffee cups multiplied exponentially on our table as we talk, moving from one topic to another, and another. When we hit three cups each, I interrupt our easy conversation. "Whoa! Too much caffeine! Must stop!"

Xander laughs a little. "Yeah, I hear you." His smile fades suddenly and his eyes look sad all of a sudden. "I don't want to go. I have never talked with anyone like this."

I want to say that I don't either, but I know that if we keep going, it will only get us deeper into something I can't have right now. *I can't get too involved.*

He must see my reaction and see it as rejection because he says, "And now I feel like an idiot."

"No, don't please. I...I just remembered that I have to be somewhere. Home. I'm sorry, but I have to go."

Xander smiles softly and nods. As we walk out of the coffee shop, I'm cursing everything that has happened to shift my life from normal to chaotic over the past two months. This guy is charming, attractive, and kind, magnetizing even and I can't get close to him, can't get involved. We walk back to the store in an awkward silence, stealing small glances at each other along the way.

Suddenly, I feel a warm hand cover mine. I look up at Xander who is looking down at his hand. My gaze follows his to see his fingers linking with mine. My pulse speeds up and instead of pulling away from him, I intertwine my fingers with his. I look up at him slowly, checking his reaction to my response. He keeps his eyes on our hands for a moment, and then a huge smile spreads across his face. It is contagious, damn it, and I have to smile too. He looks away quickly, covering his mouth with his hand to hide the ever expanding smile. I turn away and look at a shop we are passing, hiding my expanding smile and swelled heart. Neither of us let go and the silence settled between us is no longer empty and awkward, but full and comforting.

THIS...this is a perfect moment. *It is a moment that can't last. Damn it!*

We stop in front of the bookstore and we slowly unlock our hands.

"So Xander, where are you headed now?"

Xander pulls out his phone and shows me the home screen.

251

Missed text (4) Sam
Voicemail (2) Sam

Xander smiles. "Guess I will be returning these. Probably something to do with work. You?"

I reach into my pocket. My phone buzzed numerous times at the coffee shop, but I ignored it. I look at my home screen.

Missed text (2) Ezra
Voicemail (1) Ezra

"Guess I'll be doing the same."

Xander walks over to his car leisurely. "So how are you getting home?"

"Walking."

He turns to me, resting his forearms on the roof of his car. "Let me give you a ride home. You shouldn't be walking around a big, strange town by yourself so close to dark."

For a moment, he sounds like Ezra. It makes me smile. "I don't mind, really."

Xander raises his eyebrows, presses a button on his keychain to reset his alarm, and walks around the back of his car to me. "Well, then. May I escort you home?"

When he reaches me, he formally puts his arm out for me to accept.

Without hesitating, I link my arm through his. "Yes, you may, Xander."

I'm prolonging this between him and me, only making it harder. I can't help how wonderful it feels to be with him though.

Xander starts up the conversation as we walk. "So, Jes, what small town in Georgia are you from, anyway?"

"Marietta."

I look up at him, checking his reaction to my small Georgia town.

***

Xander

My smile melts away a little at her response. I nod and clear my throat.

I can tell by the weight of her stare she is gauging my reaction. She asks boldly, "What?"

I'm quick on my response. "Nothing, It's just…I have been there before."

I look down at her hoping that my response it accepted without any other curiosity.

She smiles and I feel at ease again. "Really? Well, I guess it is not that small of a town after all. So, what were you doing there?"

Anxiety creeps back in upon her continued questioning.

"I was there for business a few weeks ago. I was…doing research on a local university. Advertising stuff."

I watch her reaction again, but instead it is posed with another question. "Was it Southern Polytechnic State University?"

I want to lie to her. Tell her it was another university, but I don't. Honestly, I think I want her to find me out in a way. "Yeah, that was it."

Jesca starts talking about campus and how she misses the atmosphere and the people. I slip into my own thoughts for a moment. The festering of the familiarity of Marietta has started in my mind and is working overtime now.

Is she the girl? Is she the one I needed to find?

What are the chances, though? All those girls on campus wearing the same collegiate paraphernalia complete with a baseball cap and backpack. I must have bumped into handfuls of girls while shadowing Ezra Kahn. How could I be sure it was or wasn't her? Sam was still searching for a name and more intelligence on the girl when he abruptly called me back to Florida.

***

Jesca

I notice a serious look on Xander's face all of a sudden. "You okay?"

I elbow him slightly to regain his attention.

Xander blinks and looks down at me. "Yeah. Yeah. I was just remembering the campus and being on it. Sorry."

I stop and turn to him. "Well, this is me."

We are at the gate to the entrance of the Cloisters.

Xander's eyes widen. "Wow."

I feel myself tense up and pull my hand away from his. "I'm staying with a friend while I'm here in town. A close family friend."

Xander sees my reaction and he changes the subject. "Well. I enjoyed talking with you over coffee, Jesca Gershon-Sera. Thank you for accepting my invitation." Xander extends his hand to me.

I extend mine and put it in his. "I enjoyed talking with you too, Alexander Crest."

We hold each other's hand longer than necessary.

This is it. I will never see him again.

Xander's look becomes more intense. "Have dinner with me, Jesca."

I feel warmth extend from my hand, up my arm, into my chest, then to my toes. "I would like that." I slowly slip my hand out from his and turn to enter my gate code.

Xander's face lights up. "When? How about tomorrow night?"

The gate opens, and I turn back. I can't say anything. I'm not playing hard to get, even though it appears to be that way to him, I'm sure. I am physically incapable of answering him, literally. I can't get myself to push the words out of my mouth.

There must be a reason, Jes. You are hesitating for a reason.

I bow my head and close my eyes to focus on speaking. I tense and suck in a deep breath. "I'm not sure."

"Ah. That's not the answer I'm looking for."

I look at him and grin. His eyes are set on mine, like magnets. My eyes are equally, if not more, set on his. The words escape me quickly now. "Let's enjoy spontaneity, shall we? You know where to find me."

Xander steps closer as the gate closes behind me. "Yes, I do, Jesca Gershon-Sera. Jes."

His eyes are so warm and safe.

I turn and start walking along the cobblestone walkway to our villa. I feel him watching me, a heavy and intoxicating weight. It is a bewitching feeling. Even though we are no longer physically together, his presence is still bound to me like a cosmic link.

Chapter 38

I read both of Ezra's texts and listen to his voicemail as I walk along.

"Where are you? We need to train tonight." Ezra's voice sounds worried.

I text him as I walk.

"Heading to the house now. In the Cloisters."

I just finish sending the message when I feel someone approach me quickly from my right. She takes me off guard with her enthusiasm.

"Hey there! I wanted to introduce myself a couple of days ago, but I haven't had much of a chance to catch you!"

She has medium-length, curly, red hair. It reminds me of Elisha. *I miss her.*

"Uh, hi."

"I'm Corinna Cain, your neighbor!"

I don't reply, just smile.

"So is that guy living with you your dad? Or is he your 'daddy'?"

Yep, just like Elisha. She genuinely makes me laugh with that question. "No! I mean. He is my dad." It feels strange telling her that Ezra is my dad.

"Name. What is your name?"

"Jesca Gershon-Sera. Jes."

"Jes. Great. Where are you from, Jes?"

It comes to me so easily. "East coast. Dad had a career opportunity, so here we are. I'm taking some courses at the nearby community college."

"Cool. Hey! What are you doing right now?"

Her question surprises me. "What do you mean? Like, this moment?"

"Yeah! I'm heading out to this boutique clothing store on Cutler. They're having an open house from six to eight. Kind of a sneak peek for frequent clients like myself. Wanna come?"

I want to. It sounds like fun to have some girl time.

My phone buzzes. It's a text from Ezra.

"Where are you, Jes?"

I sigh and look up at Corrina. "I would love to take a rain check on hanging out. Tonight is not good. Dad needs me to do some things around the house tonight."

Corinna nods with a huge smile on her face. "No worries. I understand. I'm house-sitting my mom's villa for the spring while she travels around Europe with her fiancé, Francois. My to-do list around the house is nagging at me also."

Corinna's smile slowly disappears. Then an awkward silence comes between us.

I break the silence. "So, what are you doing tomorrow afternoon?"

Corrina's smile returns instantly. "No plans. Do you wanna catch lunch and the beach?"

I feel myself light up inside for the first time since home and Elisha. "That sounds awesome."

"I'll come by your place around noon tomorrow, all right?" Corinna turns and jogs up her walkway. "Bye!"

I smile at her quirky demeanor. "Bye."

I walk through the front door of our villa.

Ezra is sitting at the table. "What happened to you?"

Feeling self-conscious, I look down at myself. "What?"

"Your face. What is that?" He looks over his reading glasses and points with his index finger in my direction.

I touch my face and wipe my cheeks. "What? What do I have on me?"

Ezra smirks. "A smile. You should wear it more often."

I growl at Ezra. "You freaked me out!"

My frustration doesn't last long. I am still bubbly from the girl-time I briefly shared with Corinna. I head to my room to change for training.

Ezra and I take to the beach. Our side of the beach is very private, away from the public eye. So the military crawl in the sand from the beach to the back door of our villa is not going to draw attention.

I tell Ezra about meeting Corinna and how she reminds me of Elisha. I tell him about her and me hanging out tomorrow.

"I think that's a great idea. Just remember not to put yourself in a position that could jeopardize you or anyone around you."

I catch his drift "Yes. I know. I won't put us into that position."

I know how important it is to keep our identity as vague as possible. We can't confide in anyone for fear that they may be a Sondian spy. Or worse, confiding in an innocent person that discovers us and then becomes a target for the Sondian guardians. It is dangerous for us and for the company we keep.

Over the next few days, Corinna and I are inseparable. When I'm not at the bookstore with Ms. Olivia, or training with Ezra, I'm with Corinna. We go shopping, check out the local coffee shops, have lunch, and just hang out.

* * *

Corinna and I are at the beach. She is reading a magazine, and I'm resting my eyes.

"Hey, you want to check out this club down on the coastline tonight, Jes? I met the owner a few days ago, and he asked me to come out and bring friends. He is absolutely gorgeous. He has these eyes. They are so, so wow! Anyway, you gotta come with me!"

I open my eyes and look at her. "Do you want to check the club out or the guy?"

I feel my phone buzz. "Ugh."

It is Ezra texting me.

"Head home. I have an update."

I look up at Corinna. "Hey, can we head back? Dad needs me to break down boxes and finish unpacking the garage with him."

"Sure. Do you think you can sneak away later? I mean, I don't mind going to the club on my own. I just really want to have backup just in case anything creepy happens."

I sense Corinna's apprehension. It's the first time I sense her feeling anything but charisma, joy, and positive energy. It feels like a burning in my chest.

"Yes. I will."

Something about Corinna's words and feelings make me want to be there. I can feel an energy building up, like the feeling you get before lightning strikes.

Chapter 39

I don't expect to see Ezra sitting at the kitchen table with files scattered.

Ezra stops reading and looks up over his glasses. "Jesca."

Just the sound of my name sounds serious in this instance. I carefully put my things down on the entry table and walk over to him.

He nudges a chair with his foot. "Take a seat. We've got something to talk about."

I feel the house narrow down to this single table with a soft light above it. Everything else around us is gone. My hands start to tingle, so I start wringing them together.

Is this the lightning strike?

Ezra gets up from the table as I sit. "Do you want something from the kitchen?"

"Uh. No, thanks."

I glance feverishly from one file to the next, trying to catch a glimpse of something that could give me a clue on what Ezra is going to talk with me about.

One picture catches my eyes. It's woman in a bed with a contorted face. A priest is standing over her. Another picture, a young man is levitating over a bed while a woman covers her mouth in the background. Some of the pictures have the word MISSING across their faces.

Ezra walks up next to me.

"What are these, Ezra?"

Ezra waves his hands over the files. "This is what I have been working on since we got our territory."

I point to the picture of the woman and the man. "What happened?"

I can't look at the woman in the picture very long. She is disfigured so badly, she doesn't look human. Her black eyes were obviously staring at the camera lens when this was taken.

It looks like, like demonic...

Ezra finishes my thought. "Demonic possession."

My mouth goes dry. "Yes. Her face, its face. It doesn't look like a woman. It looks like something not of this world." I have to look away again.

The woman's eyes are sunken and bloodshot to the point of hemorrhaging. Her cheekbones are pronounced, and her mouth is stretched into an angry scowl with sores developing around her lips.

I get up and walk to the kitchen to put some distance between me and the pictures.

Ezra is shuffling pictures and files, suddenly, he realizes the emotions the photos are bringing out in me and starts collecting them into a stack.

I try to get the thought out of my mind, but I can't. The reoccurring nightmare of my parents, my mother convulsing as my father prays over her, holding her. Her face changing, contorting. I close my eyes and take a sip of the Coke that I just popped open.

Wash away the image, Jes.

Ezra calls to me, "It's not demonic. What if I told you that for centuries what people have thought to be demonic possession of the body and mind was actually an alien possession resulting from abduction."

I choke on my Coke. "What? Alien possession? There is no such thing. That's crazy, Ezra!"

Ezra retorts, "As crazy as demonic possession?"

He has a point. For hundreds of years the argument of demonic possession being real or not has been fought.

Ezra starts, "In the Bible, possession did occur, and it is referred to as demonic. How do we know that the demons in the Bible were grotesque-looking animal-like mutations from a realm called Hell, rather than beings with different physical attributes and chemical properties from another world named Hell? How do we know that those possessions were not the beginnings of abduction of the human mind and body to eventually be marked and probed? And by marked I mean physical implantation of a communication device, much like a marine biologist would tag a group of migrating whales in the ocean, to keep track of the tagged and in this woman's case, to use her as a vessel for communication and monitoring of our world by another. To watch and observe us, like a window into our world, to communicate their desire to learn about us and co-exist with us."

Once again, Ezra amazes me with the possibilities. I can't resist the argument, though. "And priests?"

Ezra responds matter-of-factly, "Students of God and teachers for us. Teachers of prayer and spiritual communication with Him, the Lord. And teaching a splash of psychology for good measure and the balance of science and religion in our universe," Ezra sighs and continues while he puts his files together. "Who better than a human host to be the medium between intelligent, extraterrestrial life and our world? A way for them to enter our world and dwell among us."

I walk back to the table and sit. I look directly at Ezra. "You're serious." I am not questioning, but searching his eyes for solid assurance that he truly believes this.

Ezra looks back at me with intense seriousness. "A theory that is totally a possibility and is logical. As long as you are of both the faithful and logical, science and religion."

I ask, "So how does this connect with what's going on here?"

Ezra changes the subject. "It started dull and is getting stronger now, isn't it?"

The humming.

I reply flatly, "Yes, but I'm fine."

Ezra is a little agitated by this. "Yes, Jesca, you are fine. But you need to keep me in the loop. I need a warning as well. And you are the only warning we have. Your gift is unique and one that I don't have. Work with me, okay?"

At this point, his anger has turned to a plea.

I understand.

"You're right, I just wanted to keep it quiet until I knew for sure that something was happening."

Ezra mumbles, "You are not a one-man army, Jes. Don't even attempt to try it. Promise me."

The concern on his face prompts me to try and ease his nerves. "I promise, Ezra."

Ezra sits and gestures for me to come back to the table from the kitchen counter. "Initially I was sent to participate in the research surrounding the Bermuda Triangle and the Einstein-Rosen bridge theory link. We were to blend in and adapt to the community. In addition to my 'day job', I was being sent documents from global Dobrian intelligence."

Ezra points to the files in front of us. "These files are real people from all walks of life all over the world. This is proof that extraterrestrial marking, implantation, possession, and abduction of humans on Earth is happening. Not only that, it has been occurring steadily in one location for the last six months."

Ezra begins to restack his files and sighs. "When you look at the reports of abductions globally, the largest numbers reported in the past two years have occurred in Japan and North America. We have Dobrians everywhere to track and document this kind of intelligence: hospitals, institutions, churches, doctors, lawyers, nurses, pastors, priests. The list goes on.

"Now, within the last six months alone, we have received multiple reports targeting an area that has absorbed a large amount of missing people, mental illnesses in people where there is no familial history of illness, and priests and pastors working with individuals that think they are losing their minds or think they are possessed."

I put my head down and blow my lower lip out. "Let me guess. Right here in Florida."

266

Ezra nods. "And all of them have similar episodes and speaking in one particular language. An ancient language, Aramaic. From here to Japan, the translators have confirmed that the human victims are all focused on one specific event: the collision of The Milky Way and Andromeda galaxies.

Chapter 40

It is surreal to say out loud. "So, these people are being…abducted, marked, and used to warn us?"

"Well, it is more of an announcement, a revelation, that a collision of our two galaxies will occur."

I have so many questions, but I am so overwhelmed I don't know where to start. Thoughts start racing through my head. *When will it happen? What will it do to our world?*

Ezra senses my thoughts. "Imagine bubbles floating in the air. The wind shifts the directions of the bubbles, and two begin to float into each other. They either join, intersect, or they become one bubble. In our situation, we have two galaxies. The thing that is drawing these two galaxies to each other is the cosmic links that have been created first by Sebastian's travel, connecting Earth to Dobria, and then continued cosmic linking by Balthazar's travel, connecting Earth to Sonde."

I feel resentment emanate from Ezra briefly before he blocks me.

"A gravitational shift has begun. Our galaxy and Andromeda have been set into motion to collide, like two bubbles. And what that collision will create is not known to us yet. But fellow Dobrian scientists, climatologists, and biologists have been reporting changes in our world that are showing the Earth's vulnerability to the movement that is occurring: shifting of the polar caps, weather patterns becoming unstable and volatile, natural disasters occurring with greater frequency. When will it happen? Within months. Will we intersect and become one or collide and be destroyed? Only God knows."

We both become quiet to take in the possibility of this unavoidable event.

Ezra continues, "Balthazar has been working very hard for years to form an alliance with the inhabitants of Sonde in preparation for this intersection, Jes. Not only that, he has been traveling to multiple worlds in both our galaxies and in Andromeda for the same purpose. He is obsessed with the power he has experienced from each of these worlds he has visited. Through valuable sources, Sebastian has learned that the inhabitants of Sonde are unhappy with what Balthazar is doing, the alterations he is making in other worlds."

I think about that for a second. Alterations?

Ezra continues, "There have been rumors of a revolt against Balthazar and his team in Sonde. They are not planning the revolt until the event has occurred."

I finish his thought. "Because they want to inhabit Earth." I bite my lip as I think about the repercussions. How will this play out? What will our world become? Questions are whirling in my head. I start to feel the adrenaline pumping faster.

I look Ezra square in the eyes. "Well, what are we supposed to do, Ezra?

"All we can do is be ready to protect the humanity in our world from those that may want to destroy it," Ezra sighs in relief. "The good news is that Dobria is in the Andromeda galaxy. We have an ally over there."

I know that Ezra is working hard to change the growing wrinkle in the middle of my forehead. It's not working, though. I know that we have to do something now.

"All right, who are we looking for? Who is the one that has been causing the abnormal growth of victims in Florida?" I am digging because I know that is where this conversation is headed. There is one person pulling the strings here for Balthazar. "S. C. Who is S. C.? From the files back at the facility."

"His name is Samson. He is the right-hand man for Balthazar. He has a young assistant. I don't know who he is yet." Ezra looks away.

My adrenaline is boiling over, and I let the questions loose. "Where is his location? When do we plan to attack? Are we to capture or kill?"

"Whoa, girl! This is heavier than what the team originally thought when you and I were sent here." Ezra shakes his head. "We are in over our head, Jesca. We need backup."

My anger gets the better of me. "What? Ezra, we are ready for this. We have spent a month preparing, with endless scenarios and plenty of combat practice. You and I can do this. Stopping this Samson guy would put a huge hole in Balthazar's plan. Who knows? That might alter the collision."

Ezra puffs out his lower lip. "I have been advised to call in a partner for us. A partner for you."

I feel my pride take a punch in the stomach. "A partner? For what? To hold my hand!" My mouth starts going dry. *I can't believe they are doing this now. They didn't even give me a shot on my own.*

Ezra feels the need to explain more. "Sebastian and I both agree. He has already put in the order. Sebastian and I know what we are up against, Jesca. Don't let pride get in the way of your judgment."

I shoot back. "You know what I am capable of." I look up at the ceiling and yell. "And you know too Sebastian, where ever you are!"

I look back at Ezra and point at him accusingly. "You said it yourself. You have never seen someone with so many abilities gifted to them. And I know how to use them."

Ezra nods in agreement. "And they are getting stronger by the day. That is precisely why you need to be paired with someone who can be your balance. You do not know everything you are capable of, Jesca. You need another to balance your abilities." Ezra looks defeated all of a sudden. "Someone other than me."

I turn on my heels and grab my backpack. "This is crap."

I am seeing red and need to get out of here as quickly as possible before I explode.

Ezra's voice becomes stern. "Where are you going?

I am packing my bag with anything I can stuff in it—my wallet, spare clothes, shoes, and a toothbrush.

"Out. I need to cool off. I can't believe Sebastian. And you! Of all people, you! You didn't give me a shot on my own!"

Ezra argues back. "We are trying to keep you safe!"

I don't back down. "I am safe. Too safe. Too safe to stop anyone on my own, apparently."

I zip my bag and slam the door to the villa behind me. My chest is tightening. I try to breathe deep, but I can't slow it down. I close my eyes and concentrate on slowing everything down. I take a deep breath to think about where I am heading. I don't have many options. I shift the weight of my bag and head for Corinna's.

Chapter 41

Corinna is in the bathroom, curling her eyelashes, when she hears the knock at her door. "Ugh. I hate having short eyelashes. Short and straight. Coming! Be right there!"

Corinna tosses the curler into her makeup drawer and skips to the front door. The living room is a wreck. She trips over a beach towel, picks it up with a sigh, and tosses it over a kitchen table chair on her way to the door.

Corinna opens the door with a huge smile. "I knew it would be you!"

My face must show the anger I am still feeling.

Corinna's smile fades to concern. "What is up with you?"

God, she sounds so much like Elisha.

I smile a little and roll my eyes. "What's up with me? What's up with you? Are you going to that club tonight or what?"

Corinna's eyes light up again, and the excitement comes out in her high-pitched voice. "Yes! Are you done at your house?"

"Oh, yes. I am done for the night." I don't have anything "club worthy" in my bag. "Do you have something I could borrow?"

Corinna grabs my hand and pulls me into the villa. I reach to shut the door behind me as she pulls me along.

"I have the perfect outfit for you, Jes. A royal blue, sequined tank with tight, black, leather pants. You've got the body!"

I stop listening after the tight, black, leather pants. *What am I getting myself into?* I always knew what fun trouble I would get in with Elisha. For the first time since home, being with Corinna felt the same way.

After clothes and hair, Corinna was ready to work on makeup. She takes me into the bathroom and gets to work.

I make conversation while Corinna works. "So, what are we doing tonight? I mean, I know we are going to a club. Are we meeting anyone there?"

Corinna studies my face as she brushes here and brushes there on my forehead and eyelids. "Club Helion. Lots of friends from campus have gone and have been trying to get me to go. I have been stand-offish about the whole club scene since the recent negative publicity it has been getting."

This gets my attention. My eyes open to look up at her. "Negative publicity? Like what?"

Corinna rolls her eyes while she speaks. "A few night-clubbers have gone missing over the past couple of weeks."

I stop Corinna's hand mid-brush. "Corinna! Why are we going there?"

Corinna defends her decision. "All of the missing turned up a day or two later, Jes! Unharmed for the most part. Reporters speculate there were drugs involved since they could not recall where they went and who was with them. And by the looks of these people, they were probably real wack-jobs in the first place."

274

I can't help but think of Ezra's conversation with me about the abductees. I found it too coincidental to not be related. "Were the victims okay after they were found?"

Corinna stops brushing my eyelashes with mascara. "Well. I think so. I think a few of them needed some additional medical attention."

I close my eyes while Corinna continues to touch up my eyes. If Ezra and Sebastian were not going to give me a shot on my own, maybe this is my chance to do a bit of investigation by myself. This may or may not be a lead. But I am going to take it. If it turns out to be nothing, I will be hanging out with Corinna, forgetting about everything for a little while.

Corinna taps me on the head with the tip of an eye-lining pen, like she has worked magic.

I open my eyes and smile. "So did you work a miracle on my face, friend?"

Corinna snickers. "Ha ha, friend. You didn't need much work. You ready?"

"Yes. Let's go."

I don't bother looking in the mirror. I don't want to see how much makeup Corinna has used on me. Since I am a no-makeup girl, any amount is too much. I am anxious and curious. Will I uncover a key player in these possible abduction cases or have a thrilling time with a new friend away from the crazy path my life has taken?

Corinna stops me as we pass her room. "Hey. Can you help me put on my bracelet?"

It is silver with small amber stones all around it. I comment as I put it on her. "It is so beautiful."

"Thanks. My sister, Isabel, gave it to me for my birthday last year."

Corinna smiles as she recalls the event in her mind. It reminds me of Bethany.

"I miss my sister Bethany a lot, too." I look down, recalling the sibling rivalry as well as the friendship we had as kids.

Corinna reaches for my hand. "I'm glad that we found each other here, Jes. I mean, meeting you and becoming friends so quickly. That normally doesn't happen to me."

"It doesn't happen to me either."

Corinna says, "Uh! Listen to me. I sound so sappy."

I put my hand over hers. "No. Not sappy at all."

Corinna pulls her hand away and flutters them in the air to remove the imagined sappiness from the atmosphere.

"All right! No more talk! Let's get out of here!"

We both smile and head out the front door.

Chapter 42

Sam is sitting in a dimly lit office in Club Helion, waiting for Xander. He has a tumbler of scotch and water in his hand.

Xander pulls up to the club in his 2011 Porsche Panamera. He smiles at the valet as he tosses the keys to him. "How's it going, man?"

The valet replies, "Great, sir. Busy tonight!"

Xander walks past him into his club. On his way through, he shakes a few hands and exchanges embraces, smiles, and waves. He is making his way through gyrating bodies toward his office in the back of the club. His mind is on the meeting that he called with Sam. Since meeting Jesca, Xander hasn't been able to get the familiarity of her out of his mind. He needs to know if she is involved in that trip he made to Georgia. And lately, the way Sam is acting with the clubbers is questionable and drawing concern among the regulars. Sam is becoming very comfortable with taking some of the late-night clubbers to 'private parties'. With the recent news about young night clubbers who have been at Helion and Meridian going missing for days and then resurfacing, it looks really bad for the clubs' reputations. The secrecy behind so many things that Sam is doing lately is wearing on Xander. He needs to talk to Sam and find out what is going on.

About six weeks ago, Sam started giving Xander lists of VIP people that he needed to meet and invite to the club for personal tours of the club scene, only to be given by Sam.

Xander thought the lists to be harmless the first two times Sam presented them to him, like a promotional thing. Sam was very particular with Xander's presentation of the invitations to these VIP people. It was almost like a courtship initially, to gain their trust. The latest invitation is to a girl from the Cloisters, Corinna Cain. She is supposed to stop by tonight. After a couple more weeks of lists from Sam, then meeting Jesca, Xander feels like something else is going on; he doesn't like it.

Xander scans the club one last time before entering the office, but doesn't see Corinna. Xander remembers her as a sweet girl. Christian and Xander met her for lunch one afternoon to deliver her invitation. Until he knows exactly what is really going on with Sam, he doesn't want to get her involved by being here. He hopes she won't show.

Xander opens the door to the office. Sam turns in the chair to face Xander with a smile.

"Xander."

Xander doesn't return the smile. "Sam."

"Oh, c'mon. Don't sulk. Why are you sulking?" Sam walks over to Xander and pulls him in for an embrace. "How have you been, boy?"

Xander slowly pats Sam's back. "Good. Just keeping up with the club. It's been kind of crazy lately. Where have you been? You have been hard to pin down the past couple of days."

"Aw. I've had investors breathing down my neck. And entertaining the VIPs that have been coming into the clubs. They have demanded quite a bit of my time."

Xander looks at him straight on. "Really? I was under the impression you were taking those VIPs elsewhere for private gatherings?"

He is digging for an answer. Xander knows he has every right. His name is on the line as well. He isn't going to let Sam smooth-talk his way out of this without a solid, justifiable explanation. Not this time.

Sam slowly sips his drink, and then turns his wrist to swirl around the contents. Sam doesn't speak, just stares at Xander. Whoever speaks first would lose.

Xander says, "What's going on? What are you involved in, Sam? What are you getting me involved in, with beefing up the personal invitations to the clubs?" Xander feels a burning in his head as his heart begins to race faster.

Sam sits his tumbler down on the side table from where they are standing. "What is going on has been happening since before I picked you up at Cutler St. My involvement has always been the same. Now, I'm preparing the path for you, Xander."

The crease between Xander's eyebrows increases. "Preparing a path for me? Do you know what is being said about the clubs around town, especially ours, lately? Are you involved in what is happening to these people that are missing for days, then resurfacing days later? I am getting heat, and I need to know what is going on."

Xander looks at Sam with pleading, but determined eyes. Determined to get answers.

Sam rolls his eyes and uses his animated hands to show how frivolous the claims are. "The heat will die. It will pass.

It's just the latest media feasting on a few kids that had a little too much fun, got loaded, and passed out at friends' houses."

Xander puts his head between his hands as he leans forward. He runs his fingers through his hair. "No, these kids have names that I know. I personally invited them. I screened them for you. They were clean people. I feel responsible. And you should too."

Sam huffs. "Xander, we provided the entertainment. If we worried about every person that walked through our doors and left our doors..." Sam trails off to a pause. Sam continues in a calmer tone, "The point is, you are not responsible for what another consenting adult decides to do."

Xander smirks and turns away from Sam.

Sam jumps. "What, Xander? Spit out any other accusations you may have!"

Xander turns back to Sam. 'That's the thing. I don't think these people are deciding anything."

Sam moves closer to Xander. "What are you saying, Xander?"

Xander's eyes do not leave Sam's. His patience is running thin now. "Corinna Cain was the latest invitation. Who is she? Why her? What are your intentions with her because she is a nice girl, Sam."

Sam shifts in his seat and lets out a cackle and mimics Xander's words. "What are my intentions with her? She is a nice girl. Please, Alexander. Let me tell you something, kid. You have no idea what my intentions are." Sam's face begins to redden. "You want to know? All right. Think back as far as you can. Past the first time we met. Think back to your grandmother. Your parents. Can you remember them?"

Xander's blood begins to boil. Sam is being cruel. Xander looks down at his hands that are resting on his hips. "No, Sam. I was very young. I don't remember my parents." Xander can't help to feel a bit deflated from the low blow.

Sam takes advantage of his moment of weakness. "Well, let me give you a brief history lesson, son. Your parents were part of an organization, a fellowship. One that I have been a part of for the greater part of my life. I knew your parents. The organization was established by a man named Balthazar Onoch."

* * *

Sam details the history of Balthazar, Sebastian, Sonde, Dobria, and the intersection. Xander is astounded. It all seems fake. How can he believe anything Sam says at this point? Slowly puzzle pieces of his life that never matched up in the past, start snapping into place. Unsure if he wants to know more or not, Xander cautiously asks, "So how did you and my parents know each other?"

"Your parents were both physicists at the University of Miami. They had been involved in ongoing research of the Bermuda Triangle and wormhole theory applications. Balthazar was impressed by their level of knowledge and their own supporting ideas of the correlation between wormholes and the Bermuda Triangle. So, he introduced them to the world of Sonde, knowing that they would not be able to resist the invitation." Sam pauses awkwardly after he says the last word, 'invitation'.

He continues, looking down at his tumbler. "They traveled with Balthazar to Sonde. I met your parents there. I was there researching. Months went by and your parents, Rebekah and Paul Sera, were enthralled by their accomplishments on Sonde, especially with the use of their knowledge in the development of a mechanism to sustain an open portal from Earth to Sonde for an extended amount of time.

"Even though they loved the endless learning, research, and experimentation that they were a part of in Sonde, they wanted to come back to Earth. They wanted to stabilize the mechanism here on Earth. Rebekah and Paul were also eager to have a family, a child. They were truly invaluable assets to Balthazar. Balthazar planned to send them home to Earth so that they could continue processing the mechanism from here while having the life they desired. Before they left, you were born."

Sam pauses and looks at Xander. "Months later, when you were old enough to travel, the finishing touches were being made on the mechanism here on Earth. When you were only a year old, your parents were prepared to link the device on Earth with Sonde. Dobrian spies infiltrated the research lab where Rebekah and Paul were working. Unfortunately, Rebekah and Paul were caught in the crossfire between the Sondian and Dobrian guardians, and they were murdered at the hands of the Dobrians.

"From that point, well, you know the rest. Your grandmother, God bless her, kept you safe, protected, and loved. When I saw you, Xander, when Balthazar told me that you were the one who was going to be a key component in the collision of our galaxies, that you had a purpose beyond his, mine, and your comprehension, that I needed to keep you, raise you, and teach you…I was intimidated. Intimidated by what you could become as a man."

Sam looks down at his folded hands. "But I myself had lived my whole life for work, not for making friendships or a family. I wanted to be a part of another's life at the very point in time that I met you." Sam's face becomes softer suddenly.

Xander shifts and crosses his arms over his chest.

"As life progressed for you and I, Balthazar kept me informed of what steps needed to be taken and when."

Xander's expression changes. A light goes off in his head. "The investor is Balthazar, isn't it?"

"Yes. He is the investor. He is our guide. He is the one that will give us unimaginable ranking when the collision occurs."

Xander breathes out a large sigh. He is trying to grasp all of these fantastical images running through his head. He looks over at Sam again. "Is he the one that ordered the invitations of these people I'm bringing to the club, like meals on a platter for you?" Xander can't resist the sarcasm. Sam deserves the dig after keeping as much from Xander as he has.

Sam looks at Xander with serious eyes. "Xander, it is not like that. These people were chosen to become very important vessels, prophecies of the collision."

Xander looks at Sam like he is crazy. "Vessels? And you think that it is okay for Balthazar to just use them?"

283

"They have been chosen to be a part of the multitude when the collision occurs. They are the first phase. These average humans have become communication vessels if you will; the eyes, ears, and voice of the beings that will be coming to our Earth."

Sam wipes his hand over his mouth and moves closer to Xander. "I took these vessels and sent them to Balthazar with the help of the mechanism your parents created, a Copula. The vessels were then implanted with a second generation Copula. This device interacts and synchronizes with the human's central nervous system, allowing extraterrestrial access to the vessel when they are elsewhere, like on Earth, for instance. It is almost like this vessel has become possessed by the extraterrestrial. That is why these people disappear for days. When they return, they have no recollection of the journey. The journey has been blocked from their minds. It is for their safety."

Sam is stating all of this so bluntly, cold even. Xander is floored. He runs his hands through his hair and starts pacing in front of Sam.

"Safety? Are you kidding me? Listen to yourself! Michael at the door was telling me that two of the people that have been found had to be institutionalized. They are going crazy, Sam! Another was exorcised by a priest. This is sick, Sam!"

Sam shows no emotion as he looks at Xander. He looks vacant. Xander knows Sam is already in too deep; he is lost.

Xander stops pacing and stands in front of Sam. "I'm done! I'm not going to be a part of this, Sam!"

Sam throws his glass against the wall. Sam is so close to Xander, he can feel his breath on him.

"Did you not hear me? This is part of your purpose, Alexander. The collision is inevitable. You will have a direct hand in this one way or another. We will be protected, given safe haven, power, and resources. You are a Sondian by lineage, Alexander. It is what your parents wanted for themselves. And it is what they wanted for you! If you are not a part of our purpose, then you are a liability, and I will not be able to keep you safe."

Xander walks to the window. A loud thundering knock on the door interrupts them.

Xander answers, "Yeah, Come in."

It is Michael and Cecil, the front doormen.

Cecil says, "Mr. Crest, your guests have arrived. Corrina Cain and her friend. I'm sorry, but the friend did not disclose her name."

Sam speaks over Xander. "Thank you both. We will be right behind you. Please escort them to the lounge and set them up with some drinks."

Sam holds his smile until Michael and Cecil leave the office.

Xander walks over to Sam. He grits his teeth. "I'm not going to put Corinna and her friend through this!" Xander puts his drink down on the desk and starts toward the door.

Sam grabs Xander by his shirt and turns him around to face him. He pushes Xander against the wall. "No, you aren't, Xander. But you are going to introduce me to the girl that has given you a conscience."

Xander glares back at Sam, not backing down. He is beyond that now with Sam.

Sam sees this and softens his hold. His expression instantly changes to that of a soft smile. He begins to smooth out Xander's shirt. "She must be a pretty amazing woman if she moved your emotions like this, my boy."

Xander's stoic face does not change. "Actually, Corinna wasn't the cause. Do you remember my trip to Georgia? For the investor?"

Sam walks to put his sports coat back on, still listening. "Yeah. The research on the professor there. Ezra Kahn."

Xander nods. "Was he the only reason, though?"

Sam pauses and looks up at Xander.

Xander senses the tension brewing in Sam.

"I mean, I don't believe in coincidences, and a week ago I met a girl from the same town in Georgia I was sent to. She attended the same university as the one Kahn taught at. And to top it off, I think I might have seen her before last week, bumped into her on campus. I wasn't sure, though. So I did some digging in the university's records. And wouldn't you know it. She was coincidentally specializing in Ezra Kahn's department."

Xander smiles and looks down. "I couldn't get her out of my mind from the moment I met her at the bookstore. Jesca Gershon-Sera is here in Florida."

Sam's skin slowly loses its color from his shock at the familiar name. He puts his phone in his coat pocket and crosses his arms. "Jesca is another important component. She is a Dobrian guardian. And I can only guess that she is here

286

because she was sent here to eliminate any Sondians in her way."

Sam steps toward Xander one final time. "Be sure of this, Xander. She is not an ally. Be cautious, and keep your distance."

Xander looks down and turns to retrieve his phone from the desk. Who is Sam to dictate who is an ally or enemy? Xander isn't sure where Sam stands in his mind right now.

Sam doesn't budge and continues to watch Xander's expression. Sam's eyes widen all of a sudden. "Don't tell me you're falling for her? Don't go weak on me now, kid! We have too much at stake."

Xander stiffens as he takes in everything he has learned: the collision, his purpose, Jesca's purpose, and Sam's intentions. He needs time to absorb it all and work it out in his head. In order to do that, he needs to fake his loyalty to Sam, find Corinna and her friend, and get them out of here. Xander puts his phone in his coat pocket and inhales a huge breath.

Sam smiles coyly and puts his arm around Xander's shoulders to lead him to the door. Xander lets him. They are going to walk out there and meet Corinna and her friend; that is inevitable. But he isn't going to let anything happen to either of them.

"C'mon, Xander, introduce me to Corinna Cain and her mystery friend. And don't even think about making a scene, my boy. You are being watched. And those watching you are being watched. Remember, always watching." Sam's hand tightens on Xander's shoulder as he moves him toward the door. Xander resists just for a moment to show Sam that he would not give in to his bullying. Enough resistance for Sam to release him and let him move on his own accord.

Chapter 43

Xander

I lead the way out of the office, with Sam close behind, watching my every move. I can feel the weight of Sam's eyes and the proximity of his body close behind him. My eyes scan the dancing bodies from one side of the room to the other. I pause at each sentinel-like figure strategically positioned throughout the club; Sam did this.

They are watching us.

The vibration of the music increases as the music changes, becoming louder and more technotronic. With Sam right behind me, pushing me along, we start up the staircase to the VIP lounge. It overlooks the dance floor and the DJ. The club is packed; too many people at risk if things get rough. The lounge has multiple clusters of bodies toasting, celebrating, and mingling above the melodic chaos below.

Sam greets a few of the groups and welcomes them to the club. I ignore their pleasantries, focusing on finding Corinna and her friend. I see the flash of red hair and latch on to the girl; it's her. And to her side, an unforgettable presence. *Jesca.*

I'm frozen, immobile. I am in awe and devastated all at once. She is the friend that Corinna brought. I'm not sure I can follow through with this now that she is here. I can't let anything happen to her. *I won't. She is too important.*

Sam steps ahead of me now that his targets have been revealed. He looks back at me and grins. "You didn't know they were friends? Ah, c'mon. Even I did enough research to know that my boy."

My blood boils with this revelation. *Sam knew Jesca was the friend coming here.*

What is Sam going to do to her? My body goes rigid at the thought of him near Jesca.

Sam watches my reaction. My mind works through what Sam has planned for Corinna and Jesca. The urge to strangle him right now is strong, but I clench my fists to hold my anger at bay until the right moment. Sam's smile fades. His volume increases as the music starts to thump louder. "You got it now, Xander? Thanks, son. You made this so much easier. The capture of two Dobrians and a key component, Jesca. But you've known in your heart that she has been the key all along, haven't you? Balthazar will be ecstatic!"

I feel pure betrayal by the man I have grown to call father. And Jesca, what is she the key for?

Sam turns and heads toward Corinna and Jesca. I lunge toward him, grab his forearm and turn him to face me. Cecil puts his heavy hand on my shoulder and squeezes, warning me to not take this any further. "Sir, don't do anything to jeopardize all of these people." Cecil nods toward the sentinels below us, their eyes fixed on the scene we are creating. Their hands are discretely resting on their waists, suit coats pushed back.

On the trigger.

I grit through my teeth. "I won't."

290

I pull away from Cecil roughly and continue behind Sam, contriving his next move. *Plans have changed.*

Sam reaches the ladies. "Corinna Cain? I'm Mr. Crest, the owner of this club and Xander's father."

Both Corinna and Jesca turn toward the entourage behind them.

Jesca's eyes immediately lock on mine. I see the shock radiating from her now.

***

Jesca

I am frozen stiff. *Xander? What is he...?*

My brain slowly begins to work again. Crest. Samson Crest. Sam, from the text on Xander's phone. He is on Sam's side!

My heavy stare on Xander breaks to Sam. "Are you Samson Crest?"

Sam moves toward Jesca and takes her hand in his.

I notice Xander tense up as soon as Sam touches me. His touch, it is cold and dry. I want to pull back, but I know it would ruin my chances of finding out more. I need more information before I react and try and take out Sam. *And Xander.*

Sam smiles widely. "Well, I haven't been called Samson in ages. Yes, I am, dear. And your name is?"

I'm slow to answer, needing to digest the shockwave of having this sadistic man standing in front of me and a man I was falling for being his side kick.

I need backup, damn it! How am I going to let Ezra know? I can't break away right now! Damn it!

Corinna picks up on my silence and answers for me. "This is Jesca Gershon-Sera."

Play along! Don't give yourself away. I need to let Ezra know, but I can't open my mind to communicate with him right now. Sam might get in, then all of this will explode, and I will lose him and Xander.

Corinna leans across Sam to hug Xander. "Hi there, Xander. Where is Christian? He is such a nice guy."

As Corinna hugs Xander, his eyes shift to look at me, my reaction. *Son of a....what the hell is that. Did he try and woo her too?*

Pissed as all hell, I glare back at Sam.

Out of the corner of my eye, Xander releases Corinna, moves passed her and toward me extending his hand. "Hi. I'm Alexander Crest. Xander."

I look at his hand, and then glare up at him. The jerk gave me the identical introduction from when we first met. I wanted to kick him in the... ugh. Two can play this game, and I am game right now. I jut my hand out to him and push the words through my clenched teeth. "Hi. I'm Jesca Gershon-Sera. Jes."

I want to not feel anything when our hands meet, but it is impossible. The touch is not sinister, but benevolent rather.

292

***

Xander

The conversation I had moments ago with Sam comes flooding into my mind.

She is a Dobrian guardian. She is here because she was sent here as a spy. She is a Dobrian. She is not an ally.

I have to touch her, remember what I felt the last time I was with her. I have to know that she is not the one I should be fearful of or fighting against. When our hands touch again, I feel vulnerable in her eyes all of a sudden. *What is she looking for? Does she think I'm the enemy? Does she think I'm involved in Sam's plan?*

I feel Sam studying my reaction to her. "Well, isn't this a pleasant surprise. When Xander said that Corinna was here with a friend, I didn't know it was going to be a beautiful force like yourself, Jesca."

Sam's words are the knife that breaks Jesca's and my hands apart. Without our eyes parting, we both blink as if we were woken from a trance. When Jesca breaks our gaze and shifts it to Sam, she looks like she is going to claw out his eyes. I can't look away from her though.

Sam continues talking. "Just look at you two girls, beautiful and so intelligent. We are honored to have you at our club this evening."

Corinna giggles with excitement at his compliment. Jesca's smile is reserved as she looks from Sam back to me briefly. She wants answers. Answers that I want to give her.

***

Jesca

My eyes lock back on Xander. *He is a Sondian! Son of a...*

A Sondian approaching me at Ms. Olivia's store in broad daylight. Then taking me for coffee? Why didn't he just kill me then? I should kill him right now!

I suck in a huge breath, knowing that my anger is spiraling out of control right now. *Calm down Jes. Don't lose it!*

Sam interrupts my spiraling. "Hey, Corinna, will you join me downstairs. I'm famished and would love for you to do the honor of picking out some appetizers for us for to partake in. Our chef is extraordinary."

Corinna is mesmerized and hangs on Sam's every word. "Of course, Mr. Crest."

The show makes me sick.

Corinna looks at me for confirmation that it is fine if she leaves for a while. Corinna is evidently smitten with Sam's good looks and charm. Something that he obviously has used to his advantage during the abductions. I close my eyes, feeling the bile rise in my throat. *Settle down Jes.* This may be my only chance to take down someone in the Sondian fellowship that is single-handedly pushing along the collision of our galaxy and Andromeda. Taking him down might stop the advancement of the collision.

Corinna comes close to me and whispers, "Jes?"

I tighten my fists, open my eyes and look at Corinna for a moment, contemplating letting my friend go with the enemy in order to trap him.

She is not bait, Jes.

I shake my head and clear my throat. "I love seafood. Pick something interesting, okay?" And there you have it, I let her go. I just threw Corinna out there like bait.

She'll be fine. This will be over in minutes. As soon as I kick Xander's ass and all of these other Sondians, I will kill Sam.

Corinna hugs me quickly and dashes away with Sam on her arm. I watch her walk away briefly, and then return my heavy stare to Xander.

***

Xander

She is going to kick my ass, try and take out all of these guys, then go after Sam.

Sam leans over to me as Corinna and Jesca make their exchange. "I promise I'll have her back in a flash, Xander."

My body instinctively stiffens at the sound of his voice.

Sam wraps his arm around Corinna's waist and holds her other hand to escort her down the stairs. Xander's and Jesca's eyes follow Sam and Corinna until they are out of sight. Jesca doesn't waste any time as she lunges at me. I sense her attack before Cecil and the others notice anything wrong. I cover her attack by grabbing both of her arms and holding her to me. Having her this close to me makes me want more and I lean in, burying my mouth close to her ear, grazing it with my lips.

295

I try to keep my voice low. "Don't do anything! They are watching. They will kill her and all of these people if you make a move!"

Jesca tries to shift out of his grasp as she hisses. "You bastard! You are a Sondian!"

I grab her tighter and walk her backward slowly; she resists every step of the way. I finally back her against a marble column. "I didn't know Corinna and you were friends."

Jesca spits out, "Funny, I didn't know you were friends with Corinna."

I hear the jealousy in her tone. I shake my head. "This is not the time to be jealous."

Jesca's cheeks start to feel hot against mine now. She scoffs, "Why the hell would I be jealous?"

"This invitation was Sam's doing. I was just the messenger."

I am not involved in this, Jes. I didn't know about any of it until twenty minutes ago.

Jesca goes rigid and sucks in an audible, ragged breath. "What did you just say?"

Did...did she just hear my thoughts?

Jesca tries to pull back and being a little taken aback I let her.

***

Jesca

I feel a shiver run through my body. I just heard his thoughts! How is that possible!

"Why did you invite Corinna? Why her?"

Xander's body stiffens at the question. He pulls back and looks into Jesca's eyes. "I met Corinna after leaving you at the gate of the Cloisters a few days ago." He pauses and lowers his voice. "She's a good girl, Jes. I didn't know this is what was happening. Please believe me. If I knew what Sam was doing…"

The familiar humming vibration instantaneously spikes in my head. I lean back against the column as Xander moves closer to me. I grab onto Xander's shirt quickly try to hold onto something solid as everything starts to spin.

Xander brushes my fallen hair away from my face and holds my chin with a gentle hand. "Jesca. Are you all right?"

The spinning slows and I open my eyes and look into his hazel orbs. I can't deny the safety they give me. The safety is brief though.

Corinna.

I turn to look below us at the sea of dancers. I scan the floor and see a flash of red hair by the main entrance. Corinna looks worried, anxiously looking around her. I swear I can hear her quickened breath and racing heart from here. Sam is by her side and is no longer smiling.

He's taking her!

"Where are they going?"

Xander pulls me along with him toward the stairs. "Damn it!"

Xander has his arm around my waist and is pulling me along until I feel myself again and regain my footing. Together, we skip every other step down the stairs and reach the front door in a blink.

Xander looks at me in disbelief of our speed together.

I hear him think. *How did we do that?*

He has the ability of speed and he can hear my thoughts.

Xander turns and refocuses on Sam and Corinna as they get into Sam's Porsche and drive away. Cecil and Michael are closing in behind us. Xander pulls me out into the night and into his car. Before my door is shut, he starts the car and guns it. Xander yells, "Son of a…"

"Xander! Where is he taking her?"

Xander's jaw works. "He is taking her to Club Meridian. We need to catch them before he…before it is too late."

"He is going to hurt her."

Xander answers huskily, "Yes, he is. Damn it!"

My chest burns with worry and adrenaline.

Xander shifts gears and weaves through traffic. "Sam and I work for this investor. He has been using me to invite people to the club. Sam has been having me introduce them to him, and then he takes it from there."

I can sense his feelings; disgust, pain, sorrow, hate.

Xander hits the steering wheel with his hand and my eyes snap back to his pained face. "He is sending them through a portal. They travel to another world, Sonde. They are implanted with a Copula. It's like a transmitter. Balthazar is building an army with them! They are being used like slaves, Jes."

Xander looks straight ahead as he continues to weave in and out of traffic. His eyes are tearing up. Not from sadness, but from rage. He blinks once, and the tears fall. "God, I'm so sorry. I had no idea he was doing any of this."

He swerves in and out of more traffic, faster and faster. "He used me for all of this! God, I am so sorry!"

I have to touch him, let him know I believe him. I place my hand on his shoulder and squeeze. "I believe you, Xander."

The humming vibrations subsided and I am able to think more clearly now.

I want to be honest with him, too.

"I'm a Dobrian."

I look at him to see his reaction.

His eyes are a bright, iridescent green from the tears. He answers softly, "Yes. I know."

The remaining time in the car is silent except for the moist wind coming off of the ocean.

The silence is ended as Xander hits the steering wheel again with his palm. "Damn it!"

I can't sense if he is cursing the situation or the fact that a very thick line of opposition

has been drawn between him and I.

Chapter 44

Xander pulls into a side parking lot next to Club Meridian. Sam's car is already parked in front. Xander and I walk quickly toward the door, both determined and worried about what we will find. As we cross the street and are a few feet from the door, we are blocked by two bodies.

Nate and Ezra.

Nate reaches for me and grabs me by the wrist firmly but gently. Ezra stops Xander with his palm planted on his chest. Xander looks at him, not with hostility, but inquisitively. Xander knows him somehow.

I feel my body go numb. I can feel my jaw hanging open and quickly shut it, as I stare at Nate in shock.

I snap. "What are you two doing here?" I look from Ezra to the crowd in line a foot away from us. I don't want to draw any attention.

Xander looks from them to me. "Of course, Kahn and his sidekick?"

Nate's head snaps from me to Xander.

I quickly step between them toward Ezra and speak quickly. "Sam Crest has Corinna. He is going to teleport her to Balthazar if we don't stop him. We can't lose another to him, Ezra."

My voice cracks a little. "Especially her, Ezra."

Ezra thinks quickly. *We aren't prepared, Jes.*

I hear his thought and move past them. I push through the line and the doormen with intensity. The doormen don't put up much of a fight. It appears to be more like a welcoming to me.

Ushering in all its glory.

Xander, Ezra, and Nate are close behind me. They scan the crowd for anyone that might prevent our progress. I know exactly where they are.

The back room off the hallway.

Ahead, two black suits block my path toward the hallway. I charge the two, striking one dead center in the nose. He stumbles back against the wall. Nate is on him within a millisecond. I turn to the other suit grabbing me by the back of the neck. I grab onto his arm with both of my hands and swing my left leg up and around. My foot strikes his head with such force he hits the wall and is immediately unconscious.

Nate releases a thought. *Show off.*

On that thought, my head whips around to Nate. "I don't need a damn babysitter, Nate!"

Nate just glares back. I turn on my heels, heading down the long hall to the last corridor. Nate waits up for Ezra and Xander, who are carrying up the flank.

* * *

Xander

When all appears clear from behind us, I start on a dead run down the hallway, passing everyone, including Jes. Woah,

301

how did I do that? I feel the hairs on my arms stand on end suddenly. *What is going on with me?*

Jesca pulls on my shoulder, stopping me from advancing. All of them, Ezra, Nate, and her are looking at me strangely.

I hear Jesca's voice in my head. *"I heard him. Did you?"*

She looks to Ezra. He nods then looks to Nate. *"Did you?"*

Nate nods and glares at me. *"Yeah, I heard him."*

I pinch my eyes closed and whisper urgently, "How the hell can I hear you guys in my head?"

A struggle coming from the other side of the door brings us out of our internal thoughts.

Corinna whimpers, "Help!" Her voice is so slurred and weak.

I don't waste time. I start pounding the weight of my body against the door. It only takes three lunges to unhinge the door from the frame. As I break through, three more of Sam's bodyguards appear on the other side, ready to attack.

Nate grabs one and throws him like a rag doll against a mirror within the office.

Ezra has two ganging up on him. He sends one into a wall head first. Ezra simply snaps the other one's neck with a quick twist of his hands.

Jesca combats the fourth with quick precision, taking him down hard and fast. All of this achieved in a matter of seconds.

***

Jesca

Silence. The only sound in the room is curtains flapping in the wind. We all scan the room quickly to see multiple windows open, sending curtains high up toward the ceiling. No sign of Sam or Corinna. There is a leather sofa, disheveled desk, toppled over lamp, nightstand, rumpled sheet on a cot with restraints, an empty vile and syringe. I move closer.

Ezra's thoughts are apparent to everyone in the room. *He knew we would come here. He sedated her. He has taken her somewhere else.*

The shift of a door in the corner of the room sets us on guard again. Ezra's and Nate's eyes immediately dart to the far back corner of the expansive room.

The familiar growl of a sports car's engine sets me running past them all and down the stairs.

Corinna.

Nate, Xander, and Ezra are right behind me. All we can do is watch the car speed off.

My heart sinks. I mouth an inaudible whisper, "No."

I run back into the office. The cot shows signs of a struggle. I can feel my eyes fill up with hot tears. "I shouldn't have let her go with him!"

I see her bracelet on the bed. I sink to my knees and raise my hand to pick up the delicate keepsake. The tears are clouding my vision. Frustrated, I roughly wipe my eyes with the back of my free hand. I put the bracelet in the front pocket of my jacket.

Xander kneels next to me and puts his hand on my shoulder. The moment his hand touches me, I flip him over and pin him to the ground. Nate instantly tries to pull me off of him, but I shove him back and lock my eyes on Xander, needing to take out my pain on someone. Xander whispers raggedly. "I won't fight you Jes. It is my fault. I'm sorry Jes."

I feel the hot tears flowing freely from my eyes and pooling under my chin.

Ezra grabs a hold of my shoulders now. "Jesca, stop! He is just a pawn. This is all Sam's doing. Balthazar's doing. He didn't know."

I want to do something, throw him across the room. Instead, I release him hard against the ground, his head making a thudding sound as it hit. I jump up and turn on Ezra, still needing to release the pain and guilt I am feeling.

"Sam Crest! We could have saved all of those people, Ezra! Protected them!"

Xander sits up, rubbing the back of his head. "I know where he's going."

Nate yells at him. "Where?"

Xander slowly rises and staggers to the back door, ignoring Nate's question. He quickly rights himself and starts running down the back stairs. Nate starts to run after him, but Ezra heads him off at the top of the stairs, stopping him from taking chase. "No, Nate, let him learn the truth."

Nate looks at Ezra urgently. "We need to follow him! We need to try and save Corinna!"

Ezra grips his shoulders hard. "She is gone, Nate! Let Xander learn who he is and who he will need to become!"

Chapter 45

Xander's car speeds through the streets on the hilltop lined with estate homes. He knows Sam would head to the house. Sam's car is in the circular. Xander pulls next to it and runs to the front door.

The house is silent. Xander feels Sam's presence. His skin is crawling, and he gets a chill.

The basement.

As soon as Xander gets to the bottom of the stairs and is about to burst through the door, Sam opens it. "Hey there, Xan."

He sounds so calm, normal.

Xander rages and pins Sam to the wall. "What did you do, Sam?"

Sam pushes Xander off of him and against the wall behind him, pinning him there. "Don't."

They are both breathing fast.

Xander struggles to remove Sam's hand with no success.

Sam turns his head to reveal a huge gash. "This one put up a fight. Redheads!" Sam snickers and clicks his tongue. "So feisty."

Xander's anger is uncontainable now. He pushes Sam against the opposite wall and punches him.

Sam smiles and yells, "Yes! That's the spirit, my boy! We will make a fighter out of you yet!"

Xander releases him and starts up the stairs.

Sam sighs. "Where are you going? To her? Jesca Gershon-Sera. The Dobrian?"

Xander keeps walking.

Sam pushes off of the wall and follows after him. "I saved you, Xander. You are my son. Where are you going to go, huh?"

Xander is at the top of the basement stairs when he turns to face Sam. "I need to think."

Sam stands with both hands on either side of the staircase railing. He calmly smiles. "Of course. Cool off. Think. Then come home. Being a misfit in the world without a guide is like being blind without a walking stick. We can work through this together."

Those words would have made Xander sick to his stomach if he had not become numb to everything Sam stood for now. Xander knows it is easier to just nod in agreement, even though he has no intention of returning.

Systematically, Xander walks up the stairs, enters his room, packs, and is out the front door and pulling away in a half hour.

Chapter 46

Balthazar looks at Sam, who is sitting in the chair opposite him in front of the fireplace.

"Alexander is catching on quickly. It is time to entrust him with his abilities."

Sam feels like he is being stabbed in the gut. "I did everything you said. I can't read him, but I know he still thinks that his parents were Sondian guardians murdered by the Dobrians. I can keep him focused on our purpose."

Since he first met Alexander, he could never get past his mental block. Sam couldn't understand how he could maintain this block without knowing about his abilities. It made him feel inferior in comparison to Alexander's strength.

"Sam, I still need your help."

Inside, relief washes over Sam. "Thank you, Balthazar." His grin quickly turns to a thin line. "Jesca Gershon. I'm sorry, I didn't—"

Balthazar interrupts him. "The attempts to retrieve her in Georgia were also unsuccessful. The woods. By the diner." His words are not angry. Just a reminder of Sam's failures.

Balthazar reassures Sam. "Xander would have been lost to us if you had taken them both at the club tonight. You did award us with another Dobrian, though."

Sam releases a small smile. "Corinna."

Corinna Cain. Part of a long Dobrian line. It is no wonder why she and Jesca sought each other out so quickly upon Kahn's and her arrival."

Sam thinks for a moment. "What about Kahn?"

"Leave him. His demise after the collision will only make your revenge sweeter, Sam."

Sam nods in agreement, but bites his lip, wishing he could have taken immediate vengeance.

"You are receiving a new child to groom, Sam."

Sam's visions of vengeance turn to confusion. "What about Alexander?"

Balthazar answers after a pause. "He needs his space. He told you that himself. I will keep an eye on him and intervene if necessary. I need you to groom Corrina Cain when she returns to Earth. She will be yours. She will have no recollection of her life, lineage, or family. Only that you saved her from the abductors that have been plaguing the night clubs. The suspects have been caught. An hour ago to be exact. The press was alerted that the two thugs with a laundry list of offenses and warrants are in custody. These suspects were caught with a slew of pharmaceuticals that would render a victim helpless. Then they subdued the victims long enough to empty their bank accounts and steal other valuable possessions."

Sam runs his hand through his hair and grins at Balthazar's quick work.

Balthazar's smile now turns serious. "Someone is always watching, Sam."

Sam blinks his eyes, and he is awake in his suite. Sam lies there taking in Balthazar's last words.

Someone is always watching.

Chapter 47

Jesca lets the shower run down her sore arms. She hangs her head under the stream. Her hands start moving over her body, searching for damage. Her hand finds a tender spot on her right side above her hip bone. She opens her eyes to take a look. The gash is about six inches long. The lower part of the wound is open, like a butterfly'd fillet. It is oozing blood and clots are being washed from it under the warm stream of water. She continues the inspection. Bruises on her left elbow, remnants of the blow to the first body guard at the club.

Thoughts of Corinna come flooding back into her mind. A lump develops in her throat. She tries to swallow it back. Jesca shuts off the faucet and gets out of the shower, grunting and wincing at every movement.

She doctors the wound as best she can with the gauze she finds in the medicine cabinet. She doesn't want to bother Ezra or Nate with it. They have not spoken since Xander took off after Sam.

* * *

Nate sat next to her on the drive back to the house. Jesca's eyes were closed, but she could feel his eyes watching her closely.

She overheard Nate and Ezra planning ahead. "Get her in the house. Watch her closely. She is in shock."

Nate said, "Yeah, I will. Where are you going?"

Ezra replied, "I need to get in touch with Sebastian and tell him about the Cain girl. Her family needs to know what has happened."

* * *

Jesca turns off the bathroom light and opens the door to her bedroom across the hall. She is able to slip on her undergarments and a long, button down night shirt. The nausea from that small amount of exerted energy is instant, and she needs to lie down. She starts to cross the room to her bed, when Nate knocks on the door and comes into the room carrying a tray. She is taken aback by Nate and shifts into a defensive position. She winces at the pain that surges to the wound at her side. Jesca reaches for her hip and sucks in her breath.

Nate sees her reaction and quickly sits the tray down on the dresser and walks over to Jesca cautiously. She is leaning against the bedpost now, breathing quickly.

Nate stands near her. "You're hurt."

Jesca snaps, "I've already bandaged it."

Nate ruffles his wavy brown hair and blows out a breath. "It's not nothing, Jes. I can…"

Jesca grimaces. "Yeah, I know. We are still linked, aren't we? The moment I saw you I knew it wasn't broken."

Jes, let me heal you. Nate looks at her, desperate for her permission.

Jesca feels his eyes on her heavy now. She winces again feeling defeated. "Fine."

Nate helps her around to the side of the bed.

Jesca sits slowly with Nate's help. She feels pain and immediately reaches her arms around Nate's neck for support. "Ouch, Ouch!"

"It's all right, Jes, I've got you."

Jesca lets her body go limp in his arms. Nate lowers her the rest of the way onto the bed. Jesca is breathing deeply, trying to control the pain with every breath. Nate sits on the bed and starts to reach for her. Jesca's eyes snap open.

Don't, Nate.

His eyes don't leave hers. "Jes. I'm trying to help."

Nate reaches for her night shirt cautiously. Nate lifts her shirt far enough to see the wound on her hip.

Jesca feels her cheeks flush. Anticipation both of the pain and of Nate's touch. Nate touches her skin, and she shivers. Jesca winces.

Nate whispers, "Sorry."

Jesca nods, letting him know she is fine.

He peels back the gauze bandage and pulls the shirt back away from her skin a little more to reveal the extent of the wound.

"Damn it, Jesca! This is not a small wound!"

She immediately feels what he is going to say next. "I was being careful. I was totally expecting the bodyguards. I was not expecting you and Ezra. Especially you!"

Nate looks at her briefly, then back at the wound. "Ezra called me in. Sebastian's orders. Things are heating up with the collision timetable apparently. Look, Jes, I get that you think you can do it all. Just remember what the mentors told us in the facility."

Jesca knows in her heart that he is right. Beyond her super-sized pride, she was glad to have backup. Jesca repeats what they learned at the facility. "We are stronger together than we are on our own."

There is no denying that both Nate's and Jesca's abilities are heightened when they work together.

Nate slowly shifts to kneel in front of Jesca. He puts his left hand on her elbow, swollen and bruised, and his right hand on her wounded side. His eyes look up into hers. "Put your hands on mine."

Jesca takes in a deep breath.

Nate winks at her. "Don't' look at me that way. I promise I won't try anything."

Jesca smiles sarcastically and closes her eyes.

"Not unless you want me to, that is."

Jesca eyes shoot open, and she tries to push his hands away. She winces from the brief strain. "Ugh!"

Nate smiles and puts his hands back in place. "Sorry. Sorry."

Jesca continues to glare at him. This time she puts her hands on his just to make sure they stay where they are supposed to. Jesca's eyes move back to his. His eyes are so comforting, like home.

Okay, Nate. I'm ready.

They both close their eyes.

Nate inhales a long breath. Then exhales. Jesca feels a surge of warmth course through her body. It is a steady flow. Jesca's breath quickens. Soothing warmth centers in her core, her arms, her side, her legs. It radiates so quickly, she starts to feel light-headed. Jesca leans forward into Nate. He leans into her. Nate slips his arms around her waist, his hands on her skin, in an embrace. She can feel his breath on her neck now. Jesca begins to feel the energy melt away until everything is still.

Jesca and Nate don't move. Not wanting to break this spell.

Nate speaks into Jesca's ear. "I asked to come here."

Jesca shifts to pull back and look at him.

"Since the facility, I have felt numb, Jesca. California is stable and has very little need for intelligence right now. I don't think you need to be babysat." Nate unexpectedly leans in and kisses Jesca's cheek. His lips linger. He whispers, "Especially by Alexander Crest."

Jesca pushes Nate back enough to look at him again. "Really! That was not necessary!" Jesca looks down. "I don't think Xander knew what was going on. I don't think he knew anything until tonight. Sam kept everything from him. And back at the club, when we felt and heard Xander's thoughts at the door. You felt and heard him too!"

Jesca's eyes start to well up at the thought of rehashing Corinna's abduction. "He was as surprised as we were. I mean, he has abilities that Sam obviously has not told him about."

Nate looks down briefly. Thinking through the logic. He doesn't want to admit it. "I think you're right. Just...be careful. He has had loyalty to Sam for so long and that is hard to break. And I'm sure he is confused about where he belongs."

Jesca looks into Nate's eyes. "I won't. I will be careful."

Nate sighs and starts to stand. "After healing those nasty wounds, that line doesn't hold much water with me, Jes."

Jes grabs his hands and pulls him back to eye level. "I mean it. I just feel that Xander has not been told so much. The way things truly are. I just hope he finds the truth soon."

Nate touches her chin softly. It surprises Jesca.

Nate's voice is soft. "That! That is what I missed. Your strength, faith, and hope."

Jesca laughs a little. "Strength? Yeah, I really showed that today."

Jesca's smile is too brief as she remembers Corinna, and the knot forms in her throat again. Jesca tries to hide her expression, trying to maneuver around Nate.

Nate puts his hands on her hips to stop her from rising. He moves closer to her again. "Don't do that! You have amazing strength. What happened to Corinna, you were caught off guard, it wasn't your fault. Too many other factors were working against you."

Jesca turns her head away from Nate to hide the tears. Her voice cracks. "This is too much. I can't...I can't handle all of this." She looks up at the ceiling quickly, trying to hold the tears in.

Nate moves his hand to her face. He brushes her cheek with his thumb. Nate's voice is strong and determined now. "You will, Jes. You can handle this. I will help you. I will be here for you. We can do this. Remember our strength together, back at the facility?"

Jesca nods quickly as she sucks in her breath. "Yes. I remember."

She is breathless all of a sudden. Jesca remembers their time in the facility.

The kiss.

The thought slips out before she can block it.

Nate's determined face softens. For a moment, he studies her. His hand still on her tear-streaked face. Nate leans closer, then pauses. First, to see her reaction, and second, to think about what he is starting again.

I can't be without you, Jes.

Jesca's hands go to Nate's chest. Nate pulls her body into him. His lips touch hers softly at first. The kiss instantly deepens and becomes intense. Jesca feels Nate's heart pounding under her hands as she grips his shirt and pulls him onto the bed with her.

I need you, Nate.

Nate pulls back for a moment and looks into her eyes. Jesca puts her hand around Nate's neck and pulls him to her. Her mouth crashes into his. Nate's hand runs along her face and down her neck. The kiss is deep and reckless.

A knock at the door catches them off guard.

Ezra calls from the other side of the door. "Hey, Jes, did Nate bring you food?"

The spell is broken. Nate rolls onto his elbow and climbs off the bed. He quietly moves toward the door. Jesca quickly sits up and shifts her nightshirt back into place. He looks at Jesca for a moment and sighs. He turns and opens the door.

Ezra looks up at Nate, then over at Jesca.

Nate clears his throat. "Yes. I brought her food. And I healed her."

Nate looks down and puts his hand to his lips. He looks at Jes and speaks in a low voice. "I will check on you later."

Jesca nods. She doesn't speak. She is speechless. Her heart is still pounding out of her chest.

Nate turns to leave. Ezra shifts one way and Nate the other as he tries to get out the door. "Sorry."

Ezra enters the room and closes the door softly behind him. "So. You and Nate okay?"

Jesca's cheeks flush. "Uh, yes. Much better."

"Well, I'm glad. You know you may not realize how great of a partner Nate will be for you. You and he share so much strength. You two together, it is…"

Jesca cuts him short. "I know. I mean, I know we are stronger together."

She clams up again. She is still resentful about Ezra not telling her about Sam being the key to the operation earlier. She knows now that it won't make her any stronger fighting with Ezra.

"I'm sorry I didn't give you all the facts, Jes. I was trying to protect you, and I wound up leaving you more vulnerable."

Jesca looks at him. "Please. Don't keep me in the dark anymore. I'm a big girl. I can handle it."

Ezra puffs out his upper lip and runs his hand through his hair. He takes off his reading glasses and places them on his head in one motion. Jesca knows he is holding something back.

"You're right. You aren't a child anymore." Ezra walks over to the bed, pulls up a chair from her desk, and sits in front of Jesca. "I have something else to tell you."

"What is it? Hit me with it."

Ezra looks at her wearily. "Everything is part of a grand blueprint. But there are always key players. And I know I have withheld many of those from you. You must know that I was only withholding them to protect you, until the right time."

Jesca has heard this so many times before from Ezra.

What is he going to tell me now?

"Your biological mother, Anna, was a high-ranking Dobrian. Her role was set into motion when she was your age. She was sent on a mission to infiltrate the Sondians by going undercover and learning as much as she could about their plans of the coming intersection. At that time, there was strong belief that we could stop it since the gravitational pull of the Earth had not shifted much."

Ezra looked down. "She had to become involved with a Sondian, Sam Crest. Son of Rein and Victoria Crest. They both were Dobrian captains for years and worked as spies. They were slain by the Sondians they infiltrated when Sam was fourteen. Sam was taken under Balthazar's wings. He groomed Sam in the Sondian fellowship."

319

"Sam's parents were Dobrians? Why didn't Sebastian save him? Why would he let him be captured?"

"He didn't let it happen. Balthazar got to him before Sebastian could." Ezra pinches the bridge of his nose. He looks tired all of a sudden.

Ezra's voice becomes agitated. "Anna. She went undercover. The deeper she went undercover as a Sondian, the more she lost herself. The line between which side was the right one began to blur for her. And she began to fall in love with Sam. Seeing Anna's wavering patriotism to Dobria and the temptation of a charming Sondian, Sebastian sent in a partner. Her life was in such great jeopardy. One slip of Sam or Balthazar discovering she was there to destroy the second generation Copula and Balthazar would have her killed without a second thought.

"A partner went in and worked on getting Anna back. He slowly got Anna to refocus on her mission. In the same breath, Anna and her partner began to fall in love with each other. They began a love affair. Sam was a very territorial and possessive man. When Anna's undercover routine began to change in the slightest, Sam knew something was wrong. One day, he followed her and caught her meeting with her partner, a known Dobrian. He was enraged to catch Anna with another man, let alone a Dobrian. Being a vengeful person, Sam was not going to make this easy for Anna. So Sam waited to approach her."

Jesca feels like she is missing a part, a hole in the story. "There is something you aren't telling me."

320

Ezra raises his voice in irritation. "Well, I'm not finished yet! So there is a lot I'm not telling you if you don't sit there and be quiet!"

Jesca throws her hands up, claiming her impatient attitude. She sits back and waits for Ezra to continue.

* * *

Sam waits for Anna the next day after the weekly debriefing at headquarters. "Anna, can you walk with me for a minute? I have something important to ask you."

Anna is hesitant, but accepts Sam's request. "Yes. Just for a moment. I have some things to do across town."

They are walking on the north lawn of headquarters when Sam stops her by holding her arm. Anna turns toward Sam and looks up at him.

"Anna. Marry me. I have fallen in love with you."

Anna is stunned by his proposal. She has to think quickly to not throw him off. "I don't know that we are ready for that step, Sam. We are so young, and we have not known each other for very long. I'm sorry, but I can't. I'm not ready for that yet."

Sam watches her reaction, and he gets his answer with her response. "Is it because of him? The Dobrian you were with yesterday."

Anna is taken aback by Sam's bluntness and discovery.

Anna turns and starts to walk away. She puts her hand in her purse and turns the safety off on the gun she is carrying. She is hoping her partner will surface since she is meeting him a few blocks away. As she expects, Sam hustles after her and a confrontation ensues. He pulls her purse from her arm and tosses it. He forces her into alley between headquarters and a parking garage.

Sam yells accusingly, "Who the hell are you, Anna? Days ago we were inseparable. Now you're shacking up with a Dobrian. If I didn't know better, I would think you to be a spy." Sam snickers and clicks his tongue against the roof of his mouth, "Tsk, Tsk. Anna the spy."

He has Anna pinned against the wall now, with his hand around her throat, squeezing tighter and tighter.

Anna thinks quickly and kicks him in the groin. She runs beyond the parking garage and through the alley. She gets to the end of the alleyway when she hears screeching tires and a horn honk; it's her partner. The car pulls up, and she gets in. Before she can close the car door, Sam is trying to pull her from the car by her hair. Anna swings her elbow back and catches Sam in the nose, leaving him splayed out on the street with blood running down his face.

Anna and her partner need to hide, go underground. Sebastian has a package waiting for them at a Dobrian safe house nearby. The packet contains everything they need to get out of the country for a while.

Within hours, they are on a flight to Nassau.

Within months, they are married. And a few months after, they have a child.

* * *

Jesca snaps out of the story for a moment. "A child. Me."

Ezra looks at Jesca, calculating how the words to follow will sit with her.

Jesca's mind is working. "My father was the partner. What was my father's name?"

Ezra leans in and sighs. "Ezra Kahn. I'm your father, Jesca."

Chapter 48

Jesca is speechless. She stands and begins to pace. She pulls her hair back into a bun and folds her arms as she stalks back and forth.

Ezra just watches, waiting and letting her take it in.

She says the words in an accusatory manner and points to him. "You are my father."

This is the reaction Ezra anticipated, hostility. He knew she would hold it in until it boiled over. He could feel it.

Sensing Ezra's thoughts, Jesca responds, "No. Not hostile yet!" Jesca continues to pace and think.

Ezra knows she is methodically backtracking the events of her life: in Georgia, the university, at the facility, in Miami. Searching for clues that she might have missed to discover this. Ezra knows that she won't. He was very careful.

Jesca never thought she would react this way. So many times she played it in her head. She anticipated a cold, emotionless conversation with a man of slight resemblance to herself in a neutral environment, most likely a coffee shop. They would be so caught up in the uncomfortable nervousness of their first meeting that the idea of pursuing a deeper relationship was the furthest thing from their minds.

Jesca stops in front of him. "I'm not going to deck you, but I am pissed. Your only salvation is that for the past fifteen minutes I have read every emotion and thought going through your mind and soul. I know that you wanted to tell me so many times over the years as you watched from afar." Jesca's voice begins to crack. "I know that for selfish reasons you could have, but for my safety you didn't."

Ezra's eyes reddened slightly.

Jesca jumps at Ezra with such force, she knocks him back a bit. Ezra immediately responds by returning his daughter's embrace. Jesca steps back from Ezra first. Both look down at their matching soaking wet shoulders. Ezra hands her a tissue from the side table and takes one for himself.

Jesca clears her throat and sits back on the chair. "Okay. What happens next? I mean, Anna and you."

Ezra sits back on the chair and continues, "Anna and I were asked by Sebastian to start preparing a training program. Between the two of us, we had to put together a team of mentors to train future Dobrian guardians. Around this time, Sebastian was commissioning an architect to draft the design of a new facility that would be used for the training sessions. Within weeks, a contract crew was hired to begin construction on the facility.

"Three years later, we completed the set-up of the training program and were instructed by Sebastian to return to the United States, Colorado Springs. Before leaving Nassau, Sebastian told Anna and I that you, now three years old, had signs of multiple abilities and that we had an enormous responsibility to nurture and grow them with you. When we got to Colorado, everything was set up for us. We had a home, a car. We walked into the house, and it was fully furnished, baby toys and all.

"We had a community of friends immediately. All of the mentors that we knew as family had relocated to the area as well. It was like a huge reunion."

Ezra looks off with a smile at the memory of it all.

"Anna had been so busy with training the mentors, monitoring the facility, and making sure you were watched over in the midst of it all. We had to maintain the cover of being an average, working-class family, so I settled into a job. I took on a job as a professor at a local community college. Astronomy. One Saturday I wanted to give your mother a break, so I offered to take care of the grocery shopping while you napped and your mother relaxed.

"I was halfway down the canned soup isle when I felt a surge of dizziness. I grabbed the handle of the cart with both hands. I had never felt such vertigo before. I heard a scream, then a cry. It was you. It sounded like you were right there in the aisle of the grocery store. But I knew you weren't. You were trying to reach me. Even at the age of three you were using telepathy and trying to astral project to safety. I left my cart and ran out of the store and to the car. I called Lucius and Mary Sera, Nate's parents. I told them to get over to the house. That something was wrong.

"By the time I got home, Mary was outside waiting for me to pull up. Lucius was standing at the doorway, blocking my entry into the house. I pushed past him. It was a wreck. There was a struggle. The lamp next to the sofa where I left Anna had toppled over onto the floor. Anna's slippers were still on the floor next to the edge of the sofa.

"I called for you as I stalked through the house, knowing in my heart that you were not there.

"Lucius pulled at my shirt and said, 'Ezra. It was Sam Crest. He did this. Sebastian has trackers on them. He has them both: Jesca and Anna.' Those words 'Jesca and Anna' were all I heard. Lucius and the other mentors took me in a caravan to track Sam. Sam had been spotted by trackers heading into the foothills toward an old run-down cabin.

"Dusk was coming too quickly. We were headed to a heavily treed area about a mile away from the cabin. We traveled the rest of the way on foot to keep from alerting Sam of our presence. We were about a quarter of a mile away when the vertigo hit me again. You were yelling and crying, 'No. Mommy! Leave her alone!'

"I could feel pain in my arms and legs. I could only think that I was feeling what Sam was doing to Anna through your mind.

"As we stood waiting for the others to get into position, I told Lucius that we needed to move now. He said that we were not to attack yet. It was too soon since we were still trying to cover the back of the cabin. I escaped his grip and ran for the cabin. I ran so hard and fast the others couldn't catch up.

"Seconds from the door, I heard a bloodcurdling scream from Anna. My heart was on fire. I kicked open the front door to the cabin."

Ezra pauses and puts his hand over his mouth for a moment.

"What I saw broke me. She was sprawled across an armchair. Her eyes still alive. Blood streamed from her chest. I went to her, untied her arms and legs, released her from the chair, and embraced her. I looked into her eyes once more. She didn't speak, but thought, *I love you both, Ezra. I love you both. Keep her safe.*

"I said, 'I love you too. Stay with us, Anna.'

"The life slipped from her eyes as they became still. I covered her with an afghan. Lucius and the others entered the cabin. I heard one of the mentors call from the backyard, 'He's on the run!'

"I couldn't leave Anna and you to chase him. Lucius and the others ran through the cabin and out the back door after him.

"I started to search the house for you. I found you in a playpen in a guest room, sitting with your blanket to your small face. You were whimpering. I picked you up and checked every inch of your body for injuries, bruises, anything."

Ezra clears his throat. "Sam was gone. Night set in, and the team couldn't track him any longer.

"You and I stayed with Lucius and Victoria for a few days until we got instructions from Sebastian. This was when you and Nate first met. He was so sweet with you. He was five at the time. The moment we walked through the door that night, Nate held your hand and led you to the guest room where he tucked you into bed. He covered you with blankets and stayed with you all night. He said that he was supposed to protect you. Even then, he was healing you, Jes.

"A couple of days passed, and Sebastian sent word through a vision. He told me that I had to separate from you. You were in danger and needed to be in a safe place away from me. After seeing what happened to your mother and what could have happened to you that night, I wasn't going to fight it. I couldn't put you at risk."

Jesca says, "So that is when I came to Georgia to live with Mom and Dad."

Ezra nods. "Yes, you did. And I was never far away. I did make that a condition. I would live and work nearby. Watch over you from afar. Never to approach you or let you know who I was until it was essential for your safety. I became a professor at the university. The Sera's updated me faithfully over the years through letters and pictures of you. When they told me you were going to attend my university, I knew the time was getting close."

Jesca smiles at the memory. "And then, that one day freshman year. I ran into you, literally. I was looking for my next class, and there you were."

Ezra smiles.

Jesca puts her hand on top of his and squeezes it. Jesca is the first to pull away and stand. Now completely recovered from the healing, Jesca walks quickly to grab her running shoes, shorts, tank top, and iPod. She is heading for the door, hands full, when Ezra stops her.

"Whoa! Where you going?"

Jesca stops and turns to him, hand still on the doorknob. "I've gotta think. I need to breathe after all of that. Work things out."

Ezra raises his voice. "Jes, it's almost midnight. You need to rest after everything that has happened."

Jesca nods in agreement. "I know. I'm just too wired to sleep. I'll be fine. Promise. Well-lit streets, okay?"

Ezra leans back on the bed and huffs. He knows she needs to put everything into balance, so he doesn't push any further.

* * *

She is dressed in a flash and opens the bathroom door, running straight into Nate's chest.

Jesca steps back. "Sorry."

Nate smiles and holds her arms to stop her from moving away. "Wait. Where are you going? It's late."

Nate brushes a stay hair off her face. Jesca looks down the hall nervously to make sure certain eyes didn't catch that.

Ezra.

Nate senses her thought and looks back, then turns to her.

"Um. I'm going for a run."

His voice grows loud. "Now!"

Jesca looks at him and whispers hard, "Yes!"

Nate leans forward and puts both of his hands on either side of her against the wall, blocking any escape. Jesca's heart quickens. "I'm going with you, Jesca."

Jesca senses he is afraid to leave her alone. Jesca puts her hands on his chest. "Nate. I'm all right. I just need to figure things out in my head."

She stretches up on her toes and kisses him softly. She pulls away slowly; her lips linger near his. Nate's hands move from the wall to Jesca's face. He pulls her into him, capturing her lips with his. In this moment of weakness, Jesca slips away from him and walks quickly down the hall. Nate leans his forehead against the wall. Just then, Ezra walks out of Jesca's room and down the hall toward Nate. Nate stands straight up and leans his back against the opposite wall.

Ezra stops to look at Nate. "What are you doing?"

"I'm, uh, taking a shower." He rolls his shoulder off the wall and into the bathroom, shutting the door quickly.

Ezra looks at the door for a moment and mumbles, "Okay. Acting a little strange tonight, Nate."

The shower turns on.

Ezra speaks over the shower. "Goodnight, Nate."

Nate hollers back, "Goodnight."

Ezra heads to the master bedroom. "Weird kid sometimes."

Chapter 49

Ezra's eyes are heavy. He doesn't fight it. His eyes close.

"Ezra, I have told Corinna's parents and sister, Isabel. They did not take it well."

Ezra turns to see Sebastian standing in the bedroom in front of his bed. Ezra sits up and leans against the headboard. "Figured as much. Is it time for Isabel?"

"Yes. Her parents, Felix and Caroline Cain, are against it after what has happened with Corinna. But Isabel is ready, now more than ever."

"All right. Do you want me to put Siobhan on it?"

"Siobhan is the best fit for her."

"I will be in contact with Siobhan first thing in the morning to debrief her on Isabel."

Chapter 50

I turn my iPod up loud enough to drown out the sound of my feet hitting the pavement and my rhythmic breathing. I move in time with the music. I exit the gates of The Cloisters and head north. Shadows fall randomly on the sidewalk. The streetlights dance above the overhanging trees and branches.

This is what I needed. The breeze to carry away the chaos and bring clarity to my thoughts. I can't help but think of Corinna's family. The loss her parents must feel. The emptiness. Her sister, Isabel. It makes me think of my own sister, Bethany.

Will she be called upon to be a guardian someday?

All of a sudden I'm hit with a knee-weakening vibration. Something fast moved behind me.

I can feel him.

I sense something in the shadow ahead a few feet, beyond the lamppost. I stare hard, trying to confirm what my heart already knows.

Xander.

I blink and Xander is in front of me. I shuffle backwards and crouch, ready to strike.

Xander puts his hands up, surrendering. "Wait! Wait, damn it!" His eyes are full of pain, confusion, and rage. "Please just listen, Jesca. Then I will leave. I promise."

I feel the honesty in his voice. I straighten my body and fold my arms across my chest. My eyes are watching his every move.

Xander's sigh is painful sounding. He looks exhausted.

"I am so very sorry about Corrina, Jes. I know you loved her. If I knew what was happening, I would have stopped him. But Sam. Sam betrayed me. I can't trust him any longer. I don't know who to trust right now."

Xander looks at me, then down at the ground. "I don't know what I am! Who I am! I don't understand all of these things happening to my mind and body."

Xander's voice is rough and tired after his ranting. It reminds me of myself months ago.

"Sam says I'm a Sondian. That Dobrians murdered my parents. But I feel it in me, in my mind, in my bones, that Sam is keeping things from me. He used me like a puppet, Jesca. And he made me do things that I am so ashamed of."

Tears are falling now on either side of his face.

I move closer to him slowly. "Xander, I know that you have been used. You need to find out who you really are. You need to learn the truth. Get away from here. From Sam and everything. Find yourself."

Xander reaches for my hands and grabs hold of them. He steps closer and puts his arms around my waist. He pulls me to him. "Come with me, Jes. I don't know if I can do this on my own."

In that moment, I want to go with him. I can feel every ounce of sorrow and pain weighing on his heart. I want to take it away from him.

Xander leans in and kisses my lips so tenderly. I lean into him and put my hands on his shoulders. Xander's hand touches my face as I pull back. His eyes are looking at me with intensity. His thumb brushes over my lips as he holds my chin with his hand.

I whisper breathlessly, "Xander, I see the good in your heart. I want to help heal you. I am tempted to leave here with you right now."

Xander silences my words by brushing his lips against mine again, more passionately now.

I'm tempted to stay here in his arms and let him carry me away with his intensity. I pull back. "But I can't."

I open my eyes to see Xander close his and lower his head.

"I care about you, Xander. But you have to do this on your own. You need to find yourself. You need to find your purpose."

I try to get into his head. But he has blocked me.

I let him in.

I hope your path leads you back to me someday.

Xander acts quickly and pulls me in to him again. His kiss is intoxicating this time. I grab his shoulders and lean into him. His arms are encircling me, molding me to him.

Then, everything material, his touch, his lips, his presence evaporates into the ethereal.

He is gone.

Epilogue

Miami…

I close my eyes. My breathing slows and takes on a hypnotic rhythm. I listen to every measured intake and release of air. Then I feel serenity wash over me.

My throat constricts with panic. I open my eyes, and I'm sitting in a living room on a sofa. A man with graying hair is sitting in an armchair across from me. His legs are crossed. He is well dressed in a suit. He looks like a psychiatrist studying me.

My voice is thick from sleep. "Am I still sleeping?"

The man responds, "Yes, you are. I'm Sebastian. You are having a vision, Jesca."

I remember Ezra telling me back at the facility that as I grew as a guardian, Sebastian would begin to visit me in visions as well. I become concerned about the purpose of the visit. Terrible thoughts start racing through my head.

"Why?"

Is it Ezra? Nate? Are they okay?

Sebastian puts his hand up to stop my noticeable panic. "They are fine. I have come to you because it is time for me to show you."

"Show me what?"

A surge of light flashes and blinds me. I rub my eyes after the flash dulls to try and refocus. But everything is dark.

Then, I see two separate, distinct cosmic waves heading toward each other.

The collision of our galaxy and Andromeda.

As they collide, a pulse of light ripples between the two galaxies and spreads within them, through the worlds contained within them, and radiates out beyond them.

Another flash, I'm standing in a city street. I look up to see an orange haze creeping across the sky and a ripple of light trailing behind it. I focus my eyes on the street again. I see Ezra standing across the street motioning for me. He is saying something, but I can't hear anything. He has a look of panic and fear in his eyes. Someone pulls on my hand. Nate is standing next to me trying to pull me toward Ezra.

I look back to Ezra and see Xander standing in the middle of the crowded street, blocking my view. He is reaching for me to come to him, but I can't move.

I look down to see what is holding me in place: Corinna. She is holding on to my leg. Her face is contorted, sunken, with hollow, black eyes. She begins to convulse. I reach down to help her, but Nate pulls me from her. We start to run down the street away from all of them. Then there is another flash. I'm back in the room with Sebastian, except I am not sitting. I am perched on the arm of the sofa ready to pounce.

I'm breathless. "What the hell was that?"

"A glimpse of what is to come, Jesca." Sebastian gets up to leave the room.

"Wait! What do I do now? What does it mean?"

Sebastian turns to me. "You will know, Jesca. You will sense it in every ounce of your being."

Sebastian opens the door and leaves.

My heart feels like it is pounding out of my chest. The vertigo starts, and I feel like I'm going to throw up. I fall down onto the sofa from dizziness. The spinning of the room increases. I have to shut my eyes.

As soon as I feel a warm hand on my forehead, my eyes open.

I look at Nate. He is sitting over me, holding my hand.

My whimper turns to a sob.

Nate crawls into the bed with me and holds me. "It's all right, Jes. You're okay."

I practically attack him with an embrace. I need to hold onto something real, tangible. Nate is real. Nate is my link.

"No, Nate. It was a vision. It's not all right."

Nate pulls back and looks at me with concern. Both of his arms are holding my shaking body steady. I know he feels my fear. I'm letting him feel it.

Nate puts his mouth on my forehead. "I'm afraid too, Jes."

We hold on to each other tighter, knowing that reality right now is limited, and the altered reality that is to come has no boundaries.

Please continue reading for a sneak peek at Book 2 in the Piercing the Fold series, Surfacing the Rim.

Acknowledgements

To my family and friends for always encouraging me to never give up, to my husband and children for understanding my passion for creating through the written word, and to God for gifting me with that passion. I strongly believe it takes a village to raise a child. It also takes a village of supporters and fans to raise up an author. I have had some amazing people believe in me and the Piercing the Fold series. BIG thank you to my publishing house, Crushing Hearts and Black Butterfly, along side of Hot Ink Press and Vamptasy Press; One House United...what an amazing family of authors! Love ya'll! (Yep, I said ya'll...I'm from Texas). Thank you, thank you to all of you for raising this author :).

With that being said, I absolutely love to hear from the readers. Make sure and keep up with my projects, events, giveaways, upcoming releases, or just to chat on my wall by visiting and liking my website and social network pages. Would love to hear from you!

www.venessakimball.net
http://www.facebook.com/VenessaKimballAuthor?ref=hl
https://twitter.com/VenessaKimball

About the Author

In 2010, Venessa Kimball was struck by an idea, a story that needed telling. Having always been passionate about the written word, Venessa embarked on writing what would become her debut novel, Piercing the Fold: Book 1; a mature young adult/ adult crossover, paranormal, science fiction series. July 2, 2012, Venessa Kimball independently published the first book in the Piercing the Fold series. Book 2, Surfacing the Rim, released March 14, 2013.

In August of 2013, Venessa joined the publishing house, Crushing Hearts and Black Butterfly. The Piercing the Fold series will be re-published with them beginning with Piercing the Fold: Book 1 on September 3rd. Surfacing the Rim: Book 2 will be re-published on September 24th and Ascending the Veil: Book 3 will be released for the first time on October 18th. The final book in the series, Book 4 (Title TBD) will release in 2014.

As for the future, Venessa is already filling her Work-In-Progress folder. Two of her future projects are adult contemporary fiction and will reflect her diversity as a writer in other genres. When Venessa is not writing, she is keeping active with her husband and three children, chauffeuring said children to extracurricular activities, catching a movie with her hubby, and staying up way too late reading and writing.

Sneak Peek of Surfacing the Rim:
Piercing the Fold, Book 2 Chapter 1
Jesca

I am still in bed. I should be in my car, heading to Ms. Olivia's in an hour to open the store.

For someone with an acquired ability of stealthy speed, I'm moving like a snail. The sleep issue has gotten worse since leaving the facility and moving to Miami.

Ezra told me the visions would come back with intensity when we left the facility. Being underground at the facility had its perks. He said to tell him when they got bad again, but I haven't mentioned it to him.

Because of our link to each other, Nate's the only one who knows how bad they've gotten. Ezra says that we are linked, or coupled, because of our abilities. I'm not sure about that, but I know that Nate and I have become inseparable since he became my partner.

When Corinna was taken by Sam, I made sure to let Ezra and Nate know that I didn't need a babysitter, but I'd do my best to accept a partner. I know that I'm completely capable of protecting, defending, and guarding myself along with those around me. But, I also know that since Nate has been here I've felt less vulnerable and less anxious.

After knocking, Nate whispers, "Can I come in?"

I smile a little and whisper back, "Yes."

It's still dark in the room with the first light of dawn slowly creeping through the window. Nate peeks around the open door.

His hair is rustled, and he's wearing a long-sleeve unbuttoned shirt and a pair of boxer shorts. His lean abdomen is peeking through the open shirt. He's gorgeous, even first thing in the morning.

How can guys do that? He looks amazing and beautiful without even trying. I must look like the Bride of Frankenstein.

I self-consciously brush my hair to the side. He walks over to me, sitting on the side of my bed. He leans in to me and kisses my forehead.

His lips linger on my head. "You do not look like the Bride of Frankenstein, Jes."

I laugh a little, embarrassed but also humored, because no matter how hard I try, I can't block my thoughts from him. It just might be that I don't want to block Nate anymore.

Plus, we're linked to each other for a purpose. We have to keep our link unaltered and uninterrupted for our safety and for the safety of those around us. Ezra explained it in Ezra-terms, but the gist of it is that we are strongest and safest when we are open to each other's thoughts.

Nate reaches up to my face, brushing hair away from my forehead. I look up into his eyes—those beautiful blue-green eyes.

Since the night Sam took Corrina and Ezra revealed that he is my father, Nate has been watching over me like a hawk. He doesn't treat me like I'm a fragile basket case though—

mainly because I told him I hated his hovering after enduring it for a week. From then on, he's been subtle.

Nate whispers, "How did you sleep?"

I am slow to answer and look down briefly. "Okay. You?"

Nate glances down, scratching the top of his head. "Alright."

I turn my head slightly toward his. I know that he's had just as bad of a time as I've had, sleeping across the hall from one another for the past two months. We can feel each other's vulnerability. It can weaken us quickly if we let it.

Sometimes, I hear him call out in the night within seconds of me waking up from one of my intense, vivid nightmares. On the nights that I beat him to it, I tiptoe to his room and sit on the side of his bed. I put my hand on his chest, whispering that we will be okay.

Ezra said that our premonitions and telepathy will develop at a quicker pace now that we are trained and use our abilities daily.

As guardians, Nate and I have come to terms with the fact that my lucid dream world will seep into our real world at some point. The lucid dreams always leave us breathless with fear. I don't think that will ever get better. If anything, the dreams are intensifying.

Nate rubs his eyes, and then he reaches for my hand to reassure me. "I'm good, really. I don't get all of the images you get. I just get your feelings and thoughts. It's not bad. I'm listening rather than being a physical participant. I think that's a lot easier than what you have to see."

Nate yawns and gives me a shove to scoot over. Moving aside, I give Nate some room on the bed. He lifts the covers back, and I feel a cool draft touch my legs.

The weather has turned cold lately. It's been cooler than what you would expect for Florida in early fall. Ezra said that we would start seeing some climate changes before the collision and intersection of our galaxy with Andromeda. We don't know what kind of effect the intersection will have on us. Our world could survive or die when the intersection occurs. Ezra likes to play the devil's advocate, warning us to be prepared for the worst.

I can't imagine what worse would look like though. All of a sudden, I feel a bang of dread.

After Nate settles the covers back over us, he turns to face me. His eyes are focused intensely on mine.

Self-consciously, I ask, "What?"

Nate holds my hand. "Don't try and wrap your mind around it, Jes. I have tried and failed. It just is."

I look at him, smirking. I know he's right.

I try to joke. "Wow, look at how smart you are, Nathaniel Sera!"

He lets out a low chuckle. His smile fades a little as he pulls me closer to him, wrapping his arms around my waist.

In a soft voice, he says, "Don't do that. You do that when you want to make light of something you're feeling. It's alright to be scared."

I'm about to argue with him when he puts his index finger on my lips to hush me. My breath catches with the feel of his touch. Nate leans in, and our lips touch lightly. With his arms still wrapped around my waist, I move my hands to his shoulders, finding the collar of his unbuttoned shirt. My hands quickly slide under it, touching his skin. I push the shirt off of his shoulders, and Nate reacts with quick movements, getting his shirt out of our way.

My hands move to his face, running across the stubble along his strong jawline. With my touch, the kiss deepens instantly. I feel Nate's hands tighten with urgency around me. My heart feels like it's pounding out of my chest.

Nate pulls back. He's as breathless as I am. His hand cups my chin, keeping me from moving too far away.

My breath is fast and uneven. "What?"

His eyes are on my lips. His stare reveals a yearning that makes my heart ache.

Nate's voice is ragged and breathless. "Ezra. He's coming to your room."

Before I can respond, I hear a knock at my door.

"Jes, it's Ezra. I need to talk with you."

Nate pulls back from me. His eyes are still intense.

My voice cracks a little. "Um, just a minute."

Ezra would definitely freak out with the current situation. Nate slowly and quietly stands, picks up his shirt, and moves behind the door.

"Uh, I need to get dressed. I'll be out in ten minutes, okay?"

Ezra says, "Okay. Hey, have you seen Nate? He wasn't in his room."

I answer quickly, "Nope. No, I haven't. Maybe he went for a run."

Nate is standing behind the door, rolling his eyes and smiling at my nervous response.

Grabbing the closest thing to me, I throw a tennis shoe at Nate, hitting him below the belt.

He mouths, "Ouch."

I put my finger to my mouth, gesturing for him to keep quiet.

Ezra asks, "Are you okay in there, Jes?"

I jump off my bed and sprint toward the door instantly, knowing Ezra's next move.

Ezra starts to open the door, and I lean against it, shutting it back in place.

I look at Nate while I respond to Ezra. "I'm fine. Just stubbed my toe. I'm getting dressed right now. Hey, I have to get to Ms. Olivia's pretty soon. Will this take long?"

Ezra responds, "I called her to let her know that you and Nate wouldn't be making it in today. There's been some development, and we have a change of plans. I'll meet you in the kitchen."

As Nate and I continue staring at each other, I hear Ezra walk away from the door.

I peek out the door after a couple of seconds. The hallway is clear. Nate and I shuffle around each other, so he can leave the room. Before he leaves, he wraps both arms around my waist, pulling me into him, and he kisses me deeply, desperately.

He inches back just enough to look into my eyes. "Good morning, Jes," he whispers.

Our physical proximity leaves me breathless—again. "Good morning, Nate."

The corners of his mouth turn up in a smile.

I push against Nate's chest. "Go, go, go."

He tiptoes down the hall, and I quickly shut the door behind me, leaning against it. My hand immediately goes to my lips, replaying our encounter.

* * *

For the past two months, Nate and I have been treading on uneven ground. As Nate and I grow more dependent on our link to help each other, we become more addicted to each other physically. The simplest touch sends us both into an intimate frenzy.

It's like I crave more of his touch. It's been one of those things that Nate and I know could potentially bear a problem, but we don't want to talk about it. Part of me doesn't want to let go of how safe and secure his touch makes me feel, and I know I make Nate feel just as safe in my arms. But, I worry that the physical security will blur into something that could get one or both of us hurt.

I push the thought out of my mind, and I think about Ezra's interruption this morning. *What could he be up to?* I dress quickly and head to the kitchen.

Ezra is sitting at the table, reading the paper. "Morning."

I head straight to the coffee machine and mumble, "Morning."

I'm stirring creamer into my coffee when Nate walks in. His hair is still wet from the shower, making it appear darker than it really is. I can't help but think of him in the shower. *Ugh, Jesca!* I add more sweetener to my cup and stir vigorously to distract my drifting thoughts.

Ezra asks, "Nate, where were you? Your door was open when I came by to find you this morning."

Nate grabs the cereal from the cabinet and turns to the refrigerator to get the milk. I feel his eyes on me the whole time.

"I went for a run. It was amazing."

I briefly glance over at Nate, who is leaning against the countertop now. Nate winks discreetly at me. I fix my coffee to quickly distract myself from him.

Ezra eyes are still glued to his paper. "That is not breakfast, Jesca."

I quickly finish mixing up my coffee, creamer, and sweetener and have a seat. "It is until I hear what you have to say, Ezra."

Nate moves around, sitting next to me at the table.

Ezra puts his paper down and looks up at me. "You look terrible!"

I respond sarcastically, "Thanks so much. You say the nicest things, Dad!"

Leaning his arm on the table, Ezra props his chin on his hand. "Why haven't you told me the visions have gotten worse?"

"Visions? More like nightmares." I take a long sip of my coffee.

Nate interjects, "They're getting worse."

Clearing my throat, I roll my eyes at Nate's comment. "Thanks, Nate."

"Sorry, Jes, but Ezra needs to know." Nate's eyes dart back to Ezra. "They're becoming more intense and vivid. They're premonitions, aren't they?"

Ezra's eyes never leave mine. "Yes, they are. Jesca, with regular training, your abilities will grow. Lucid Dreaming, Telepathy, Qi, Astral Projection—all of your abilities are becoming stronger, and their strength has spawned a hybrid. Your Lucid Dreaming and Telepathy are melding to create an outlet for these premonitions to come to you."

I get up to refill my empty mug. "Awesome. Just perfect."

As I come back to the table, Ezra's voice fills with worry as he says, "Jes, you need to tell us what's going on with these lucid dreams. Your mother, Anna, had lucid dreams and premonitions of the future before her..." Ezra stops speaking.

I turn to look at him. His eyes are reddening, shining with fresh tears.

He's right. I need to stop being so flippant with the images I'm getting in my dreams. They can help us.

I put my hand on top of Ezra's. "Okay, from here on out, I'll tell you about them. You're right. They might be able to help guide us when the collision comes."

I tense when the word "collision" leaves my mouth. *It's surreal that our world might end within my lifetime because our galaxy could collide with Andromeda.*

350

Ezra reads my mind. "I already told you, Jes. Our scientists have confirmed that our galaxy and Andromeda will collide and intersect without destroying us."

I sigh. "I know. It's just what happens *after* the collision that has me worried."

* * *

Within a week after Sam Crest took Corinna Cain, the imminent collision of the Andromeda galaxy with ours was leaked to the mainstream news. Months prior to the leak, scientists had speculated that the climate shift and other global events might have been a result of a gravitational imbalance in the Earth and its atmosphere. They had said a polar shift might be occurring. Then, a reporter from CNN accessed information that confirmed the collision as a scientific fact. He reported that the collision between the two galaxies was inevitable.

Nate insinuated that someone had gotten sloppy, but I could feel that it was someone on the inside—a Sondian. Ezra thought the same, too.

For the past two months, we stayed in the villa, awaiting intelligence from the fellowship's scientists while we compared notes with the local, national, and global news. Rebel factions already started to sprout up all over the world. Civil riots and protests for government assistance caused worldwide governmental departments to be on high alert. They started shutting down borders between nations, trying to keep the chaos contained within their own countries.

As guardians, our job of protecting humans on this Earth—while also trying to safeguard ourselves—became a million times harder because of this insider leaking information. It was intended to intimidate us. And, it served its purpose. We are only a few saviors in a sea of frightened and confused civilians.

* * *

Ezra shakes his head, stiffening his lips.

Dangerous thoughts start stirring in my mind.

Nate tries to save us from our thoughts by changing the subject. "So, what's up?"

Ezra looks up at both of us. "Sebastian is sending us on a mission."

I feel a knot form in my stomach.

Nate sits back, moving away from his cereal. "What about our mission here?"

Ezra sighs. "Well, the mission here has fled Miami and is now in Tokyo, Japan."

I ask, "Are we going to Japan?"

"We need to get a fellow guardian on board with us and take care of some housekeeping at MIT first. Sebastian hasn't confirmed, but I think that's where we're headed." Ezra pauses, nervously tapping a pen on the table. "This fellow guardian. He may be…resistant."

I start probing with a million questions. "You said *he*. Who is it? Why would he resist? What do we need to tell him that could make him resist?"

Ezra sighs, throwing his glasses down in frustration. "Damn it, Jesca!"

Ezra doesn't do frustration often, so I know my heavy line of questioning has definitely gotten under his skin.

The feeling I get just before lightning strikes is creeping in. *This is not going to be good.*

Ezra closes his eyes for a moment. With Ezra being Ezra, I know he's trying to regain his composure before he speaks. Nate and I remain quiet and wait.

Ezra's voice becomes even again. "Because I have to tell him things that could change everything he thought he knew about himself." He looks down. "Things that *you* may resist."

I lean onto the table, looking directly into Ezra's eyes. "Us? Resist? I highly doubt that!" I sit back and cross my arms. "Try me."

Ezra breathes deeply and looks from Nate to me. "The implantation of the second-generation Copula."

Nate breaks in, "Yeah? What about it?"

Ezra holds up his iPhone. "A device similar to this was used prior to travel to send a surge of electricity directly to the Copula. The surge acted as a harness between the body's copper and the Copula, working together to open the wormhole, but this device wasn't just a Copula defibrillator. It had multiple purposes.

Looking away, Ezra continues, "It was a miniature computer. This device recorded neurological and physical changes within the body during and after travel. As protocol, after every mission, Sebastian's associates collected the data to check for any changes or abnormalities. Across the board, the data showed increased levels of copper in those who were implanted. The levels of copper contributed to alterations within the body, making those implanted superior."

Nate questions, "Superior? In what way were they superior?

Thoughts start firing in my head. *Alterations in the body making the implanted superior. Alterations.*

Ezra's voice is filled with worry. I tune back in enough to hear him say "...physical strength and speed. Psychic abilities, such as clairvoyance, telepathy..."

His mouth is moving, but I'm not listening anymore. *Are we implanted?* I almost speak the words, but instead, I quickly shut my gaping mouth.

Nate guardedly looks at me. "Jes?"

Ezra's gaze focuses on me. He's just sitting there, waiting for me to ask.

I don't ask the question sitting on the tip of my tongue, wanting to leave my lips. If I do, I'll slip below the surface of reality, sinking into a sea of new truths that I will have to surface from. I don't know if I can handle that. I don't know if I'll be able to surface once I hear the answer to the unspoken question lingering in the atmosphere.

Ezra sits back in his chair, crossing his arms in front of his chest. His voice is soft when he speaks. "You are both implanted with Copulas."

Yep, I'm slipping deep below the surface. I feel every hair on my body stand on end. My throat constricts, and I can't get enough air.

I push my chair back and stand slowly. Nate reaches out to hold my arm and steady me, but I pull away from his grasp. *I need to get out of here.* I charge quickly to the coat closet and grab my sweatshirt.

Nate calls after me, "Jesca, wait! Where are you going?"

Ezra reprimands Nate, "Nate, let her go!"

I ignore them and run out the back door.

CPSIA information can be obtained
at www.ICGtesting.com
Printed in the USA
FFOW02n2013201114
8863FF

9 781939 769374